STRAINS OF INNOCENCE

A DCI MCNEILL NOVEL

JACQUELINE NEW

www.jacquelinenew.com

STRAINS OF INNOCENCE
DCI MCNEILL Book 2

Cover design: The Cover Collection
Interior Formatting: Jesse Gordon

Visit the website **www.jacquelinenew.com** to sign up to the no-spam NEW CRIME CLUB. You'll get news, updates and more.

Never miss a new release.

PROLOGUE

ALONE IN A NONDESCRIPT FLAT, nestled among countless identical, soulless boxes in a drab tower block, he sat, immersed in his critical task. The walls, paper-thin, whispered secrets from adjacent lives: a TV's muffled dialogue next door, the sharp crescendo of arguments from above, doors slamming in frustration and anger. Below, shadowy figures with hoods and masks congregated in groups on the bleak concrete outside. This cacophony of life, echoing through the walls and floors, served only to emphasise his solitary confinement.

As he worked, he seethed with a quiet rage. This wasn't his world; he was an outcast, forced into a new existence in sharp contrast to the exalted status he'd once held. The room he sat in now was bleak and unadorned, a daily affront to his former life of respect and privilege. It held only the essentials: an old camping table with rusted joints, a tangible symbol of his descent, and a sleek, new Wi-Fi router, an incongruous beacon of modernity in this god forsaken space. The pedestrian car-

1

pet, stained and threadbare, was another testament to his current, dismal circumstances, so at odds with the polished floors and richly hued luxury of his past. Every corner of this meager existence was a bitter reminder of what he had lost, fueling a resentment that continually simmered beneath his methodical calm.

Condensation wept down the windows, blurring the outside world. The persistent moisture gathered in droplets, slowly pooling on the sills, where it would foster patches of dark, creeping mould if he didn't scrub it daily. On the table, a collection of boxes and packages lay in wait, each marked with the impersonal precision of QR and barcodes. Under the harsh glare of a single bulb, he prepared for his meticulous task.

At a second table, scrubbed clean and reeking faintly of bleach, a plastic box of cleaning supplies nestled beneath. Half the table's surface was occupied by a collection of petri dishes, each labeled with painstaking care. The other half held a padded envelope, identical to the others he had collected earlier that day.

Donning sterile latex gloves with exacting precision, he lifted the package, placing it before him with reverence. He painstakingly scrutinised every millimetre of its surface through a magnifying glass, his bald head and bare brows reflecting the stark light, his smooth jaw and cheeks obscured by a medical-grade mask.

The search was methodical, almost ritualistic. If fruitless, the package would join the discarded pile. But today, fortune favoured him. A single hair, partially ensnared by the sealing tape, glinted like a precious jewel. With the patience of a surgeon, he wielded scalpel and tweezers, liberating the hair, its follicle the ultimate reward for his patience and dedication.

He sealed the hair in a petri dish, then, with a marker pen, inscribed a name and address in neat, precise block capitals. Hours at the table had etched pain into his back, neck and legs, but it was a trivial price to pay for his triumphs this evening. His gaze lingered on the six shallow, transparent, lidded dishes he'd filled that night–six lives, six souls, unwittingly ensnared in his macabre collection. He nodded with a shiver of pleasure, a small, sinister smile crossing his lips as he contemplated the next phase of his plan.

CHAPTER ONE

THE HAND WAS PALE AND DELICATE. Female. Palm up with slender fingers curled inward. Small dark areas marred the otherwise perfect and blemish free inner hand and wrist. Mac frowned. Indentations? They looked like teeth marks. Behind him he could hear the Scene of Crime team labouring up the hill carrying the tent and their bags of equipment. The sky behind the mound of Arthur's Seat was lightening, but this side was still in deep shadow. The ground was sodden beneath his feet, and he was glad the call had come through on a weekend. It had found him away from home and dressed for days out with a friend and her daughter. Hiking boots, jeans, and a fleece. His black hair was tousled. Dark eyes lidded and intense. With his attention focused on the scene his face was closed, permitting no intrusions. The uniformed officer guarding the clump of bushes that concealed the latest horror gave a perfunctory nodded salute and stepped aside.

For a long moment, Mac looked at the hand. Then he

crouched and moved aside the stiff branches of the bushes. An arm was revealed to the shoulder. Obscene in its nakedness. Mac had donned latex gloves as he walked up the long path from the car park. He felt moisture through them now. Checked and found no blood. Just dew on the foliage then. Or rain from the night before.

"Help me with this," he said.

The uniform stepped in and grasped a sizable portion of the bush, carefully pulling it to one side and holding it down. Mac stared at the newly revealed body. A young woman. Naked and covered in stab wounds. Face round with short dark hair. There was a smear of blood against the side of her nose. Mac took his phone out of his back pocket and switched on the torch. A ragged hole in the side of the right nostril was revealed. As though a piercing had been torn out. A policeman's pessimistic mind read that as trophy taking. It could have been torn out in a struggle, but he looked for the darkest explanation as a matter of course. There was cut under her chin and two either side of her nose, slashing, straight lines. He quickly counted the wounds he could see. Most were above the waist and below the neck. Thirty or so. Frenzied attack then. But done quickly. Not much bruising that Mac could see. Had the girl had time to fight back there would be defensive wounds on her arms and hands.

He saw no such signs on the pale, delicate flesh. An attack that happened so quickly she had no time to react and didn't need to be restrained. He looked back over his shoulder to where two uniforms stood with a woman in all weather gear and a woolly hat. She had a golden retriever in a harness which was going from one officer to the other, receiving pats and fuss. Its tongue lolled and tail wagged. Mac stared. He knew the dog. It had belonged to a family in a previous serious crime case. He was glad it had found a good home.

"Did she find the body?" Mac asked the uniformed officer.

"Yes, sir. Dog found it. She said it got the hand in its mouth before she realised what it was and got it under control."

Mac nodded. They *were* bite marks on the hand and wrist, as he'd surmised. At least he now knew where they came from.

"Guv. Dressed down today?" Kai's voice drifted to him over the chill air. Too bright and cheerful this early in the morning. Especially considering the reason they were up here.

Mac looked back to where DC Kai Stuart was hurrying up the path, long overcoat held shut by hands in the pockets. He wore a suit and looked the part of a detective, right down to his styled, short hair.

"Got the call away from home," Mac replied.

"You're the one with the dry cleaning bill," DS Nari Yun said.

Kai half turned and Mac saw the slender, petite Nari behind him. She bore a cardboard tray with three takeout coffee cups on it. The Scene of Crime Officers were waiting to erect the tent over the body, already in their paper suits and masks.

"Who's our pathologist today?" Mac asked.

"Stringer. He's not liking the hill," Kai replied.

Mac could just make out the portly shape of the SOCO team leader, forensic pathologist Derek Stringer. In the last year, he'd added to the padding around his middle along with another chin thrown in for good measure. Mac wondered if he was ill. Or just getting old. Mac hadn't exactly been treating his own body like a temple lately. Too many takeaways at

Clio's or drive thru's at the insistence of thirteen-year-old Maia who was a calorie burning machine. He straightened and stepped away from the body, indicating to the SOCO team that they could proceed. He stepped well clear and held out a hand for a coffee. Nari smiled as she handed him a cup.

"Chai tea," she said.

"What?" Kai snorted. "Going middle class on us, guv?"

Mac sipped the spiced, aromatic liquid. "Expanding my horizons," he replied.

"What are we looking at, guv?" Nari said, handing a steaming over to Kai and taking her own.

She looked directly at Mac, holding his gaze in a way that made him slightly uncomfortable. Too intense. Too... something.

"Young woman. I'd say in her early twenties. Naked and stabbed. Could be a sex attack. Not much sign of blood, so I'd say she was dumped here."

"It was chucking it down last night," Kai said. "And freezing. Not the weather for dogging."

"That woman down there found the body. Kai, go and talk to her. Make a fuss of the dog and she'll be your friend for life. Persuade her to go over whatever statement she gave to the first responders and take notes. I want as much detail as she can give."

"On it."

Kai was all leading man toothless smile as he approached the witness. Enough to put her at ease without being disrespectful of the circumstances.

Mac stood with Nari as Stringer trudged up the hill, his feet crunching on the red gravel. Edinburgh was a toy town below them. A net of streetlights lay across a jumble of buildings that looked as though they'd been thrown in the air and left where they landed. He sipped the drink that was supposed to be relaxing and felt his stomach clench. In his peripheral vision, he noted Nari kept glancing at him. He ignored it. He didn't want to get into a conversation about his weekend, or anything other than the dead girl a few feet away.

"Morning, Inspector," Stringer huffed out, finally reached the scene.

"Morning. Looks like a multiple stabbing," Mac said, eager to get on.

Stringer sighed as he secured the mask over his face. "I hate the messy ones."

"You're in the wrong job," Mac told him as they approached the tent together.

"Oh, there's all kinds of neat and tidy murders. Strangulation. Suffocation. Poisoning. Now, I had a case just recently, you might have heard about it. Fast-acting poison that clears itself and…"

He glanced at Mac as he lifted the tent flap, observed his jeans, boots and fleece, then pointed to the camping table that had been put up adjacent to the tent and piled with spare forensic suits. Mac nodded, dressing as Stringer ducked into the tent. By the time he followed, Stringer was crouched over the body. A SOC officer was combing the branches of the bush with tweezers, using a square magnifying glass. Another was photographing the scene from all angles. Mac squatted next Stringer, keeping his hands carefully away from the ground or the body, hanging them loosely over his knees.

"I take it back. Someone has been very neat and tidy with

this one," Stringer said, his educated Edinburgh accent barely Scottish at all. "Lots of wounds made by a very sharp, narrow blade. They don't look deep, so I'd say maybe two or three inches long. A scalpel or Stanley knife maybe. But, the body has been cleaned up. And despite the multiple wounds there was one killer. Here."

He pointed to a cut beneath the girl's left breast.

"That's very precise for a frenzied attack," Mac said.

He hadn't noticed that particular wound amid so many. He revised his initial assessment. One blow delivered with surgical precision to kill her. Then thirty or so more.

"Precision first. Frenzy after," Stringer said, his eyes met Mac's in a quick gesture of mutual professional respect. Stringer always appreciated police officers who could read a crime scene almost as well as he could.

"I'm not sure what to make of those three cuts on the face. Difficult to get such neat cuts if your victim is alive. Unless anesthetised, of course. Underneath the chin like that. And to achieve such straight cuts either side of the nose. Again the placing is very precise. I'm going to go out on a limb and say it might very well have been done post-mortem. I'll know more when I get her back to the lab."

"There's a lot of blood somewhere," Mac observed.

"There is. But not here. We'll need more SOCOs. The killer may have carried her up the path here or may not. There's any number of routes up the hill to this point," Stringer observed. "You notice the wound at the side of the nose, I take it?"

Mac nodded curtly. Stringer sighed.

"You'll need a lot of bodies to find it out here. Assuming it's on the hillside somewhere and not in someone's pocket."

Mac's grin was a mere showing of teeth. Stringer was just as inclined to the worst possible scenario as he was. How could you work around dead bodies for a living and not be? He remained crouched, eyes roaming over the girl. Her eyes were open and blue. A startling blue.

"From the flexibility of the limbs, I would say death occurred no more than two to three hours ago. No sign of livor mortis, but I wouldn't expect to see lividity where the body has been lying, apologies I should say placed, in a prone position. Feels cold to the touch but then it is very cold and she is naked. So, death occurred between two and three this morning. Make of that what you will, Inspector."

Mac nodded, his mind already working back to what a young girl like this might have been doing. She had dark eyeliner and painted nails. Not the most made up girl, but some students didn't go in for makeup by trowel. Then again she could have been attacked in her bed. Or someone else's.

"Well, you'd better let me get on. You'll have my report as soon as possible," Stringer said, a slight note of testiness creeping in.

Mac stood and left the tent. He crunched down the path a ways. It wove in and out of trees and bushes, up from the road far below.

"Quite a climb with a dead body," Nari observed, offering her refreshments again.

"Why bother?" Mac said. "You can't hide a body up here. Not with the amount of people coming up here every day."

"Maybe they wanted the body to be found?"

Mac stripped off the gloves, balling one up inside the other. He dropped them into his tea after draining half of it in one mouthful. There was a litter bin beside the path and he tossed both cup and gloves into it.

"Maybe."

There was a pause. "You came dressed for the occasion anyway," Nari said.

Mac wasn't about to go into the details of his Saturday. How he and Clio had taken Maia walking into the Pentlands. It wasn't the kind of pastime he would ever have said he liked. But Clio had become a good friend since the horror that had led to their meeting. The Celtic Killer, so named by the tabloids. And, though he wouldn't admit it to anyone, Maia had him wrapped around her little finger. Uncle Callum. He felt a smile tug at the corner of his mouth at the notion and forced his thoughts back to the present. Nari was looking at him, the ghost of smile daring to show itself on her face.

"I'll speak to Reid about the extra officers we'll need to comb the hillside," Mac said brusquely. "I want you and Kai covering witnesses, CCTV, motorists. Anyone we can place in the vicinity that might have seen the body being carried up here. That would have been from about two o'clock this morning onwards."

The fingers of one of Nari's hands were dancing across the screen of her phone. She glanced at her coffee and tossed it as Mac had done, then went back to note-taking.

"We'll base ourselves out of HQ at Hillside. I've already called Melissa; she'll take care of reassigning any cases you have. This will be the priority."

He began to walk back down the slope towards the visitor's car park a quarter of a mile below. As he did, his mind recalled a conversation he'd had the previous day with Doctor Clio Wray. Initially a consultant he had recruited to help solve the case of a serial killer, now one of his very few friends.

CHAPTER TWO

"SHE'S EXHAUSTED and as happy as I've ever seen her," Clio said, wearily walking down the stairs.

"I don't think she wanted to leave," Mac replied, holding out a glass of white wine.

He held a bottle of Bud in his other hand. Clio took the wine and they went into the living room. Mac dropped into an armchair while Clio sat at the end of the sofa nearest the chair. She tucked her feet up under her and let her head flop back against a plump cushion stuffed into a corner of the sofa. Mac felt at ease in Clio's house despite its marked difference to his own. She lived among clutter and bric-a-brac. He lived among stark lines, minimalism, and cold function.

"She didn't. Classic case of FOMO," Clio replied.

Mac frowned with a quizzical smile. For a moment, his eyes narrowed, then he shook his head and took a swig from the bottle. The liquid was crisp and sharp with cold, washing away the weariness of a day spent in the kind of activity he hadn't engaged in since...No, he'd never done any of the things he'd done today with Maia and Clio.

"I can't even guess at what that means," he said.

Clio grinned. "Easy for a parent. Every child suffers from it. Fear of Missing Out."

Mac chuckled, seeing it in Maia's reluctance to admit she was done in, not wanting to go to her bed despite the late hour.

"Especially when it comes to you," Clio went on.

"Me? I don't get it. Why me?" Mac replied.

"What don't you get? You're a hero cop. You're mysterious; practically an alien, as far as Maia is concerned. She knows you do things on a daily basis that she'll never find out about because they're not safe for a child to know. And that makes it the single most intriguing thing in her entire world. Compared to you, my job at the university is a yawn-fest."

Mac ran a hand through his hair, feeling even more confused.

"I thought she would be scared by me. Well, not by me exactly, but by what I do. I mean, Serious Crimes don't get called in unless there's been just that, a serious crime. Someone has to do something brutal to someone else before I'm asked to investigate."

"And she knows that, but she's also sneaked a look at TV and movies she shouldn't have. Bypassed my parental locks or just watched it with her friends. So she knows that people are horrific to each other and when they are a policeman like you sorts it out. She thinks you live in a world of car chases and shoot outs. That the cops always get the bad guy in the end. Good versus evil stuff."

"Maybe pre-internet. But surely kids these days are more switched on?" Mac protested.

"Kids like Maia think they are, but she's been somewhat sheltered. I've made sure of it as best I can. I can't control 100% of what she sees online but she's still sheltered from the worst of life's atrocities. She's still a child, Mac, and I want her to have a happy childhood for as long as I can without real world horrors tainting it. She'll get enough of that when she's an adult."

Mac nodded. "I can think of kids who are not sheltered at all. I've seen them, and the adults some of them turn into."

"Exactly," Clio agreed, taking a sip of her wine. "You're a glimpse into an exciting world she knows she's been protected from. And you are a good man. She knows that and idolises it. Take it as a compliment,"

Mac nodded, feeling embarrassed to be the subject of hero worship. He thought about the interactions with Maia over the past year. At first he'd found himself speechless in her company, mind blanking at the prospect of holding a conversation with a child. He knew Maia was way too old for baby talk, but what was the proper level of conversation.

"I will. I'm glad I've made a good impression. I have to admit, I've felt a lot more relaxed around her these last couple of months. I don't take to people quickly. Never have."

"I've noticed," Clio said. "When you first met her, I don't think you spoke directly to Maia at all, just to, or through me. But I expected it."

Mac raised an eyebrow. "Expected it?"

"Yes, a man like you. I knew it wouldn't be easy for you to make friends. I was surprised how quickly you and I seemed to click, to be honest."

Mac looked directly at her. It was an unusual experience to find his mind completely blank, unable to fathom a meaning. Usually, he spent his time in a constant state of analysis and hypothesis, reviewing data and coming up with theories to fit the evidence. But he had no idea what Clio might be driving at.

"I'm lost."

"Really?" Clio said, sounding genuinely surprised.

"Really. What do you mean a man like me? A policeman? A workaholic? Middle-aged?"

Clio looked at him in a strange way. It was the kind of look that said Mac was being deliberately obtuse, refusing to acknowledge something obvious. Mac spread his hands, laughing.

"I'm serious. No games. What are we talking about? I'm curious."

"I just mean someone who is on the spectrum," Clio said.

"Spectrum?" Mac was genuinely confused for a moment. Then it dawned on him what she meant. "Seriously? I don't have Autism, Clio."

"No-one does. It's not a disease, Mac. It's a neurotype. Maia is neurodivergent too. She's ADHD. At least that's the label society gives it. She's just Maia Wray as far as I'm concerned, but you have to have a label before institutions like schools will offer support or make allowances. She probably inherited it from me. I'm undiagnosed ADD, Attention Deficit, I don't have the hyperactive part like she does. I felt sure after you and I met that you were on the spectrum. It's never been discussed with your parents or in your school days?"

"Never. I think you must be wrong. I mean, I don't know much about it other than the name, but don't autistic people..." he hesitated, suddenly aware of his ignorance and not wanting to resort to generalities.

"It's called a spectrum for a reason. From what you might describe as mild, right up to extreme. From the day we met, I can count the number of times you've held eye contact with me on one hand. I bet it's physically uncomfortable for you. Am I right?"

Mac swigged from his bottle, taking a long swallow, and realised he wasn't looking Clio in the eye while she spoke. She'd zeroed in on something he'd always known about himself and had labelled as a silly weakness. He forced himself to meet her eye. She was smiling gently and after a moment he laughed, looking away.

"You don't have to be embarrassed. I've taught hundreds of autistic students. It's just the way your brain is wired. Not an illness or a defect. You think differently, that's all. Maia thinks differently. So do I."

"Neurodivergent," Mac said slowly, trying out the word.

"Yes. But I bet you can look at the minutiae of evidence in a case and see details everyone around you overlooks. Finding patterns in apparent chaos. A real superpower for a policeman."

Mac nodded, genuinely interested. His mind was already racing along a new path, examining traits of his thinking and behaviour, holding them up to this new lens.

"Hyper focus," Clio continued. "Maia does it when she is genuinely engaged in something. Excludes the outside world totally. Sound familiar?"

"You could stand beside me and shout into my ear. I wouldn't hear it," Mac said. "Some of my colleagues used to make jokes about it when I was first promoted to CID. The fact that I could be in a world of my own. Then I started seeing connections in cases that the most experienced detectives missed. And I started getting picked for big assignments by ambitious senior officers like Kenny Reid. And I rose in the ranks."

"I told you. Compared to a neurotypical mind, your ability to see the detail is a superpower. I wouldn't be surprised to learn a lot more successful police officers are neurodivergent. But, as with everything in life, there are good and bad parts to it. Like you mentioned not getting along with people very quickly. I know you're not a social guy. You avoid hanging out socially with your team and don't miss having a lot of friends. It's not important to you."

"Or friends at all," Mac said. "And no, I don't miss it. How do you miss something you've never had, or for that matter needed? But I don't feel anything about it one way or another. It just is. And I do have some. A few. One." He smiled sheepishly.

"Two," Clio corrected.

"Two," Mac agreed.

He wasn't convinced, not completely. But it was uncanny that Clio had been aware of character traits she wouldn't have had an opportunity to observe, but knew were there. The fact she could tell him he didn't have many friends could have been deduced the same way that he, a detective would. By talking to those who knew Mac and investigating him, trawling his digital footprint, what there was of it, and basic observation. But none of that would reveal what he thought about it. That he didn't have a lot of friends could be discovered easily. That he didn't miss it or care one way or another?

"I've been told in evaluations by some of my commanding officers that what I do is good work. But how I do it needs improving. People don't take to me. They think I'm arrogant..."

"Aloof? Unfeeling?" Clio asked, pointedly.

Mac nodded. "Exactly. So, you're telling me you think it's because I'm on the spectrum?"

"I'd put money on it," Clio said. "I care about my job, the teaching aspect, not just the academic part. I try and understand all I can about my students and how they think in order to understand how they learn. I've done a lot of research and taken a lot of courses over the years relating to neuro-divergence in young people."

"And middle-aged men," Mac said.

Clio blushed. "I'm sorry. I've just realised how completely inappropriate this whole conversation is. I shouldn't be just telling you what you are. I'm like a sledge hammer sometimes. That's the ADD for you right there. Impulsive."

"Like leaping to help a detective who shows up at your office looking like he's been given a good going over by a street thug?" Mac said with a rogue's grin.

"Exactly," Clio lifted her wine glass to drink, but it was empty.

Mac got up and took it from her, walking back into the kitchen and pouring another. He took a fresh beer from the fridge and dropped the dead one into the plastic box inside a cupboard where Clio kept the glass recycling. He still wore the jeans and t-shirt he'd donned to hike through the Pentlands for most of the day though his new hiking boots were on the door mat in the porch. Clio's house was a familiar place to him after just a handful of visits, somewhere he felt comfortable. It came down to the people who lived there. He realised he had felt at ease with Clio almost immediately and was now learning that Maia was a human, not some unfathomable being from another planet. Knowing that she looked up to him made Mac feel more relaxed about her. The only people he'd felt this comfortable with before had been Siobhan and her daughter Aine.

Thoughts of Siobhan still brought a stab of pain. A sense of loss that came suddenly, cored out his very being and then faded away with a whisper. It left a deep, pervasive melancholy which he tried to shake off. He didn't want these feelings to ruin a great day and evening.

"I'm sorry if I've overstepped. I just thought a man as perceptive as you would already know this about himself."

Mac shook his head. "Don't be. I'm genuinely fascinated. Carry on Clio."

"I prefer Camping actually," Clio said, as he handed her the fresh wine.

Their fingers touched around the cold glass, but Mac missed the moment, thrown once again by her comment.

"I don't feel too much like the brilliant detective when I'm around you sometimes," he admitted.

"Carry On?" Clio said. "Come on; don't tell me you've never watched the Carry On films?"

"Oh, right. No. Not my thing," Mac said. "Aren't they just completely sexist and outdated though?"

"Of course they are. But you might notice that the girls always get the upper hand and the old lechers always get what's coming to them. I used to watch them with my granddad. That's really why I have a soft spot for seventies toilet humour and sexism. It reminds me of him," Clio admitted.

"Lots of things remind me of my old man," Mac said. "None of them good. My brother, on the other hand. I used to think of him every time I had to break up a pub fight."

"He was a drinker?"

"He used to beat me up," Mac said. "Until I got big enough to give as good as I got."

He shifted in his seat, took a swig of his beer as a shield between them and changed the subject with the subtlety of a brick. Clio smiled to herself but didn't protest. They talked about Maia and her troubles at school, about the visit Mac said he'd try to arrange, to talk to the kids about being a policeman. He relaxed, realising that tension had begun to rise in his shoulders at the personal nature of the conversation. He laughed at her jokes and at her reaction to his kind of music when he demonstrated one of his playlists for her.

As yawns replaced words more often, Clio made up the sofa for him and, before going up to bed, grabbed him in an impulsive hug. Mac felt the urge to pull away, an instant and visceral response. Autism? Was that really the answer?

CHAPTER THREE

"MUM, ARE YOU AND CALLUM sleeping together?"

Clio choked on a slice of toast. Maia sat opposite her at the small, round table in the middle of the kitchen. She grinned around a piece of toast of her own. Like she knew what a hand grenade she had just thrown into the room.

"First of all, none of your business. Second of all, no. No. How do you even...?"

Clio stopped at the raised eyebrow from her thirteen-year-old going on twenty. She had the same dark hair as Clio but her father's eyes and nose. Dark eyes that could look like bottomless pits when she was angry or Bambi eyes when she wanted something. A young woman sitting in the place of her baby girl.

"How do I even know about sex?" Maia asked.

"I know, I know. Stupid question. But you still shouldn't be asking." Clio said, clearing her mouth of crumbs with a mouthful of cold coffee, which she'd forgotten she'd even made for herself.

"As far as you're concerned, he's just your cool uncle who doesn't set boundaries. Which is why you like him so much. I'm the bad guy that makes you do your homework and says no to McD's."

"Anyway, I know he stayed over last night."

"Because he deserved a glass of wine after spending his Saturday with you," Clio shot back with a grin of her own. "And he slept on the sofa. He's a friend, and that's all he'll ever be."

"I've seen the way you look at him. I don't blame you. He's a hottie. For an old guy," Maia said.

"Are you actually trying to get yourself grounded?" Clio replied. "Enough."

The problem was that Mac was every bit the hottie. Tall, dark, and handsome. A cliché, but there was no more apt description of him. Brooding. Silent too often and completely unreadable. Not the kind of man it was healthy to fall for. Which Clio wasn't. Under any circumstances. Maia's eyes had become infinite pools of blackness. She didn't pout, her mouth just went straight. These days, she could flit between banter and offence in the blink of an eye. Clio sighed. Picked up her coffee mug in both hands. Remembered it was cold and went to the pot to pour another.

"Look. We both nearly died last year. It creates a bond. I was working with him and his team. We became friends. And yes, he is good-looking. But he's not available to me or anyone. Nor am I. OK?"

She kept her tone gentle, wanting Maia to be friends again. Maia shrugged and smiled. A bright grin that flashed, lighting up her face and Clio's heart.

"Sure. So, what's the plan today? Packing? Moving?"

"Packing. Thirteen years' worth of packing," Clio said with a grimace.

She looked around and felt the usual guilt. Guilt that Maia had been living for the past three months surrounded by boxes and bin bags as they tried to prepare for a move.

"I still think the landlord is a total..."

Clio decided to let the word that followed pass. In the twenty-first century, you couldn't expect a teenager not to know how to swear. And Clio happened to agree. She had rented from the same kindly old retired teacher since just after Maia was born. He had died six months ago and his daughter wanted the house back. Had given Clio and Maia four months to unpick over a decade's worth of possessions. Mac had intimidated the woman into extending that to six.

"It doesn't matter now. We've got our new place. And Corstophine is a very nice area. And much closer to the city center. You can get on a bus for free and go anywhere. So, she's doing us a favour even if she is a...cow." Clio decided to amend the swear word to something more appropriate for a parent.

"You don't have to sell it to me," Maia said, getting up and opening the fridge.

"Nothing in there that wasn't there five minutes ago," Clio pointed out.

"I'm still hungry," Maia complained.

"Have some fruit," Clio said.

Maia wandered into the living room, separated from the kitchen by an arch that had once been a wall, knocked through long ago. A duvet was folded at one end of the sofa, two pillows sat neatly on top of it. Maia sat herself next to the bedding and started typing on her phone. Clio knew that she had a narrow window of time to get her daughter engaged and moving or she would be on her phone all morning.

"I've got a delivery coming and two parcels to go out. I'm going to take a shower. Can you take those two boxes on the coffee table out to the front door and listen out for the driver? The doorbell's not working and I've rescheduled once already."

Maia grunted.

"Please, sweetie. I'll get charged if I miss another one."

Maia's sigh made it clear this was the biggest imposition on a person the world had ever known, but she rose and went to pick up the first box.

"Careful, it's heavy," Clio said.

"Okaaay."

Clio smiled as she cleared away the breakfast things. She grabbed her phone as she left the room, heading for the stairs. Maia had taken up sentry position on the bench they kept in the porch, feet up against the opposite wall. On her phone. The two boxes sat behind the door.

"You'll need to move them to open the door," Clio called as she went up the stairs.

"Uh huh," Maia replied.

As Clio went into her room, bed unmade and curtains still closed, she saw the email on her phone. Still open from the twentieth time she had been through it. It made her angry just seeing it, and she swiped it away. Who the hell did Michael Gaines think he was? To lecture her like she was one of his pupils. And to cast aspersions about her daughter. Like Maia was the only problem in her school. She dropped the phone on the bed, running her hands through her short, dark hair.

Closing her eyes, she went through her mantra for calm, holding the jasper she wore on a necklace. It was just so unfair. And she knew it was taking a toll on Maia. It was getting harder and harder to persuade her to get out of bed for school in a morning. Her mood began to descend through the course of Sunday as the new school week approached.

Mac helped. He was a calming influence and someone Maia seemed to almost hero worship. What had begun as someone for Clio to talk to about the experience they had shared last year had become a genuine friendship. To the point where Mac stayed over on the sofa. Papers were scattered across the bed and she began to gather them to take her mind off the issues at Maia's school. The phone rang, and she groaned when she saw the name, throwing herself back onto the bed, debated for a moment just letting it ring, then answered.

"Dean, hello."

"Clio, sorry to disturb you on a Sunday, but just wanted to touch base with you on a couple of things before the committee meets tomorrow," said Dean Graeme Hutchison. "And call me Graeme, please."

"Ok, Graeme. What committee is this?" Clio asked.

She hoped it wasn't within the paperwork her new boss had given her last week upon informing her she'd been successful in her appointment to the head of faculty. She didn't want to start the job by forgetting something important.

"Sorry, my fault. Was in the diary for the end of the month, but I brought it forward," Hutchison said. "One thing you'll discover about me is that I'm never not working and my faculty heads end up doing the same thing."

"I suppose it goes with the salary," Clio said, dutifully. "I'm not complaining,"

She hoped that sounded earnest and enthusiastic.

"That's the stuff. Brilliant."

The conversation swiftly turned to agendas and departmental budgets for the upcoming tax year. Clio found a pen on the floor beside the bed and grabbed a piece of paper, scribbling notes in the margins. She felt like she needed the weekend to start over. It was too much. Starting a new job, supporting Maia through her rocky start at high school and moving house, too. Insanity. After Hutchison had hung up, she threw the phone aside, covering her face with a pillow, feeling like she was about to cry. She thought of Mac. His unflappable calm and icy exterior. Tried to think like him. It wasn't her. Downstairs, she heard the door open and Maia's voice. Then a male voice answering. Getting up, she went to the bay window at the front of the room and pulled the curtain aside.

A man in a baseball cap, cargo trousers and a polo-shirt stood at the door. From this angle, she could just see Maia.

"Picking up or dropping off?" she was asking the man.

He checked his phone, which was hooked to his belt. "Picking up. Two parcels. Clio Wray," he said.

"These two," Maia said, nudging one with her foot.

Clio let the curtain fall back as the man glanced up. She got an impression of a boyish face and dark eyes, a smudge of dark hair curling from under the cap. Clio felt mildly embarrassed at being caught spying. She chuckled to herself as she began to undress, ready for her shower. Maia was a good girl. She didn't need to be told how much help Clio needed. Well, she did, but she didn't complain about being on the hook for it. Well, yes she did that too, but only a little, then did what was asked of her. Not every parent could put as much trust in their adolescent kids as she had with her daughter. Clio had no doubt that Maia would remain at her post until the delivery arrived. By which time Clio would find something else for her to do. As she stepped into the hot shower, the inappropriate question Maia had asked returned to her mind. She closed her eyes, unable to resist a moment of fantasy. Mac was handsome. Slender but strong. Dominating and very male. She shook her head, opening her eyes and picked up the exfoliating glove that hung from the wall. She began to scrub herself vigorously, thinking of work, school, house moves. Anything but Callum McNeill.

CHAPTER FOUR

MAC WOKE FEELING AS THOUGH he had been punched in the stomach. He couldn't remember the dream, but the aftertaste it left behind was visceral. A weight that pushed on his chest denying him the process of getting up, showering, dressing. All the activities that would transition him into the role of police detective. A role where action was demanded and any thought not related to the job pushed aside. With a feeling of disgust at his own weakness he threw back the duvet and swung his feet to the ground. Rain. He had a pervading impression of soaking, driving rain. That was the only semi-coherent memory he could dredge from a night's sleep that felt like it hadn't properly begun before it was time to get up. It had been a late one, right enough. The press conference had been held toward the end of day one. Just in time to make the drive time news.

A young woman in her twenties found dead. A description given of her appearance, her makeup and nose piercing.

A plea to anyone with a friend missing, a daughter, or a girl-friend. Contact the police. Reid had wanted to be by his side, but Meredith Blakely had stopped him, vaulting the chain of command like only a civilian PR expert could. Kenny Reid was less than a year out of an Anti-Corruption investigation. Reid had belligerently pointed out that it was confidential and closed. Blakeley had bullishly replied that nothing leaked like a police force. Reid needed to keep a low profile. Let Mac's smouldering looks be the face of the press conference. Mac got up, going to the wardrobe. His fleece hung on one side with some polo shirts and jeans. Sweaters piled precisely and neatly on a shelving unit beneath.

On the other side were black, grey, and white shirts. Four suits beside those, black and grey. He reached for a shirt and suit, laid them on the bed. Then he picked up his phone as he headed for the shower. An email from Talvir Sidhu. Swiped and deleted. He'd seen the notification when the email arrived yesterday and had ignored it. Further down the list was a missed call from the same person. And an SMS. This was the second day of a murder investigation. He didn't have time to attend counselling sessions just because he'd almost been killed a year before. And didn't need them anyway. It was an intrusion. He forced his mind to concentrate on the case. No ID as yet so no motive. A naked girl indicated a sex attack but there were none of the usual signs on the body. Post-mortem would confirm if she had recently had intercourse.

He stepped into the shower and closed his eyes. The water hammered at him, cold enough to raise goosebumps on his skin. Rain. Hard rain. All he could remember of that dream. Being wet, soaked to his skin and cold. Rain. He turned and fought the urge to arch his back against the sudden icy deluge. He felt the need to breathe deeply. He inhaled but it was as though he had been running. He couldn't breathe deeply enough to satisfy the craving in his chest. He took in lungful's in rapid succession and felt the pulse in his throat. A finger to his neck confirmed it was racing. Breathing was coming in short, sharp gasps now. He fumbled for the door of the shower and staggered out. His movements were un-coordinated and his bare foot slipped on the floor dropping him to one knee. It slammed into the tiles painfully. One hand grabbed for the corner of the sink but his head was spinning.

Was this a heart attack? There was no pain in his left arm, no stabbing agony in his chest. He felt in the grip of the worst fear he had ever experienced. His hand slipped from the sink and slapped against the tiles. Nausea suddenly gripped him and his stomach clenched. He heaved, unable to control the urge to vomit. Again. And again. Mac sat back, muscles like water. He pushed himself to the wall and flinched at the feel of the cold tiles against his naked back. The sensation helped anchor him. He breathed in deeply through his nose, focusing on the basic action of drawing in air. In through the nose and out through the mouth. The urge was to gasp and claw for breathe. He brutally crushed it. The ache in his chest eased. He suddenly felt as though he were getting plenty of oxygen, improving more with each breath. His heart still raced. Fingers to the neck he counted his pulse and continued to breathe.

Mac knew what it was now. A panic attack. It was bloody ludicrous. His body hadn't responded this way when running from an exploding building. Or when dangling over a stairwell six floors high, a face hidden behind a surgical mask staring down at him. Or when discovering the body of his father, half his head missing from a self-inflicted shotgun blast and foam filling his mouth from the rat poison that had turned his insides to jelly.

"You need a break," he said to himself aloud.

On shaky legs, he picked himself up, turned off the shower and dried himself. Wet towels into the hamper, dry ones folded neatly in their place. He dressed quickly, forcing his mind to the case, letting the details of it fill his awareness. He put on a grey shirt, tieless with collar open. Deep, navy blue suit, almost black and shoes the same grey as the shirt. It felt like armour. Phone into his jacket pocket, hand lingering for a moment over the top drawer of his bedside table. There was a pack of cigarettes in there with three remaining. Had been since October. Mac turned away and left the room, leaving the drawer unopened. It was half six when he left the flat and drove the Audi out of the building's underground parking garage. It was still dark and the city was quiet. Leith Walk cut a straight path through the middle of Edinburgh and the City Centre station of Edinburgh's South East Division was located off Brunswick Street. A modern building resembling a collection of boxes piled together. White with timber fronting here and there and blank, staring one-way windows.

Around it were old blocks of flats with flat roofs and tan pebble-dash around tiny windows. A forty-year-old social housing estate of similar flats faced the modern architecture of the police building, flanked by offices and a pyramid shaped apartment block of timber-faced walls and gated parking. There was fresh graffiti over the Police Scotland sign that stood amid the planted landscaping in front of the building. It was cleaned regularly and some ned went and put it back before long in a constant game of cat and mouse with the polis. He parked and went into the building through a rear entrance, swiping his ID at outer and inner doors. His office was on the fifth floor, down the corridor from Reid's. His team had a cluster of desks. As he strode past a man in overalls pushing a hoover he saw that Melissa was already in. In the pods across from his team DCI Hafsa Akhtar was talking to a DS in her own team. Akhtar wore a long coat over her trouser suit. Her dark hair was pinned up and she had a rucksack over one shoulder.

She looked up as Mac walked up the central aisle of the open plan office. Her face was long, giving her a naturally mournful expression. But her eyes were sharp, black stones that missed nothing. She was skinny with sucked in cheeks. It was appropriate. She was hungry and ambitious.

"DCI McNeill," she greeted.

"Hafsa. Good morning," Mac replied. "Mornin' Mel," he called to DI Barland.

"Morning, guv. Good night?" Melissa replied.

She was putting up boards around two sides of the pods occupied by Mac's team. There was a pile of printed crime scene pictures waiting to be tacked up. Their Jane Doe already had pride of place at the top and middle of the central board.

"Late one. Processing all the data coming through from SOCO. Anything from the search teams yet?"

He walked past Akhtar and began leafing through the pictures. She had turned back to her DS, but Mac could almost feel the woman's ears straining in his direction.

"Not yet. Kai has identified a number of CCTV sources outside of the usual traffic cameras, including a shop at the foot of the hill, almost a direct straight line up to the body, if you don't mind climbing through the bushes in between. He's been contacting owners and operators of the private CCTV systems, as you know. Nothing so far. Lots of footprints left, pictures have been taken of all within a radius of two hundred metres of the body and the possible routes someone could have taken, carrying a dead body. We'll get 3D mapping on the computer which will give us some ideas of the size and weight of the killer."

"Or the accomplice who moved the body for our killer. Let's not make assumptions," Mac said.

"Right," Melissa replied, easily.

"Well, let's get this set up. I've asked Nari to go straight to the scene and canvas witnesses so we won't be seeing much of her today. Kai will take the IT as per, but he's got orders to liaise with Nari if he gets a free moment. That leaves us holding the fort here."

He helped Melissa put up the pictures of the crime scene as the room around them filled up. Akhtar's team consisted of the same number as Mac's. A constable, sergeant, and inspector. Melissa chatted with them as they arrived, and Mac acknowledged each individual with a curt nod. His eyes swept over the board, trying to take in everything at once, to absorb the images without putting conscious thought onto any one in particular. To take it in as it existed as a whole. His phone chimed at the same moment Melissa's laptop pinged. Then Stringer was calling him.

"Derek, what have you got for me?" Mac said, pulling

Kai's seat out from the desk and sitting down. He put the phone on the desk and switched it to speaker. Melissa pulled a chair up next to him, notepad and pencil in hand.

"Mac, you should have the report through. I pulled it together last night."

"I saw it ping. Care to précis it for me?"

"No evidence of sexual assault or recent intercourse," Stringer launched straight in, wasting no time. "She was stripped post-mortem, I would say. No evidence of contusions or abrasions from clothes being forcibly removed. I found fibres in a number of the wounds. Cotton and synthetic fabrics. All conducive with the hypothesis that she was stabbed through her clothes which were removed after death. Including the killing wound which means it was either a very lucky blow or intentionally and knowledgeably precise. Not easy to hit the heart in one stroke through garments. Even if she was wearing tight clothes it would still disguise the exact point the blade needed to enter the body."

"And it was a small blade?"

"Very small. Making the marksmanship of the blow even more pronounced."

Mac nodded, staring into space but seeing the crime. In his mind's eye it was happening in a side-street, somewhere closer to the city centre but not too far from the hill. A young girl walking home from a night out. Not much money for a taxi, so she walks. Familiar with the streets and confident. She's attacked by a man who stabs her directly in the heart with a small sharp blade. Then rapidly stabbed thirty odd times more. All before she can react to fight back.

"We found a number of foreign DNA sources. Canine,

which would be the dog that found her and thought she was a chew toy. Animal sources from lying on the ground and in shrubbery, as expected. But also a very good human source."

"Semen?" Mac asked, his mind returning to the theory of a sex attack.

If the assailant was sufficiently frightening, it was entirely possible for a sexual assault to occur without a struggle producing defensive wounds.

"No. A hair complete with a follicle. Stroke of luck if we can find the owner."

CHAPTER FIVE

ZOE PHILLIPS WAS THE NAME of the victim. A scared nineteen-year-old had reported one of her housemates missing and the officer who'd taken the call had informed Mac directly. Zoe had been for a night out in town on Friday and hadn't returned home. Her housemates had all assumed she'd stayed at her boyfriend's. Until he contacted them on Sunday afternoon to ask if they'd seen her. They'd provided pictures from social media and Mac had recognised Zoe immediately. A cherubic face in a girl favouring Goth styling but unable to quite suppress her natural prettiness. She was English, from just outside Worcester. Her parents had been contacted and were travelling up to make a positive ID of the body. It was a necessary formality. Mac knew who the girl in the morgue was. She even had a nose stud in the pictures he'd seen. Kai and Nari arrived late afternoon after Mac had recalled them to the office for a briefing. His office was partitioned from the rest of the SCU floor, next to DCI Akhtar's. Mac had floor to ceiling windows to his left as he sat at his desk, facing the door. A benefit of a long history with the boss.

He was scrolling through Zoe's social media, looking for any insights he could find into her life, when there was a sharp rap at the door. It opened while Mac was still drawing breath to speak and Detective Chief Superintendent Kenny Reid looked in. He wore a suit that was a size too big to disguise the spreading stomach. Same with the shirt collar, because Reid always wore a tie but hated to feel choked by a collar. His hair was greyer than it had been but his blue eyes were as spiked as ever.

"We're ready for the briefing, Mac. Any time you like."

Mac wasn't aware Reid had planned to attend any of his team briefings, but he just nodded, stood, and walked around his desk towards the door. Reid went ahead and grabbed a seat from one of Akhtar's desks and rolled it over to Mac's area. Kai and Nari had just arrived. Melissa glanced at Mac for a second and the question in her eyes was clear. Mac gave an almost imperceptible shrug in response and stood in front of the boards set up with the crime scene pictures.

"Zoe Phillips. Twenty years old. Micro-biology student at Edinburgh University. Stabbed to death between two and three am on Sunday morning. Location unknown. Body dumped on the slopes of Arthur's Seat. Naked but with no sign of sexual assault. Tox screen came back clean for everything except alcohol," he said, speaking of the case in terms of data points, separating the person from the evidence.

It was done through long years of practice. Shutting down emotion and divorcing the horror from the reporting of cold facts. Melissa was looking at the pictures of Zoe, her compassion written strongly across her face. Kai looked impassive and Nari was typing, dividing her attention between Mac and her laptop.

"She'd been on a night out and was reported missing by her housemate Morgan Daniels. They had digs at 32 Priestfield Road in the St Leonard's area of the city."

"St Leonard's is right next to Arthur's Seat," Kai pointed out.

"Right. Zoe's house looks out over Prestonfield Golf Course and Duddingston Loch, all on the south side of the hill."

"Significance?" Reid interrupted.

"Only that she might have been taken close to home," Mac replied immediately.

Reid grunted and nodded, folding his hands across his stomach, and gazed at the floor. Head down but listening to every word. Every nuance.

"Morgan last saw her getting on a bus on Princes Street, heading for Dalkeith Road. We've got the number of the bus and we know what stops it made, right, Melissa?"

"Yes, guv. Onboard CCTV shows her getting off at Kilmaurs Terrace, which is about five hundred yards from her house."

"Me and Kai can start canvassing the houses between the bus stop and her house. See if anyone saw her," Nari said.

"No, we've got the overtime paid for. I want my money's worth," Reid put in, looking up. "Let the grunts do the legwork. We'll reassign some of the search teams we've got on Arthur's Seat to go door to door for us. Nari, liaise with Inspector Brandon, who's been kind enough to loan us his uniforms."

"Right, sir," Nari replied, glancing uncertainly at Mac.

"Anything else, sir?" Mac asked, plastering a rictus smile on his face.

He was beginning to get annoyed at Reid's interruptions. He'd never got operationally involved in any other case and gave Mac a lot more leeway than any of his other subordinates. Mac had no idea what the hell this interference was all about. Reid smiled back innocently.

"Not at the moment. Carry on, Inspector."

"Did she have a boyfriend? Or girlfriend? Friends? Someone we should be speaking to?" Nari asked.

"A boyfriend. Looking at her social media, she had friends. We'll need DNA from all of them but particularly him. DNA was found on her which wasn't hers. Or any of the SOCO team, obviously," Mac said.

"He sort of raised the alarm," Melissa pointed out. "The boyfriend. By asking her housemates if they'd seen her. But he didn't phone the hotline or 999 after the public appeal. It was her housemate that did that."

"So, why wouldn't her boyfriend be the first one on the phone to us?" Mac said.

"Maybe he's got something to hide," Kai put in. "Who is he?"

"His name is Kyle Culshaw and we have his address, digs in Tollcross. He's also a student on the same course as Zoe," Melissa said, reading from the notes she had been compiling while waiting for Nari and Kai to return. "And he's got form. Public order offenses mostly. All involving drink."

"So, when he's had a few, our Kyle has a temper?" Kai said, looking around the room.

"Let's not jump to conclusions," Mac said. "Although he's obviously a person of interest. If his DNA matches the sample we have from Zoe's body, then it really could be that obvious. But in my experience it's never that easy."

"Not every killer is a criminal mastermind," Reid rumbled. "Or a serial psychopath."

"Doesn't mean it isn't the case here," Mac found himself arguing. "Right now, we need to keep an open mind."

His eyes were drawn to the straight lines that had been carved into Zoe's face. Vivid colour and printed on glossy paper in sickening high definition so that no detail could escape. She looked so pale and young. The wounds could almost have been superimposed on her image by photographic trickery. The shock hit Mac like a sledge hammer. She reminded him of Iona. Same short dark hair. Same round, innocent face. Same tortured, sadistic death. He stared at the face pinned up on the walls. Eyes open and staring, glassy behind the corneal clouding. Lips blue but still full. About to quirk into a smile.

Iona's bedroom was in the flat roofed extension built when William and Theresa McNeill found out they were expecting their third child. Back when William Struan McNeill was a capable man who thought nothing of building an extension to his house with his own two hands. Back when he could call on the help of the Campbell's next door to assist with the roofing. Before Theresa had died and Connor ran away to sea. Before William ran away to the bottom of a bottle.

Callum sits on the windowsill of the room he had once shared with Connor and watches his sister open the window of her room and climb out. She drops soundlessly the four or five feet from the window ledge to the grass beneath, wearing jeans, a leather jacket that had belonged to Connor and a denim back pack. It's raining. The collar of the jacket is turned up.

Iona is climbing out of the window because William is in the front room getting drunk. But he won't pass out for a few hours and she wants to go out to the pub in town with her friends. But she's grounded. Callum watches and sees her look up to her big brother. The rain is plastering her dark hair around her full cheeks and rosebud mouth. She looks like their mother. Iona stands there a moment, waiting. She's wondering if he's going to tell their father. But Callum just smiles and gestures with his chin towards the road and Portree. Iona grins and blows him a kiss. She runs through the rain, around the blocky extension and over the rough ground towards the Portree road. It's the last time Callum ever sees his sister.

"Nari, go talk to the friends and housemates. Try and piece together Zoe's last movements from the people who saw her. Kai, same job, but from the digital side. Melissa, go track down our friend Kyle Culshaw…" Reid was standing and talking briskly, issuing orders to the team.

Mac shook himself, realising that he had been standing still, zoned out, for several seconds, staring at the picture of Zoe Phillips. Staring at her and remembering Iona.

"No!" he said now. "I'll track down Kyle Culshaw and interview him. Melissa, I want you to co-ordinate a list of everyone who might have come into contact with Zoe Phillips so we can start eliminating DNA sources. And I need the sample of human DNA found on Zoe run through the databases for a match."

"Well, you've all got your orders. Snap to it," Reid said, clapping his hands. "Mac, a word."

He preceded Mac into the office. Mac followed, running fingers through his dark hair, and closing the door behind him.

"What the hell...sir. I don't mind you sitting in on a briefing but..."

"Well, I'm helluva glad you don't mind me sitting in on a briefing in my own bloody department, son," Reid bit back.

He pointed at the chair behind Mac's desk. "Sit down before you fall down."

Mac refused, stepping closer to Reid as though squaring off. Both men knew it would never go so far, but neither was willing to be the first to back down, rank or not. Mac couldn't back down when his authority was being undermined. Reid would never back down to a subordinate.

"Why are you giving orders to my team above my head? You're undermining me," Mac said, quietly.

"Because you're losing it, son. You're away to Lala land in front of everyone," Reid hissed, stepping close. "You look strung out. You're daydreaming in the middle of a briefing. What the hell's going on, son?"

There was concern on Reid's face, as well as anger at being challenged. It made Mac look away, leaning back against the desk. Reid ran a hand over his chin and looked around, then pulled a chair over, and flopped down. Confrontation over. Step down.

"Why am I getting some civvie headshrinker pestering me over your failure to attend counseling? Mandatory counselling."

Reid looked at him with eyes that could chip ice, mouth hanging open belligerently.

"Sidhu?" Mac said in disbelief.

"Oh, is that his name? Is there more than one? Yes, of course him!" Reid barked. "Look, even I understand that these days you don't just go to the nearest coppers pub and get hammered every time you almost die. These days you, I don't know, talk about your...thoughts and...feelings and such. I don't know I've never done it myself. I play golf, right? But I'm not at the sharp end either. You are and the rules say you get counselling to deal with trauma. So just bloody do it, ok?"

His tone got more aggressive and hectoring as he went on. Mac could see that it wasn't a conversation he was comfortable having. His response was to bully. Mac sighed.

"Can't we just make this headshrinker go away?" he said. "You didn't send me for counselling when I almost took a bullet from a Hance Allen contract or when Strack..."

Mac stopped himself just in time. He glanced at the door and then looked at Reid for a long time. They both knew what he had just stopped himself from saying. A night years before when DCI Strachan had felt the Anti-Corruption noose closing around his neck. Mac had chased Strack down at the Imperial Dock. Cornered him. Only Mac had walked out.

"The fact you almost said what you just did tells me how strung out you are, Mac. Go talk to the doctor. He's a nice man. Very approachable. English, but let's not hold that against him, eh?"

Mac pushed his hands into his trouser pockets. Took in a deep breath through his nose and let it out through his mouth. He had faded out of reality a minute ago. Lost himself in a memory brought on by a picture. And earlier had suffered a full-blown panic attack. Over what? What the hell was going on?

"Is that an order, sir?"

"No. Quid pro quo is all. Go to counselling and I won't go to DCI Akhtar to discuss your respective caseloads," Reid said with a broad grin.

CHAPTER SIX

KYLE CULSHAW LIVED with three other boys on the second floor of a tenement house above a health food shop just off Tollcross. Mac walked through a tiled close and up broad, stone steps so old they were worn in the middle. A narrow, wrought-iron railing followed him along with the echoes of his footsteps. At the second landing, he was more out of breath than he wanted to be and he stopped for a moment. A fixed gear bike with a cooler bag bearing the logo of a fast food delivery service hung from the handlebars. There was a smell of weed from somewhere. There were two doors, but no numbers. He went to the nearest and knocked. No answer. He went to the second and thumped with the side of his fist. A chain rattled and no fewer than two locks clicked open. Then a male voice said.

"Yeah?"

Mac held up his warrant card to the spyhole. "You're supposed to ask for ID before unlocking the door, son," he said.

"Oh, yeah, right," came the reply as the handle turned and the door opened.

Mac smelled weed more strongly coming from inside. An electric fan started up. A door slammed and Mac heard the sound of a stiff sash window being forced up. In the door was a young man with a goatee beard and a ponytail pinned up on top of his head like a samurai. He had glasses and looked skinny enough to snap in two if Mac raised his voice.

"DCI McNeill, Police Scotland Serious Crimes Unit. I'm looking for Kyle Culshaw," Mac said.

"He's not here," the young man said.

"Can I come in?"

"Um, I don't know. Can you? I mean. I'd rather you..."

Mac sighed and stepped into the doorway, forcing the young man to step back without actually touching him. A narrow hallway ran to the left and right. It ended at one end in a kitchen and at the other at a door. Straight ahead was a half-closed door with cold daylight behind it. From the direction the door faced, Mac surmised this was the front room, looking out over Melville Drive, the street the building was on. He could hear traffic through the open window in there.

"Christ sake, Mark! You're not supposed to let the polis in without a search warrant," a tall, dark-haired man said, stepping out of the kitchen and closing the door behind him.

"I'm not here for any one of you boys," Mac said. "Just need to talk to Kyle Culshaw. He lives here, yes?"

"Aye," said the dark-haired man. "He does, but he's no in."

He had a swagger in his voice and his walk. Mac had done his homework, though.

"You're, Neil Meadows, second year undergrad studying

art history and this is Finlay Marsh, medicine. And the third musketeer is Kyle. He's not in any trouble but if you two keep giving me the run around he soon will be. Along with the two of you. I don't care how much weed you smoke or how much you've got in here. But I think you know that. Because you've already heard what happened to Kyle's girlfriend, Zoe."

They were visibly wilting. Meadows sagged against the wall, arms wrapping around himself. Marsh backed into the living room and almost fell over the arm of a battered sofa, licking his lips and looking as though he were about to faint. God help the country if these two were the future. Mac took the initiative and marched into the living room, throwing the door wide open. A hastily cleaned ashtray sat on a vintage coffee table. A stereo system was lashed through a daisy chain of cables to multiple speakers, including a good-looking subwoofer system. Mac saw a stack of vinyl on a shelf and perused the titles. His lip curled, eighties techno and house music. Not his scene. The air was still grey with the smoke the fan and open window hadn't begun to shift.

"If my suit ends up stinking of weed, I'm going to skelp the pair of you," Mac muttered, moving towards the window. "Where is he?"

"We don't know."

Mac was surprised that it was Marsh who summoned the courage to speak. He had sat down on the sofa and produced a tobacco tin. He began rolling with shaking hands.

"He and Zoe had the mother of all fights earlier in the week. She stormed out. He threw her clothes out of the window after her. He was drunk," Marsh said.

"So was she," Meadows said, coming into the room and leaning against the wall. "She's not a saint."

"Shut up," Marsh muttered.

"Kyle wanted to make up," Meadows said, ignoring his flat mate. "He was sorry, but he couldn't find her. She wasn't picking up for him. He spoke to one of her friends and she said Zoe hadn't been home all weekend. Kyle got scared something had happened to her."

"Couldn't find her? So he went out looking for her," Mac said, reading between the lines.

Marsh laughed. "Yeah. They were still arguing on messenger. He couldn't deal with it."

"He wanted her back. He was trying to make up," Meadows said.

"Or just tell her what he thought of her face to face..." Marsh retorted.

Then he stopped, eyes darting to the policeman who had quietly taken a notebook out of his pocket and was writing. His mouth snapped shut and Mac could almost see him replaying the conversation in his head, trying to figure out how much trouble he'd dropped his flat mate in.

"What are you writing?" Marsh said in a small voice.

"Everything," Mac replied. "Show me Kyle's room."

Meadows shook his head, kicked the sofa, and clearly meant it for Marsh. Then he opened the living room door and jerked his head. "Come on then, let's get this over with."

"I'll need swabs from both of you if you knew Zoe," Mac said, reaching into his jacket pocket and taking out two zip-lock plastic bags. "To eliminate you from our enquiries. Don't worry, we won't be running a drugs test."

Meadows swore under his breath as he walked down the hall towards the kitchen. Before reaching the kitchen, there was a set of steep wooden stairs. He plodded up and opened the door beyond. Mac was at the foot of the stairs and saw Meadows freeze. He swore again, opening the door wider and looking around.

"Jesus. When did he do this?" he whispered.

"Get back," Mac commanded, vaulting the stairs and taking his arm at the elbow, steering him from the door.

Meadows stumbled down the steps and backed away. Mac took out latex gloves and his phone, switching on the torch. The room beyond was blacked out by thick curtains. There were pictures everywhere. A4 printouts of the same person. Zoe Phillips. They covered the walls, the ceiling, the floor. All had been mutilated in some way. Shredded and torn. The light from the phone played over a carpet of scrunched paper. There was a smattering of dark liquid over some of it. It showed up red in the white light of the torch and it had been smeared and daubed over the pictures of Zoe. Mac took out another zip-lock bag and leaned forward, crouching and stretching to reach the blood. Using the bag like a glove, he picked up the nearest bloodied paper he could reach and then reversed the bag to secure it inside.

He sealed the bag and carefully slipped it into his pocket before levering himself back over the threshold. He turned the phone over and called Melissa.

"Mel, I've got something at Culshaw's place. 11 Melville Drive. I need a forensic team..."

As he spoke, he was closing the door behind him and walking back down the stairs and hallway, intending to tell the two students to stay away from the room. In fact, they would need to leave while the place was searched by a SOCO team. He passed the front door just as it opened, bumping his shoulder. Mac looked up. A young man had walked in. He had dreads hanging to his shoulders and the build of a rugby player. His eyes were wide and there were circles under his eyes, like he hadn't slept for days. He had a bulky rucksack on his back.

"Kyle!" Meadows shouted from the kitchen.

Kyle Culshaw swung his rucksack at Mac, catching him off balance and sending him thudding into the wall. Then he was away, taking the stairs three at a time. Mac pushed himself away from the wall in pursuit. Culshaw was already on the first floor landing and Mac acting instinctively. He grabbed the wrought-iron railing with both hands and swung himself over it to the next flight below. He landed on his heels on the edge of a step and pitched himself forward, catching himself half falling and half running. He hit the wall at the first landing, pushed off and attacked the final flight of stairs. Kyle was wrenching at the heavy front door, panicking, and failing to realise it had latched. Mac was halfway down the last flight when he cottoned on and managed to get the door open.

Mac had his phone in his hand and could hear Melissa shouting, no doubt demanding to know if he was OK. He ran through the door and saw Culshaw racing out into traffic, rucksack clutched over one shoulder. He chased, dodged around a taxi, then a bus going in the opposite direction. Culshaw shrugged out of the rucksack and shoved it back against Mac's chest, who was gaining on him. Mac slammed into a lamppost, his head bouncing off solid metal. He threw the bag aside and growled, continuing the chase with teeth bared. People were standing stock still in the street, staring. Drivers rubber necked and Mac caught glimpses of people in the windows of fast food takeaways and shops. His attention was focused on the man running from him towards the open, green expanse of the Meadows. He was much younger and fitter, but he was in a state of terror. Mac had one window of time to chase him down before Culshaw figured out he had Mac's measure and could outrun him if he just got himself under control. Lungs burning, Mac forced himself to a sprint. Culshaw made the mistake of looking back over his shoulder as he reached the Meadows and tripped over a protruding tree root.

He fell sprawling onto the grass, his legs tangled with Mac's and they ended up rolling over each other. Culshaw came up on top, but with Mac's hands wrapped around a handful of dreads.

"I'm a copper, you moron! You're under arrest!"

CHAPTER SEVEN

Mac watched Kyle Culshaw through the two-way mirror. Culshaw sat staring straight ahead, fingers drumming on the table top. His feet moved constantly beneath the plastic chair he sat in. Tapping. A duty solicitor sat next to him and had been talking to him for the last ten minutes. Now the woman was quiet, running through her notes. She cast glances from her client to the two-way mirror. Experienced enough to know there would be coppers watching.

"Looks bang to rights to me, eh?" Kai said from somewhere in the dark behind Mac.

"Looks traumatised," Melissa said.

"Realising what he's done," Kai suggested.

"Or wondering how guilty he's made himself look," Mac put in softly.

The evidence was enough to cross the evidential threshold. Testimony from his housemates that he had a volatile relationship with Zoe Phillips. Evidence found in Kyle's room of an obsessive nature and extreme anger. Lack of an alibi. Hopefully. But Mac wasn't about to dive in head first and eyes closed. Circumstantial evidence did not mean he did it. Mac wanted a confession, nice and neat. Case closed and justice served for Zoe. At least as much of it as he could deliver. What the KC's and the courts made of it was beyond his control.

"Sometimes you look guilty because you are," Kai said.

"And sometimes you're just in the wrong place at the wrong time," Melissa replied, reasonably.

Nari was sitting next to Kai, quiet. Mac knew that she was watching Kyle, making notes. He'd seen her observing the boy as he'd walked in.

"Any insights, Nari?" he asked, glancing over his shoulder.

"Nervous but that could be ADHD just as easily. Looks withdrawn. His solicitor gave up trying to reach him a few minutes ago; she's just waiting out the clock now. He's somewhere else and doesn't like it."

Mac nodded, tapping his lips with a forefinger. His own assessment was the same. On the surface he was guilty as hell and acting it. Underneath? Who knew. But how to play it. Take Melissa in with him, mother figure, put Kyle at his ease? Unless he had a reason to dislike mother figures. Kai? That would be a full on attack, bad cop bad cop. Nari? Sharp but lacking Melissa's experience. Liable to speak at the wrong time out of sheer over enthusiasm. On the other hand she was young and pretty. And Kyle was hetero. Or at least bi. He liked girls anyway. Old school approach to take in a pretty officer but it worked nine times out of ten.

"Nari, you want to come in with me?" Mac asked.

"Yes, guv," Nari replied, almost stepping on Mac's words.

He looked back to Kyle, hearing her get up and gather her things. Mac nodded decisively. They'd waited long enough. He headed for the door, not needing to tell either Melissa or Kai to monitor the interview and make notes. They would both be watching, taking advantage of the opportunity to observe their subject while remaining unobserved themselves. The interview rooms at Brunswick Street were located in a newly refurbished basement level. The walls of the corridor were sound proofed as were all the interview rooms. There were five of them, each with an adjoining observation room and kitted out with mics and cameras. The corridor had an industrial aesthetic, ceiling low and with steel girders on display below the gray foam of acoustic dampening tiles. The floor was carpet and the whole place smelled of cheap disinfectant and air fresheners. The only light was artificial. He didn't hesitate at the door to interview room three, the next one along from obs room three.

With a swipe of the ID card on a lanyard around his neck he unlocked the door and entered the room. A uniform officer had been standing stoically in the corner.

"Get yourself a coffee, Nick," Mac said, remembering the officer's name at the last moment.

He took a seat without introducing himself. Nari sat next to him carrying a thick binder. Mac was staring at Kyle who stared back. There was no defiance in his stare. This wasn't a militant black youth sick of being the victim of random stop and search. His stare was bovine. Uninterested and without hope. A guilty man resigned to being caught or an innocent one scared out of his wits?

"DCI Callum McNeill and DS Nari Yun, Serious Crimes

Unit," Nari had pressed record on a manual tape deck built into the table which was the room's only furniture with the exception of the four plastic chairs. "Also present are..."

"Natalie McMichael, solicitor."

"Kyle Culshaw."

"Interview commences at eleven fifty three..." Nari checked and recited the date.

"Tell us about Zoe Phillips, Kyle," Mac said as soon as Nari had finished speaking.

On cue, Nari opened the binder, flipped through several pages until she reached a photograph of Zoe provided by one of her housemates. The next page, concealed for now, showed how Zoe had ended up.

"Why?" Kyle replied.

"Because she's dead," Mac said brutally.

He'd not looked away from Kyle once, nor had Kyle himself averted his gaze from Mac. Now he did. He looked at his hands on the table top. Mac had already noted the bitten nails and the dried blood. It had been checked. It was his own. Biting and scratching from anxiety. Mac let the silence weigh on his subject. The room had a high ceiling and a number of bright, white lights set into it. The walls were dark as was the floor. All designed to be oppressive but not overtly so. Not so it could be called psychological torture. Just enough that anyone sitting in the room under pressure wouldn't feel it easy to relax. Kyle's feet tapped furiously. He pressed down on the tabletop as though trying to force himself to keep his hands still.

"Yeah, I know."

"How?" Nari asked.

"One of her friends told me. Said the police had been round going through her things."

"Doesn't mean she's dead though. Just missing," Nari persisted.

"That's quite a conclusion to jump to," Mac put in, letting Kyle hear the questions come from two different voices, letting the pressure pile up.

"You came to my house and chased me. What was I supposed to think?" Kyle responded, some energy in his voice.

He met Mac's eyes and then looked away.

"Where were you between the hours of two and three this morning?" Mac asked.

Kyle shrugged.

"Do you understand what's happening here, Kyle?" Mac said, raising his voice. "This is a murder investigation and the victim was your girlfriend. Whose blood soaked pictures we found in your bedroom today. So, how about you drop the attitude and answer the question."

"My client does not know where he was after approximately twelve o'clock last night. The last location he remembers was a club called Rock, near Grassmarket," McMichael said.

"And after that?" Nari asked.

"I don't know. I was wasted," Kyle replied antagonistically.

"See, I don't get your attitude, Kyle," Mac came back aggressively, wanting to push his subject. "It's almost like you've given up in advance and that makes me think we've got the right man. You don't seem scared to be facing a murder charge."

"Inspector, as you well know everyone's reaction under stress is different. It is not a signifier of guilt," McMichael said sharply.

"In my experience there are a range of responses to stress and what I'm seeing does signify guilt. So, I'll proceed on that basis. The Procurator Fiscal is frothing at the mouth to see this case prosecuted. She wants your client strung up," Mac stabbed at the table with his finger. This was the moment for Nari to come in with the good cop, softly softly approach. But she hesitated. Mac glanced at her and she leaned in.

"Kyle. Why don't you tell us how you felt about Zoe? It looked like there was some conflict there. Help me understand it."

Her tone was conciliatory and she smiled, putting her hand halfway across the table towards him. Half reaching out to hold his hand and half just gesturing to make a point. Mac saw Kyle shift in his seat, the foot tapping stopped. His eyes flicked up and down Nari. Her smile didn't slip. Mac sat back, folding his arms, and waited.

"We were on and off. Usually her. She cheated on me and I took her back. Then she would make an argument out of nothing. Just an excuse to dump me. Then kick off when I got off with someone else. She messed with me head."

"Were you together recently or broken up?" Nari asked.

She slid the picture of Zoe towards Kyle as though she wanted him to take it. He responded by touching it, pulling it closer. Mac saw a glint of wetness in his eye, blinked away rapidly. Remorse? Grief?

"Broken up but she'd been getting in my face online."

"So you were angry with her." Mac said.

"I didn't say that."

"We have your messages. We can read," Mac said. "You sounded angry."

Kyle looked to the solicitor who nodded. No point trying to hide an emotion he had spelled out clearly in writing.

"Yeah, I was angry. But I didn't kill her, right!"

Suddenly, Kyle went from docile to eyes wide, staring, and angry.

"We haven't asked you if you did. Just where you were and how you felt about her," Mac replied.

Kyle looked up, put a hand over his eyes, rubbing with thumb and forefinger, then put both hands back on the table, fingers drumming again.

"I don't know where I went and I've told you how I felt about her."

"Why did you cut yourself? Why do that?" Mac asked, relinquishing the bad cop role for a moment.

The blood on the pictures found in Kyle's room had been sent to the lab to be matched against Zoe's blood type. They didn't know that it was Kyle's but it was worth a punt.

"I was upset, I guess," Kyle said the sudden flash of anger evaporating. "She'd dumped me again just when I thought we were actually going to be happy. No warning. Just text me and told me it was over."

"What made you want to have it out with her?" Nari asked.

"Who said he wanted to have it out with her?" McMichael queried.

"His housemates," Mac replied.

"Hearsay and opinion, which could be factually incorrect," she responded.

"Did you go out looking for her last night? To have it out with her or otherwise," Nari amended her question.

"No. I just went out to get off my face," Kyle responded.

There was a tap at the door. Mac looked back over his shoulder as Melissa came in. She walked to him and bent low to whisper in his ear.

"DNA results have come back. You need to see them."

"Interview suspended," Mac said, glancing at a clock on the wall and giving the time stamp.

He stood and followed Melissa from the room. When Nari started to rise also he stopped her with a brief gesture, keeping it from the solicitor and her client by turning his body. He looked from her to the table and she settled herself, as though she had simply been making herself more comfortable. Outside, Melissa turned to him and produced a printed page from a folder under her arm.

"The DNA found on Zoe's body is not from Kyle Culshaw. But we've matched it to someone else. An ex-con who's just finished a five-year stretch for aggravated assault and burglary. Ashleigh Fenton."

CHAPTER EIGHT

CLIO PUSHED AT THE MAIN ENTRANCE doors to Cramond Secondary School. They didn't budge. The doors were glass with chrome handles. The building was blocky, a pile of plastic fronted squares coloured in a range of pleasant shades. Green, yellow, orange. Painted footsteps marked a path into reception, presumably for the youngest kids. Clio noticed Audis and Mercs in the car park. She backed away from the door wondering about the salaries of the teachers here. Then she saw an intercom next to the door and pressed a button. After exchanging a few words with a receptionist she was allowed inside to take a seat opposite the school's office. It was Tuesday; Maia had been withdrawn the night before, claiming to be tired and not saying much. Today, Clio got a call from the school. From Michael Gaines. Asking her to come in and claiming there had been an...incident was the word he had used. She would be taking Maia home with her.

She'd waited ten minutes when a man approached the

glass doors separating the reception area from the rest of the school building. Beyond was a high-ceilinged room they called The Street. It was bright, airy, and white with pastel coloured furniture dotted about and the walls decorated with various arts and craft works made by the pupils. Michael Gaines was middle-aged with short-cropped graying hair. An earring stud glittered in one ear and he wore an open-necked shirt, suit trousers and shiny shoes. He held a thick folder in one hand and a phone in the other, a distracted look on his face.

"Mrs. Wray?" he asked.

Clio decided not to correct him. "Yes, you called about Maia. What's happened?"

"This way, Mrs. Wray," Gaines said, stepping aside and holding the door for her.

She entered, and he led her along The Street and through a convoluted route of stairs and corridors. Clio felt on edge already and it only increased the further they went.

"Could you just tell me what happened?" she asked after a minute of walking, in which the only conversation was banal small talk.

"I'd rather discuss it in front of Maia and in private. Walls have ears, eh?" Gaines said.

Clio smiled thinly, gritting her teeth behind her lips. Eventually, Gaines opened a door with his name on it and ushered Clio into a small office with a large pot plant in one corner, a desk, and Maia. She sat with her arms folded and hands tucked away under her arms. She glanced up at Clio as she entered, then her eyes danced away again. There had been a grimace on her face. She hung her head so that her hair hung like a curtain hiding her features. But Clio had caught sight of something that made her dart forward. Sitting in the empty chair next to Maia she reached over and brushed the hair away. Maia pulled back but Clio was having none of it. She gently held her daughter's shoulder and pushed back the obscuring hair to reveal a bruise on her cheek.

"What the hell?" Clio demanded, looking at Gaines. "You could have told me she'd been hurt!"

"Just a bruise, the other girl came off far worse, I can assure you." Gaines said with a thin smile of his own.

"I beg your pardon?" Clio demanded. "That's not the kind of response I expect from a head teacher of the school when my child has clearly been attacked!"

"Mum..." Maia protested, drawing the word out.

Clio glanced at her and saw through the sullen teenage bravado. Maia was fighting to hold back tears. Clio knew that any overt maternal sympathy now might break her daughter's defenses completely. She would not do that to her. Maia didn't need to be humiliated in front of this teacher.

"Please, tell me exactly what happened, Mr. Gaines," Clio said.

"Maia struck another girl. A girl in the year above. As far as I can tell, it was unprovoked and I'm afraid we have to take a zero tolerance approach to bullying."

"I'm not the bully! She is!" Maia cried.

"Did she hit you or physically threaten you in any way?" Gaines said, sitting back and folding his hands across his stomach.

"No," Maia replied, her voice dropping to a whisper.

"Then it was unprovoked."

"Just because you didn't witness the provocation doesn't mean it wasn't there!" Clio shot back.

She was trying to keep her cool, but it was difficult. This man infuriated her. This wasn't the first school visit that Clio had been forced to make and each time it seemed like Maia was getting the blame for things that weren't her fault.

"Aren't you supposed to be educational professionals, all of you? Aren't you trained to understand the psychology and behaviour of the children you are responsible for?" Clio demanded. "Why is it that every time I'm called out here it is to respond to so-called bad behaviour which I can see has another explanation? You just don't seem willing to look for it."

Gaines actually sighed. He opened the folder he had been carrying. "Your daughter has been disrespectful and disruptive in class. Has skipped lessons, and has now attacked another pupil..."

"And older pupil. What does that tell you?"

Gaines spread his hands. "What should it tell me, Mrs. Wray?"

"That is not my name," Clio said through gritted teeth. "I am divorced."

"What should it tell me, Ms. Wray?" Gaines said in an apathetic tone that made Clio want to scream.

"That you are not looking for explanations, just bad behaviour." Clio said. "Have you bothered to speak to Maia about what's at the root of her behaviour in class? I have."

"Would you care to share what she has told you with us?" Gaines said.

Clio looked at Maia, who was hanging her head again. She opened her mouth to speak but could not find the words.

This was further trauma to Maia. And for what? To satisfy a teacher who talked only in terms of black and white, of good and bad behaviour? A teacher who immediately resorted to sending out of class children who were, in his words, disruptive. Without any attempt to understand why or change his approach to give them everyone best outcome. Clio had read a lot since Maia had started struggling. It was her instinct as an academic, to learn and to understand.

"We have no choice but to suspend Maia for the rest of the week," Gaines said. "And we will require a pupil-parent behavioral contract before she can be readmitted. Needless to say, it will be a promise by Maia to adhere to the behaviours required by this school or..."

He spread his hands.

"Will it also commit the school to try to understand why my daughter has been experiencing such difficulty?" Clio asked, sharply.

"We have to cater to the majority, Mrs....Ms. Wray," Gaines said smugly.

It came across to Clio as smug; however, the teacher actually meant it. The man had a smug face. His attitude was one of being in a position of unassailable power. Clio wondered how Mac would deal with him.

"Fine. Come on, Maia," Clio stood and went to the door.

Maia followed. Gaines stood.

"Ms. Wray..."

"Please!" Clio said, raising a hand. "Don't make me say something my daughter will regret."

She wanted to tell him how dissatisfied she was with the school and with him personally. But she didn't want to give the institution ammunition to permanently exclude Maia. Exclude on the grounds of a breakdown in relationship with the parent. The upshot would be that they divest themselves of a problem pupil, wash their hands of her. She wouldn't give them the opportunity.

"I'm not angry with you, Maia. I'm angry at them," she said when they got back to the car.

Reversing out of the space, she looked along the line of staff parking.

"Do you know which car is his?" she asked.

Maia had been silent since leaving Mr. Gaines' room. Now she burst out laughing.

"No, mum, I don't. And I wouldn't tell you while you've got that look on your face."

Clio felt a flood of relief at the laughter and she clasped her daughter's hand tightly for a moment.

"Just tell me what really happened. Not what Gaines says happened."

"She's the bully, Kelly McIntosh. She's a year above me and she's been on my case on Tik Tok for weeks. I don't know what I've done to upset her, but she just won't stop."

"You've got posts from her, messages?" Clio asked, as they pulled away from the school and into traffic, heading home.

"Yes. I tried to tell Mr. Gaines, but he wouldn't listen. He thinks I should be able to just ignore it if it's only words."

"The man's dangerous," Clio growled. "When we get home, we'll get screen shots of everything and I'll speak to Mac. Get his advice. What kind of stuff is she saying?"

"I'll show you. Most of it is about me not having a dad. Or about...what happened last year. Stupid stuff. I shouldn't let her get under my skin. She just knows what buttons to push."

Clio nodded. Once the floodgates were open, Maia talked. Clio felt relief and pride that Maia was so comfortable opening up to her mother. But then, their relationship had always been close. Maia's father had been absent from before she was born. It had always been just the two of them. Now, there was Mac as well. Maia's hero. Clio's too if she was honest. Inscrutable. Handsome. She pushed thoughts of Mac out of her mind. He wasn't her type. She would have to be a masochist to want to share her life with the police force. Clio took a longer route home then she needed to. A ten minute drive turned into thirty as she let Maia talk, then stopped at a Mc-Donalds, and tried her best to make her daughter laugh; talking about the things she knew Maia was enthusiastic about. Such as her ambitions to be a writer. Or a police officer.

That was new. As quickly as she had been thinking fondly of Mac, Clio found herself cursing him in her head. Why did he have to be so damn charismatic? She smiled as Maia skirted around the subject of how you joined the police, how old you had to be, and what it must be like to be a detective. Smiled and hoped Maia didn't notice how hard she was trying to change the subject.

CHAPTER NINE

MAC DROVE HIS AUDI through Liberton, a suburb of Edinburgh to the south. According to Clio, there were two schools of thought as to the origin of the name. The first, formerly written as Libertun, was believed to have signified Leper Town, the area supposed at one to time to contain a small colony of lepers exiled from the city. The second, more modern interpretation, suggested it meant 'barley farm on a hillside.' Mac knew which he preferred. Apparently, again according to Clio's eclectic knowledge, the area was once home to Arthur Conan Doyle, who lived in a small cottage near the Braid Burn. Far more apt, although he was no Sherlock Holmes.

Mac wore a stab vest over his shirt. Melissa sat in the passenger seat, similarly attired. Behind them came a police van with metal grating over its front windows and an armed response team in the back. Two patrol cars brought up the rear of the convoy. There were no sirens, but blue lights strobed to clear the traffic. This close to the Claverhouse Community 43-Centre they did not want to risk spooking their quarry. Ashleigh Fenton was working for a charity that was using the community centre as a base in the area for a community outreach programme. The charity was called New Covenant and Ashleigh Fenton had been granted early release in part thanks to their sponsorship of him. They'd found him a council flat and given him a job. Mac wanted to know why his DNA was found on a dead girl and if he didn't get the right answer, Fenton would lose both. A call to the community centre had confirmed Ashleigh was there, helping in the community garden.

"Next right," Melissa said, looking at the sat nav on her phone. "Then first left, and it's about a hundred yards on the right. Liberton Brae."

The area was a vast housing estate. Council houses from the sixties painted a uniform cream, stained brown where outflow pipes had leaked rust. Flats in the shape of bricks with front doors looking out at painted metal balconies and the flats opposite. Chain link municipal fences separated the gardens and cars were practically stacked on top of each other, parking on roads that had never been designed for so many. Kyle Culshaw was still in custody. Mac was holding him until the last possible second the law allowed. Despite the fact that another man's DNA had been found on his girlfriend's body, Mac wasn't yet convinced that Culshaw had nothing to do with it. No alibi. Motive. Evidence of an unstable temper. Volatile relationship with the victim. But the DNA evidence outweighed all of that.

"We've still an hour before we have to charge Culshaw or release him," Melissa said.

"Plenty of time," Mac replied. "Now we've finally found

Fenton. If this pans out, we can let Kyle go. We know where to find him if we need to."

Ashleigh Fenton had not been easy to find. The DNA had been matched to the sample held on file for all convicted prisoners. But what should have been an uncomplicated process of ascertaining where he had gone after being released had not worked out that way. It had taken most of Culshaw's twenty four hours to get an answer from the Parole Service. Under-funded and resourced. Privately run. Mac forced his clenched hands to relax on the wheel as he guided the Audi around the last corner. The community centre was obvious. A large white building with tall windows and walls of painted concrete. It had the look of sixties brutalism in its architecture, the sign attached to one wall almost unintelligible under the scrawl of spray paint tags. One of the windows was being boarded up by a man in overalls at the top of a ladder.

Another man, a pensioner by the look of him, was holding said ladder, foot on the bottom rung. As the police convoy silently sped into the car park a woman with a pinched face and a cardigan held around her like armour, hurried out of the main doors. Mac didn't bother to park but stopped abruptly in front of the main doors and got out, kicking the door shut behind him. Melissa closely followed.

"Janice?" she asked of the woman.

Mac caught a glimpse of the lanyard the woman wore about her neck, almost lost in long hair and a substantial bosom. She looked to be in her fifties, wrinkles around her mouth which was pressed into a thin line.

"Aye. There any need for all this?"

"Where is Ashleigh Fenton?" Mac demanded.

"Go around the side there and through the gate. It's an enclosed garden and the fence is too high for him to jump, so he won't be able to get away."

Mac already had his back to her, striding in the direction indicated. Before he reached the gate, the commander of the tactical unit stopped him with a raised hand.

"We'll take it from here, sir."

Mac nodded and waited as the team assembled on either side of the gate. It seemed overkill for one man but it didn't take much to recall the injuries inflicted on Zoe Phillips. If Ashleigh Fenton was the killer he had to be considered dangerous and possibly armed. The gate was tested by a brief push and proved to be unlocked. It was six feet tall and made of wooden planks, providing no view of what lay on the other side. At a silent signal from the commander, an officer with an automatic weapon kicked the gate open so it slammed into the fence. Then they went in screaming at the top of their lungs. Mac looked in as the tactical team moved between raised vegetable beds made out of pallets and sleepers. His eyes darted from left to right, dismissing the two pensioners standing with hands above their hands. Lingered for a minute on a man with bad acne and a lanyard with an ID badge. He was glowering but holding his hands to his sides. Then he saw the running man.

Ashleigh Fenton wore a grey tracksuit, black trainers and bright green gardening gloves. Mac ran into the garden as Fenton attacked the fence at the rear. He tackled it at a dead run and almost got his hands over the top. He slid down and jumped again as black-clad and masked armed officers swiftly formed a semi-circle around him.

"Ashleigh Fenton! Stand still!" Mac called over the shouted

orders from the armed response team. "For god's sake, do yourself a favour and don't give us any trouble."

Fenton turned, backing into the fence, hands spread to either side. Mac prayed he wasn't about to pull a weapon. Six automatic firearms were pointed at him from close range. A twitch would leave the fence in need of a new paint job, and Mac would never close the Zoe Phillips case. Fenton had a long, thin face and dark eyes. A scar ran from his left temple to his cheek, standing out white against coffee coloured skin. Mixed race. Looked Pakistani. From somewhere behind in the background came an angry voice, shouting to Fenton and promising a lawyer. Mac glanced back at the man with the acne who had a phone to his ear.

"I'm doing nothing wrong. You can't touch me. He's entitled to a solicitor," the man shouted, red-faced.

"Mel, see who that joker is," Mac said. "I'm not in the mood for a working class hero with a chip on his shoulder about the polis."

Melissa went towards him, smiling placidly, kindly mother mode in full effect. When Mac turned back to his suspect, the armed officers had closed in. Fenton was on his face on the ground, hands being cuffed behind him. Mac approached.

"Ashleigh Fenton. I am arresting you on suspicion of the murder of Zoe Phillips. You do not have to say anything, but it may harm your defence if you do not mention, when questioned, something you later rely on in court. Do you understand?" Fenton gave a muffled yes in response. "Right, get him in the van and down to Brunswick Street."

Fenton was hauled to his feet. He was smiling. Mac frowned as he watched him go. It wasn't the reaction he'd expected. No protestations of innocence. No sullen silence of the man who knows he's been caught. A self-satisfied smile. An alarm bell began to ring at the back of his mind.

"Did you say Zoe Phillips?" said the man with the acne.

Melissa was trying to put herself between the man and Mac, but he was dodging from side to side, looking past her. He had clearly figured out that Mac was in command.

"I did. Who are you?" Mac replied.

"Gary Kirk. I work for New Covenant. I'm Ash's supervisor and I can tell you he had nothing to do with that girl's death."

"Well, he's got nothing to worry about then," Mac said without smiling.

"Aye, I know the polis. A guy just out of jail and you want to fit him up with any unsolved cases you've got. Targets to hit, is it?"

The man was pugnaciously belligerent. The kind who automatically pegged the police as the enemy. Which meant he probably came from a deprived background, grew up around crime. Honest people were afraid of coppers. Rich people assumed the police were their personal security. Poor people were the ones who resented them because so many of their communities were taken away.

"Listen, mate. I haven't hit an arrest target in ten years. I don't fit people up. I follow the evidence."

"Aye, right. Well, I've just had my boss on the phone. He'll have a lawyer waiting for you. Ash was a bad boy but, he's found God. He's one of us. He's changed."

"Like I said, I follow the evidence," Mac responded pointedly. "If you have evidence that puts Ashleigh Fenton in the clear then I'd love to hear it."

The man smiled, revealing yellowed teeth and one black replacement. "Aye, I do actually. That girl went missing over the weekend, didn't she? I saw it on the news. Well, Ash was with me all weekend. At the New Covenant retreat out Loanhead way. We left to come here on Monday. I'm his alibi, right?"

Mac stared at him in frank disbelief. Then he looked at Melissa, who shrugged. Mac felt an urge to laugh but instead he let out a long, slow breath and ran his fingers through his hair.

"You willing to give a statement to that effect?" he asked.

"It's the truth," Kirk insisted, about to prod Mac in the chest to emphasise his words.

His eyes met Mac's, and he thought better of it, lowering his hand. Mac grinned but there was no mirth in his expression.

"Then I think you'd be perjuring yourself. And I would have you on obstruction of justice. We have your friend's DNA on a dead body, which tells us he wasn't where you say he was. Unless, the two of you abducted her to Loanhead, killed her and then drove her back into town. That what happened?"

Kirk's face paled, and he took a step back. But there was a uniform behind him, who had quietly approached from one of the patrol cars. Kirk whirled in panic as he became aware of her presence and found himself held by a forearm.

"Gary Kirk. I am arresting you on suspicion of...you know what, Mel, do the honours for me," Mac said, turning his back.

He walked away from the man whose acne spattered face had turned white. Then Kirk started shouting again.

"This is a fit up! You're lying! He was with me! As God is my witness!"

CHAPTER TEN

"GUV, I DON'T THINK we can hold Kirk," Melissa said on the drive back to Brunswick Street.

"We can't," Mac agreed. "But we know Fenton was around Zoe Phillips. So there's a possibility that Kirk is lying to protect him."

"Yes, but we don't have any evidence of that. He could end up making a complaint for wrongful arrest."

"He could. I'll smooth things over, don't worry."

"I do worry," Melissa said.

Mac gave her the roguish grin, the one that almost always worked on women. Melissa looked back at him levelly. Almost always.

"Look, I just wanted to get him secure, not running around shooting his mouth off and potentially warning anyone else who may be involved. He's the type," Mac said, suddenly all business. "We'll let him go once we've got everything we can out of him. Get online and find me everything you can about New Covenant. Addresses, people, this retreat out at Loanhead. We need to test this alibi."

Melissa nodded, taking out her phone. Mac heard the vibration of his own phone receiving a notification. It reminded him of the text he'd seen from Clio last night. He'd been working, had intended to reply when he got home, but the work had followed him and he'd fallen asleep on his sofa. Still hadn't replied. He told himself he would get back to her tonight. Without fail. He glanced down at the phone and recognised the number. Sidhu. He swore. That was something else he'd forgotten about, but this was more deliberate.

"Something wrong, guv?" Melissa asked, looking up from her own phone.

"Something I forgot to do. It'll keep," Mac replied.

It would have to. This was a murder investigation, and they had a prime suspect. The case could be closed by the end of the day. So close to the conclusion of a case, Mac was like a bloodhound on a scent. Nothing would divert or deter him from getting this thing across the line. He wanted to dispense with the few miles' drive across south Edinburgh and be in the interview room with Ashleigh Fenton. Fully prepped and ready to take apart his alibi. Break him into confessing in the face of incontrovertible evidence. Clio came back into his mind. She wasn't a texter. Usually, she only messaged him to confirm a date they'd made. Or if she needed him.

"You still see Clio, then?" Melissa asked.

The question startled him. It was as though she'd read his mind. He blinked, then nodded.

"Saw them last weekend. Why?"

"I'm friends with her on Facebook. She posted some pictures of the three of you in the Pentlands. Cute."

"Don't get excited," Mac warned her.

Melissa laughed. "Sorry, guv. Was I overstepping?" Her teasing voice. The kind only Melissa could get away with.

"Way over," Mac replied.

"I think it's good, anyway. You need someone and so does she, probably."

"Clio's pretty resilient. She doesn't need anyone," Mac said, truthfully.

"Everyone needs someone," Melissa said pointedly.

A few raindrops hit the windscreen with splats. Mac sighed.

"How's the search going?" he said without even trying to disguise the change of subject.

"New Covenant is a registered charity. CEO is a guy called Michael Fielding. Looks like Richard E. Grant. Website is very churchy. Some kind of evangelical Christian organisation working with prisoners inside. Rehabilitation through Christ. Lovely."

"You don't approve?"

"Cazzy and I have had our fair share of stick online from so-called Christians who don't think two women should be married, let alone have a baby together."

"How's that going? When is she due?"

It wasn't something he needed to know about, but Melissa was a people person. He knew it made her feel good to know he was taking an interest and filed away what she told him. As she spoke, his mind was returning to the upcoming interview though.

"Three months now and starting to show. She's well into nesting mode."

Melissa sounded happy, and Mac smiled as the rain began to pelt harder. Fenton could stew in the cells for a while. He was involved, there was no doubt. Kirk couldn't be held. The arrest had been as much to put him in his place as for any real wrongdoing. He was a wide boy and needed taking down a peg. Maybe Mac would take him to the pub down the road from Brunswick Street. It was a coppers pub but that would help keep Kirk a little on edge. While the team gathered all the information they could about Fenton, New Covenant and the alibi Kirk had given, Mac would see what he got out of Kirk himself. Play up the working class part. Mac had grown up dirt poor. He was sure he could establish a connection. Something about it was making him anxious, though. He took a breath, realising that his chest felt tight. He frowned, concentrating on the road as a feeling of dread swept over him. The wipers were flying back and forth in front of him as the rain fell in millions of bomb bursts. He was sure he could hear the sounds of waves crashing somewhere far off.

"Guv?" Melissa's voice reached him from a distance.

Mac was sweating, staring intently into the rain, and feeling as though his heart was about to stop. His face felt numb. Cold swept over him. Melissa was saying something urgently. She had turned in her seat. She was shouting. Why was she shouting? The rain was thunderous and he could hear the sea. The explosions of waves hurling themselves into cliffs. It was Skye. He could smell the peat and the salt in the air. Felt the tension of waiting, waiting to bring justice to...

"Guv, that's a red!" Melissa screamed.

Reality slammed into place in front of Mac's eyes. He was heading into a four-way junction at forty miles an hour and the lights were red. Instinct took over, and he floored the accelerator, trying to get through and out of danger before... Screeching brakes. Blaring horns. A sickening crunch and the car skewed sideways. A van had slammed into the passenger side rear, spinning the Audi, and throwing Mac against the door. Something white and smothering was pressing into his face. An airbag. He blacked out.

"Callum? Can you wake up for me?"

Irish. The cliché was true about that accent. It did lilt. Siobhan had always been an early riser and never liked to let him lie in while the day was wasting. Her words. He didn't think lying in bed next to her was a waste of a couple of hours.

"It's the weekend," he murmured sleepily.

"It's Tuesday actually," Siobhan replied. "Come on officer, I need to do some obs on you."

Mac opened his eyes and then narrowed them against the harsh overhead lights. Patterned curtains formed three walls around him. He was lying on a hospital bed. He hadn't dreamed Siobhan. She was there. In scrubs.

"Don't disappoint me with a 'where am I'," Siobhan said with a half-smile.

How did she do that? Manage to smile with one side of her mouth, making it look wry and cute all at the same time. So much communicated with such a small expression. He looked into her face. Beautiful wasn't the word. Heart-shaped.

Full-cheeked. Bottom lip with a dimple in it that made her look as though she was pouting. He focused on that remembering all the times he'd nipped it playfully. Remembering the taste of her. With a supreme effort, he pulled his mind back to the present. It was wandering, like it was still asleep and dreaming while his eyes were open.

"Do you remember what happened yet?" Siobhan asked. "I'm just going to check your dilatory response."

She bent close, put a gloved hand to his forehead and peeled back an eyelid with her thumb, shining a light into his eye. Then did the same with the other.

"Yet? You've already asked me?" Mac said.

"Aye, when you came in. You were pretty out of it. Classic case of concussion. What was it? Chasing a suspect?"

Mac opened his mouth to deny it but found he couldn't remember. Then something came back to him.

"Mel!"

He tried to sit up, but Siobhan pushed him back.

"Is fine and discharged hours ago. She's got herself a neck brace and whiplash, but nothing else. You don't remember what happened?"

"No."

"You ran a red light and got hit by a van. Didn't bang your head except into the air bag but your brain got shook up, which amounts to the same thing. Concussion. You'll be staying with us overnight for observation."

Mac shook his head and sat up, resisting the push this time. It was disturbingly difficult, but he managed to get to the point of swinging his feet off the bed. Trolley actually. Siobhan folded her arms and actually pursed her lips. Which looked hotter than hell. He ran a hand through his hair, trying to find a point of focus as his mind wandered again.

"I can't. I've got a murder suspect to interview. We were taking him to Brunswick Street when..."

"You had your accident around lunch time. It's almost seven pm," Siobhan said with firmness but compassion.

She hopped onto the trolley beside him, her feet dangling in mid-air. She was a pixie. He watched her feet swing and found himself smiling.

"You haven't changed," she said.

"Haven't I?"

"Nope. Still putting the job before everything. Even your own health. Especially your own health."

"It's important."

"So are you, Callum. I spoke to Mel before she was discharged. She said you were acting odd before the accident."

"I was?"

"Yeah, you were and don't give me those playing for time one-word answers. Even concussed, your brain runs as smooth as that Audi you just wrote off. She said you were sweating, breathing fast. It looked like you were in pain. We've checked you out and I've looked at your history. I know you pretty well. There's nothing physically wrong with you. But there was right before you ran those lights."

Mac let out a long, slow breath. Playing for time. Siobhan looked at him with dark eyes that missed nothing and allowed no escape.

"I've been...look you can't say anything to anyone. I've got it under control. I mean I will...I mean...shit." Mac rubbed his face and started again. "I've been having these...episodes. I get breathless and my heart starts to race like I'm in the throes of a heart attack. My whole body just seems to tense up. It's like I'm about to die or...something."

"Sounds like a panic attack," Siobhan said gently.

She'd put a hand to his shoulder, and that touch was electricity. He realised that his voice had been shaking as he'd been talking. There were tears in his eyes. He looked away from her, blinking and angry at himself for his weakness. She reached around, found his chin with her hand, and turned him to look back at her.

"Are you talking to anyone about it?"

Mac was about to deny there was any need, but her eyes stopped him. "No."

"You need to, Mac, or it will only get worse."

Their faces were inches apart. He could just lean in and kiss her. Did she want that? Was she making an overture? Something changed in her face, and he knew she wasn't. He grinned, the rogue. Siobhan arched an eyebrow.

"Anyone in your life? Girlfriend? Boyfriend?" she asked.

Mac looked at her.

"To talk to...obviously," Siobhan said.

"No. You?"

"I'm not the one having panic attacks,"

"That's a deflection."

"I'm your nurse."

"So is that."

Siobhan stood up, picking up a clipboard from the end of the bed. She had a flush of colour across her cheeks. She made some notes.

"I'll let you know when you can leave. I'll be back later to check on you. Don't make it weird, Mac, please. What we had is over, but there's no reason why we can't remain friends."

Mac nodded.

Siobhan went to pull the curtain aside and stopped. She looked back over her shoulder.

"You need professional help, Mac. Find someone you can talk to, okay?"

Then she was gone. Mac lay back, thinking. He smiled to himself. Half an hour later, he was heading away from the hospital in a taxi.

CHAPTER ELEVEN

HE WAS SURPRISED TO SEE HIS TEAM still in the office. DCI Akhtar was there too, listening as Nari talked. Kai was at his desk, appearing attentive, but he was the first to see Mac walk in.

"Alright, guv?" he called out.

Nari stopped and Akhtar looked over her shoulder. She was standing with arms folded. Now she turned slowly to watch Mac approach.

"DCI McNeill. I didn't think we would be seeing you tonight. Neither did DCS Reid. He asked me to oversee the Zoe Phillips case while you recovered."

"Thanks, Hafsa," Mac replied, rising above the deliberately formal greeting. "I'll take over now. Where are we with Ashleigh Fenton?"

He ignored Akhtar, who cleared her throat but Mac was looking from Nari to Kai, ignoring her. Nari glanced at

Akhtar as though seeking permission to speak. Kai wasn't so diplomatic.

"His alibi is good, but not strong. Kirk, the mouth we picked up along with him insists that Fenton was with him and others all weekend. But, when I spoke to him informally he couldn't confirm that he'd had eyes on Fenton the whole time. They all had their own rooms at this retreat and no surveillance of any kind. Kirk has been released as we couldn't hold him. But there's a garage opposite the complex New Covenant uses for its retreat and it does have CCTV. I found a white van, number plate not distinguishable, pull into the lane leading to the New Covenant complex. Then pull out again a few minutes later. That was at eleven-thirty. Couldn't see anyone..."

"But that gives us opportunity. We don't have motive and Fenton hasn't given us anything," Akhtar put in. "But with the opportunity and the DNA tying him to the body, I felt it was enough to go to the Procurator Fiscal. DCS Reid felt the same."

Mac nodded, feeling a clench of irritation that Akhtar had muscled in on his case. Fenton could have been kept in custody for twenty four-hours and then longer with the DNA evidence. It hadn't needed a new DCI to take over. Akhtar was hungry though. Ever since she'd arrived, six months ago, she'd been nipping at his heels. Mac had never felt the need to compete with his colleagues but coppers like Hafsa Akhtar treated the job like a ladder. It wasn't about catching criminals. Just advancing in the ranks. He realised he was clenching his jaw, hands thrust deep into his pockets. His lips curled into a snarling smile, teeth just bared. It wasn't like him; usually he kept his features impassive and didn't let anyone see what or who was getting to him. The thought of concussion ran through his mind. Then Siobhan's face swam into his mind just as his phone buzzed. It was a text from Siobhan herself.

'*You're a fecking idiot, Callum McNeill. You should still be under observation. Just get help will you? Remember it's not only yourself you're putting in danger!*'

He frowned. His first response was to be angry at Siobhan, but he knew that was the guilt. She was right; it wasn't just himself he was risking. Mel was testament to that. He glanced up and found Akhtar staring at him.

"Thank you, Hafsa. Great work. I didn't expect to find the case wrapped up when I got back. It's a weight off the shoulders."

She smiled thinly. "What happened? If you don't mind me asking? DCS Reid was a bit cagey."

"Was he?" Mac smiled blandly, then turned to Nari. "So, we're collating all the evidence we have for the report to the Pro-Fisc?"

"Yes, but we've got this, guv," Nari assured him, looking concerned.

"Mel's gone home for the night?" Mac asked.

"She insisted on coming in for a few hours and I sent her home," Akhtar said.

"Good shout. She needs to recover," Mac replied. "Kai, send me everything we have and any drafts. Hafsa, thanks for all your help. You can go home."

He headed for his office, hearing the affirmative from Kai, followed a moment later by Nari. Akhtar didn't reply and

Mac didn't look back. He got to his desk and sat down with control, trying to ignore the temptation to drop into the seat. His head was aching, and he felt exhausted. But he wasn't about to show weakness in front of Akhtar. She would go for the throat as soon as she smelled blood. There was an email waiting for him from Sidhu which he was about to delete before he stopped himself. Couldn't hide from it forever. Instead he clicked reply and dashed a couple of lines, suggesting a date to attend counselling. There was an email from Reid. Warning him that if he didn't book a session with Talvir Sidhu he would...deleted. An email popped up from Kai with several attachments. Then one from Nari. Another from Kai. It took effort to force himself to concentrate but he managed it. He reviewed the compiled evidence and the draft report they had been pulling together. The Pro-Fisc wouldn't like the lack of motive but DNA was hard to beat. With Fenton's history it could have been a random attack.

Tox screen said Fenton had coke in his system. Either the New Covenant retreat wasn't as squeaky clean as their Christian image suggested, or Fenton was not as reformed a character as they liked to believe. Motive enough right there. Fenton fuelled on coke and booze, breaking loose from the boredom of bible studies and early bedtime, off his face. Kills. Goes back to hide behind the crucifix but knows it's only a matter of time. It explained that smile. Mac could read a lot into something like that. Nothing that would stand up in court, but enough to tell him he was on the right track. There was a tap at his door. Nari.

"Guv? You OK for us to head off?" she asked.

Mac glanced at the time on his computer. An hour had

passed since he'd sat down. He hadn't noticed. The report was ready to be sent. Fenton would be charged and, given the nature of the crime, bail would not be considered. By this time tomorrow he'd be on remand at Saughton Prison waiting for a trial date.

"Sure, Nari. Sorry to keep you so long. Thanks for all your hard work."

"Need a lift, guv?" Kai called out, shrugging into a long, dark overcoat.

"No, I'll get a cab," Mac replied. "See you tomorrow."

"Hope the insurance company doesn't give you too much trouble over the car. That was a nice motor," Kai said.

Nari hit him on the shoulder. Mac smiled grimly. "Yeah it was."

They left. A few minutes later, the automatic lighting went off as Mac sat still. Then he lifted himself from his chair with a groan, fighting the overwhelming fatigue. The light's came on in response to his walking across the office. They went dark again as he left the room. Heading for the lift he felt his phone buzz and looked at it dumbly. The number was one he knew. It originated from this building. Custody desk down at the holding cells.

"McNeill."

"Sorry to disturb you, sir. It's Sergeant Maxwell down at the holding cells. One of the prisoners has been asking to speak to you and someone said you were still in the building."

"Only just," Mac replied, pressing the button for the lift. "Can it wait? What does he want?"

He was assuming it was Fenton. Gary Kirk had gone and

at this moment was probably preparing his complaint of wrongful arrest for the Police Complaints Commission.

"Wouldn't bother you usually, sir. But he says he knows where there's a dead body."

The lift doors opened in front of Mac and then closed a moment later. "I'm on my way," he said, heading for the stairs.

Two minutes later, he was swiping into the custody area with his ID card. Jim Maxwell was on the desk, big nose, grey hair, short and wiry. He stepped away from the desk, pulling a large key ring from his belt on the end of a flexible plastic chain. He picked out the appropriate key and led Mac along the corridor. Cells lined one wall, each door bearing the details of the prisoner including time and date they were locked up and any special medical or dietary notes. He unlocked the third one along after unlatching the pull down viewing hatch and taking a brief gander inside. Then he turned the heavy metal handle. There was a satisfyingly solid thunk of metal. Maxwell stepped into the room.

"On your feet, Fenton. DCI McNeill is here like you've been asking for. Be a good boy now. You've got what you wanted."

Mac followed the sergeant into the cell. Fenton was wearing a paper suit, like a SOCO. The remains of bangers, mash and beans were sprayed across one wall, the tray they'd been on upside down on the floor. There was a steel toilet without a seat in one corner and a wash basin which was bolted to the floor and wall with nuts as thick as two knuckles. A strip of narrow windows, the glass reinforced with wire, ran along the top of one wall. Too high to reach. Fenton was sitting on the concrete bench, which served as a bed with the addition of an inch thick mat. He looked up from under lowered brows. Mac stood looking back at him, hands in pockets.

"Just you," Fenton said.

"No," Mac replied.

If this was a guilty man trying to play games just to mess with the polis, Mac wasn't going to give an inch. If he had information, he needed to realise it had to be handed over. There was no plea bargain. A lot of cons mixed up US cop shows with real-life British policing.

"I can tell you about another murder. But just you."

Mac exchanged glances with Maxwell, whose skepticism was writ large across his face. Mac grinned and shook his head.

"I'm knackered. You're going to Saughton tomorrow. Get some sleep."

He turned to go.

"Wait, wait. You don't want to know about my ex?"

Mac stopped, then shrugged. "Not really, pal. Not if I have to play games with you to find out. Just spit it out."

Fenton had clearly been looking forward to stringing Mac along for a while. Mac suppressed a yawn. Fenton glowered, looked at the floor, and then looked back at Mac.

"Vicky McCourt, right? My ex. Did time because of her. 13 Dumbeg Park, Wester Hailes. Neighbours are probably complaining about the smell by now."

CHAPTER TWELVE

MAC KNEW HE SHOULDN'T BE HERE. He felt as though he could fall asleep standing up. But, if there was a dead body out there, a second victim, he had to see the crime scene. Fenton had clammed up after making his cryptic reference to the state of his ex-girlfriend. Mac had instructed a patrol car to head to the address and scope out the situation. Thirty minutes later, he got the call. Officers had broken into the property upon approaching it and detected the distinctive smell of corruption. They'd found a body. Mac had instructed them to vacate and seal the house. Then he'd called for a SOCO team and another patrol car to drive him out to Wester Hailes. Sitting in the passenger seat with the blues and twos in full flight, he found it difficult to keep his eyes open. He told himself that he could rest up once he'd evaluated the scene, once he'd looked over the body of Vicky McCourt, if that's truly who had been found.

Forcing his mind to focus on the available data, he ran

through a checklist in his head. Zoe Phillips killed quickly and cleanly, and then stabbed multiple times in a frenzy. Killed somewhere other than where she was found. Her face marked in that strange way. He pulled up the crime scene pictures on his phone as the car sped through the night-time streets of Edinburgh. Streetlights created a dirty orange glow over everything. Those straight lines reminded him of something, but he couldn't pin it down. It was infuriating. Somewhere at the back of his bruised and beaten mind was a piece of information that he couldn't reach. It might be irrelevant, but it might not. Ash Fenton was in custody and had just confessed to murder. His DNA had been found on Zoe's body. He was bloody involved and would be going down for it. But something was niggling at him.

"Bloody concussion," he muttered, involuntarily voicing the thought.

"What's that, sir?" said the uniform who was driving him.

Mac shook his head, then remembered the conversation with Clio again. He looked at the young man, dredging a name from his memory.

"Greg, right? Greg Menzies," Mac said.

"That's right, sir," Menzies replied, his lips tugging briefly into a smile.

"Just thinking aloud, Greg," Mac said.

He was pleased he'd been able to place the man. There was a mental trick to attaching names to the faces of people you might have met only once and then only briefly. Mac had read about it once. Didn't use it though. It was just part of a detective's mindset. Maybe they were all on the spectrum. Maybe it wasn't so much a detective's mindset as an autistic one.

"This is us now, sir," Menzies said, turning into a street lined with gray pebble-dashed houses.

They were boxes with front doors and second floor side-doors reached by steps, a flat on the ground floor and another above. Larger blocks loomed out of the dark behind, four stories but seeming squat. Fenced off areas beside the buildings housed bins and old white goods. The street was made narrow by the cars parked on both sides, parking at the properties being nonexistent. Rounding a bend, Mac saw the first patrol car, mounted on the pavement. A uniformed officer stood at the top of the steps leading to the second-floor flat in a building whose ground floor had boarded-up windows. Graffiti stained the boards and the walls. Grass and weeds dominated cracked concrete. Mac frowned, trying to bring sharpness to his mind by the physical movement of his face. Typical sink estate. Employment in a place like this would be less than twenty-five percent. Crime rate high along with levels of registered addicts. And that was just the ones on prescriptions for their methadone. Mac stepped out of the car, taking in the locals peering out of windows or blatantly staring.

Menzies was putting on his hat as he walked around the car, looking to Mac for orders.

"It's a bloody shame," Mac said, not knowing where the words came from.

Menzies glanced at their surroundings.

"Aye, no jobs, no hope. I grew up not far from here," he said.

They walked across a verge of grass towards the cracked paving that led to the steps.

"What made you join up?" Mac asked.

"Wanted to help," Menzies shrugged. "A copper helped me out once when I was in trouble. Thought I could do the same, but you know what they tell you when you go to the Castle."

Mac nodded grimly. Tulliallan Castle was the training centre for Police Scotland. The instructors there taught you one important lesson about policing places like Wester Hailes. Don't get out of the car.

"Aye, I remember," Mac replied.

"Doesn't sit well with me. Can't help the community if you're not part of it, eh?"

"What can you do?" Mac said rhetorically.

Menzies shrugged. "Don't know. Become a social worker?"

Mac started to ascend the steps. He stopped halfway and turned back to Menzies.

"SOCO should be here any minute. Set up a perimeter around the building and tell them I'm inside."

Menzies nodded. "Right, sir."

Mac turned away and hurried up the steps where an older officer waited.

"Body's in the bedroom. On the bed. Naked and pretty rotten, sir."

Mac didn't recognise the man but just nodded, taking in the information. The door leading into the building was off its bottom hinge, though it had been closed over. He noticed the officer was wearing gloves. Mac fished a pair from a pocket and put them on, along with shoe covers, before gently pushing the broken door inwards. The house was dark.

"You have a torch?" he asked.

The officer unclipped one from his belt and handed it over. Mac didn't want to try a light switch in case he disturbed fingerprints or other DNA. The small but powerful beam played around the narrow hallway behind the door. Looked clean. Tatty but scrubbed. Cheap, but cared for. The smell was appalling. Movement caught his eye and shining the torch upward, he saw the air fresheners that had been hung from the ceiling. A few were twirling and swaying in the breeze. They weren't masking the smell much, if at all. Mac reached up and caught the nearest. He stretched it down on the elastic that held it and sniffed. Not much scent left. How long before these things dried out? A couple of weeks? A month? Likely that the killer hung them to disguise the smell and delay discovery of the body. Why would Fenton want to delay discovery? He'd as good as admitted to killing her. It was another question filed away. Mac stepped carefully along the hallway to the nearest door. It led into a bedroom. There were far more air fresheners here and a strong odor of bleach.

The room was dark, curtains drawn against the streetlight outside. They were blackout curtains. Mac felt as though he was stepping into hell. The air was thick enough to bite. The torch shone on dried blood, spattered across surfaces in thick, black arcs. Signs of a struggle. A chest of drawers overturned. Something crunching underfoot. Shining the torch down revealed glass, then the metal end of a light bulb, the neck of the bulb itself a jagged ring. Looking up with the torch, Mac saw the broken light fixture. Quite the struggle. He let the torch play over the body which lay on the bed, arms at its sides. Badly decomposed. Stinking. Naked. He wasn't expert enough to hazard a guess as to the age of the victim, though he could see that she was a she. The stab wounds over the torso were plain, even amongst the putrefaction. She looked similar to Zoe Phillips. But why try and delay the discovery? What was Fenton waiting for?

An idea flitted through his mind that Fenton had been waiting for the opportunity to kill Zoe. That being caught for that killing served as a trigger for the revealing of the other. Which implied that Fenton knew Zoe Phillips and had planned her murder. Which brought him back to motive. Which Mac had yet to discover. Turning away, reaching the limits of his tolerance, Mac remembered the mutilation to Zoe Phillip's face. Steeling himself, he moved closer to the body that might by Vicky McCourt. There was a straight cut under her chin running from ear to ear, but not where it would sever an artery. Her throat hadn't been cut, rather the skin under her chin. Why? For the joy of mutilation. The line was dead straight and neat edged. Done carefully and deliberately. Mac shook his head, playing the torch around the room again, seeing where cuts had been made that severed major arteries, leading to splashes of blood emerging under pressure. He could almost trace the path of the struggle by the disruption and the blood stains. A handprint on the door jamb made him think it had started outside of the bedroom until he held his hand above the print.

It was the print of someone grabbing for the doorframe from the inside, trying to pull themselves out of the room. Vicky McCourt had tried to escape. The sound of more feet on the stairs told him that a forensics team had arrived. He left the room and met the first of them at the front door. Pointing out where the body was, he let them get on with their job. Derek Stringer was not the attending pathologist. It was a woman who introduced herself as Sandra Deaves. She was middle-aged, with a thin face and invisible lips. She spoke with the hint of a European accent. Ordinarily Mac would wait for her verdict, but the fatigue was making him feel drunk. He needed to rest. That fact was undeniable even to his stubbornness. After giving her his details and where he could be reached, he left her to it. There was enough evidence to hold Ash Fenton and plenty of time for the evidence from this crime scene to be processed. He knew he needed to sleep. Needed to show willing to Sidhu about counselling. Needed to reach out to Clio after the message he hadn't acknowledged yet. Duties and obligations crowded in on him. He tripped over an uneven paving stone, stumbling and just catching his balance. Menzies appeared at his side.

"Everything alright, sir?" he asked.

"Too long on shift," Mac shrugged. "And not on overtime. I'm a sucker for crime scene."

"Want me to give you a lift back to the station, sir?"

"No, Leith. I need to get up the road, if you wouldn't mind. My car's a write off," Mac said.

"No probs, sir. Jump in."

Mac woodenly obeyed. Once in the car, he rested his head against the seat back and was asleep a minute after the engine started.

CHAPTER THIRTEEN

MAC AWOKE FROM ANOTHER DREAM that left a sour taste in his mouth but thankfully nothing in his memory. His head was pounding. Light streamed in through the bedroom window and by turning his head, he could see a pair of golfers teeing off in the distance. The sky was a fragile blue. The sun was weak. By the movement of the trees lining the road, there was a stiff breeze that must make golf a challenge. Blearily, he reached for his phone and only succeeded in knocking it to the floor. It added a crack to a corner of the screen. They never survived long without one. It was just after midday. He groaned and forced himself up into a sitting position, then pulled up Melissa's number, hitting the speaker button.

"Guv,"

"Mel, you at the station?" Mac said, running a hand over his face.

"I am."

"How are you feeling?"

"I'm fine, just a bit sore, but nothing to worry about."

"Listen, I'm sorry about what happened."

"Don't worry about it, Guv. I'm made of strong stuff. What about you?"

"I'm fine. So, brief me."

"You sure? I don't know what happened in the car but..."

"I'm fine, Mel. It's under control."

Mel sighed. "OK. Well, Vicky McCourt was killed with a single stab wound to the heart and then stabbed multiple times. Same kind of blade that was used on Zoe Phillips. Akhtar and myself have interviewed Fenton. DCS Reid's orders. He denies killing Zoe Phillips but can't explain how his DNA could be found on her. His alibi isn't unbreakable but it's not the weakest in the world either. He was certainly at the retreat but had an opportunity to leave and come back without being missed. Question is why?"

Mac was in his boxers and nothing else. He left the bedroom without closing the door. Then he stopped halfway to the living room, turned around and closed it behind him. Entering the living room, he went to the kitchen area and opened the fridge, taking out a carton of orange juice. He put it on a place mat on the counter next to the fridge, there for that very reason. Took down a glass tumbler from a cupboard over the sink and poured himself a glass, placed on a second mat next to the one occupied by the juice.

"I've been asking myself the same question. What's he got to say about Vicky McCourt?"

"She was his ex. He went down for ABH committed against her. Revenge, do you think?"

"I get killing the ex. But why kill Zoe Phillips? Could be

random. Saw her and just decided to do it. Maybe he knew he was going down for life for what he did to Vicky McCourt and decided it couldn't be any worse for him."

Mel let out a long breath. "That's a pretty evil man."

"That's as evil as they come. Unless we can find a connection between Fenton and Zoe, I don't have anything better. Maybe they met at a club and he tried it on, got rejected."

"Then sees her again and decides to punish her. Still pretty evil."

"Then life is the right sentence for him, Mel. I take it Akhtar is pushing this to the Pro-Fisc regardless of motive or connection to Zoe?"

"She is. DNA connects them, and this prior killing demonstrates that he's capable. Then there are the similar methods."

Mac drained his glass, surprising himself with the degree of his thirst. Rinsed it with a jet of water and put it into the dishwasher. Carton back in the fridge. Mats replaced in the second drawer to the left of the sink. He ran a hand over the counter top, feeling no friction from crumbs or stains.

"How long are you off for, guv?" Mel asked.

"Off? I'm coming in today," Mac replied.

"You sure? You can't mess around with head injuries. I remember when Cazzy got concussion playing football. It took longer than..."

"I'm fine," Mac replied with irritation, then he stopped himself, took a breath. "Sorry, don't mean to snap. But I feel fine. Had a good long sleep and I'm good to go. Let Akhtar handle Ash Fenton. Sounds like it's pretty much over the line, anyway. I'll just have to live with the mystery of why he killed

Zoe Phillips. Accept that he did it and move on. We've got plenty of other work to occupy us."

"Right, guv," Mel said with brisk energy.

"I'll be in by two. Let's get the team together and review the cases we put on the back burner for Zoe Phillips. Can you pull together a pack for me? The usual, status, actions, you know the script."

"Right, guv. I'll get on it," Mel said.

Mac let her go, taking a seat on one of the bar stools next to the island separating kitchen and living room. The remote for the hi-fi sat on the island and he powered up the system and selected CD. He couldn't remember if there was a disc already in the player. A second later, and dissonant, roaring, distorted guitars coughed into life. They moved smoothly into a haunting, melodic riff that sounded like it was being recorded from the bottom of a well. He closed his eyes for a moment, letting the music wash over him, rifling its rough fingers through his mind to shake loose the tension. Then he opened them, looked down at his phone, scrolling through his emails first. A message from Reid berating Mac because Sidhu was chasing him. A polite but firm request from Sidhu, cc'ing Reid, and the Division Commander. Mac swore and quickly composed a response. Before hitting send, he stopped himself. Re-read the message. Sidhu could make trouble for him, armed with the power of Police Scotland's HR regulations.

Those sessions would be difficult enough for Mac without the man conducting the sessions being antagonised. He couldn't see anything wrong with his reply. It was factual and professional. Mac growled under his breath and hastily reworded it to remove some of the formality, make himself seem more amenable. Humbler. Then he moved on to Clio's SMS.

'Mac, could really do with talking to you. Maia's been suspended from school, but it's not her fault. She's being bullied, and it's happening online. Wanted to pick your brains about the law around that. You're cheaper than a solicitor lol. Also, I've done something silly, so knowing about the law around what you can and can't say online would be good. I might have got myself into worse trouble than Maia. Give me a call when you get a minute?'

He called her on the way to the bathroom to take a shower. Voicemail.

"Clio, it's Mac. Just read your message. Sorry, I've got two murders on my hands and a concussion...long story. Will tell you about it. On my way into the office, but I'll call you later."

It didn't take a detective to figure out what trouble Clio might be talking about, particularly if she was thinking she had committed an offence. Possibly defamation or an offence under the Communications Act. If it related to Maia, then she had possibly said more than she should online to someone. There was a teacher she had mentioned as being particularly problematic. That had started the conversation about Mac possibly visiting the school. Before stepping into the shower, he made a note on his phone to find out who the officer was assigned to Maia's school. No way could he find the time to do it, but he could see if someone was available to go over there under the guise of police-community relations, ask them to keep an eye out and report back if they learned anything. Another thread to keep track of. He felt he was in danger of losing those threads. It would never happen in a case. They took over his life to the exclusion of everything else. But he felt he needed to make more of an effort holding onto the other threads making up the complicated weave of his life. Allow them to slip through your fingers and they're gone forever.

Clio and Maia. Siobhan and Aine. He had let go of two of those threads, let them be unwound from his life. He was damned if he would lose Clio and Maia, too. Siobhan had come back into it at the most unexpected time. A chance to grab that thread again and hold on tight. Was it? Or was she just doing her job, showing compassion and empathy to a patient? That's what she said, but is it what she meant? Jesus, he was useless at reading the undertones. Too complicated. Too difficult to think about and make sense of. He needed hard facts, logic, cause, and effect. If only he could apply the same cold focus to understanding the people in his life as he did to the corpses that came across his path. Mac stepped into the shower as the bathroom filled with steam. Another thread, dropped long ago, came back to him. His sister. Her face swam up before his closed eyes. Growing up, he'd never had time for her. He had been fixated on his older brother, Connor. But then, shortly after the death of their mother, Connor had left home to join the Merchant Navy. The day Connor left was burned into Callum's mind. Slamming doors. Roaring from his father. Connor trudging away, rucksack high on his back.

Mac and Iona had watched him go. Mac had seen his sister's tears. Saw the fear on her face now that mum and Connor were gone. Fear of what was in store for them now. Twelve and thirteen years old with a father hiding in a bottle from his grief. Callum slapped a hand against the tiles of the shower. Again. Harder. He closed his eyes tight as the anger swelled in him. The selfishness of the old man who turned his back on his kids. The older brother who walked out, leaving his siblings. That was when Mac knew he had to look after Iona. Had to be the parent. She'd needed him. And he'd failed her. Four years later, she was dead. This time it was a fist that slammed into the tiles as hot water coursed down Mac's face. His knuckles stung and one of the tiles cracked. The past had always been a closed book to him. Another life that had happened to someone else. He'd divorced himself from it. But maybe not as effectively as he'd thought. He wondered if this was what he should be talking about with Doctor Sidhu. The idea made his stomach clench.

Whenever his thoughts strayed too close to the rain soaked night he'd intended to commit murder, he pulled them back. Those thoughts had to be shut away. The feel of the icy rain on his skin. The numbness from standing for so long in the cold, waiting for his victim. Iona's killer had never been caught. On an island the size of Skye, the killer had never been identified. He couldn't believe it now and hadn't been able to then. Sheer incompetence when the killer's identity was clear. Mac shut off the water and stepped out of the shower, picking up a neatly folded towel from a shelf. As he dried himself, he reached for his phone, typed in a name, curious as to what would come up. He put it down again without taking in the matches to the name Mark Souter. What if he was living a good life? What if he was married with kids or professionally successful? What if Mark had made something of his life? If that was the case, Mac didn't know if he'd be able to stop himself from going through with the job he had failed to do all those years ago. Killing him.

CHAPTER FOURTEEN

Mac was relieved the effects of the concussion did not appear to be returning. He knew it wasn't that simple. The sensible course was to take time off. But, Mac had never been sensible when it came to his job. The absence of tangible symptoms meant he could forget the injury. Walking into the office he saw a crease of concern on Mel's face, before she wiped it clean into a motherly smile. Kai raised a hand in greeting, a phone cradled between cheek and shoulder as he took notes. Nari was sitting beside Hafsa Akhtar, talking earnestly. She turned as Mac strode up the central aisle between the two clusters of desks and stood. Her pretty, delicate face looked anxious. He met her eye and then glanced to Akhtar as she said something to Nari, drawing the sergeant's attention away from her boss. Mac forced a smile, returning the greetings of his team and not looking towards Nari. It was childish, he told himself. They were all on the same side. But something in him snarled at the notion of another DCI poaching from his team. The snarl deepened at the idea that one of his people would want to transfer. Nothing wrong with that. Happened all the time. Smacked of disloyalty.

"Afternoon all. Good to see you," Mac said.

"Words say so. Face doesn't," Kai said, one hand over the mouthpiece of the phone. "I've got the path lab on the phone with post-mortem results on Vicky McCourt if you're..."

"I'll take a briefing in a minute," Mac said.

"I'd like to sit in," Akhtar put in, standing, and tugging the jacket of her trouser suit straight.

Her glossy dark hair was severely pinned back. Dark eyes like coals.

"Uh huh," Mac said with a tight smile. "By all accounts, the case is pretty much closed though?"

"Bar the shouting. But I'd like to hear the pathologist's findings so I can make sure they go in the report," Akhtar said. "I believe DCS Reid said he wanted to speak with you as soon as you come in."

"Does he?" Mac said. "First things first. Kai, when you're ready."

He pulled up Nari's chair and shrugged out of his jacket, hanging it on the back. Leaning forward, elbows on his knees and hands clasped together between them, he caught Mel's eye. She wheeled her chair to him, notepad in hand.

"Is Nari jumping ship then?" Mac asked in a whisper intended for Mel's ears alone.

Mel was aware enough not to glance at Nari, but shook her head, looking scornful.

"Behave, guv. She idolises you. Knows all the big cases

you've ever closed inside out. DCI Akhtar asked for her to come across as part of the case handover."

"They look like good pals to me," Mac said, knowing he was being petulant and unreasonable but not caring.

Seeing Nari sitting with Akhtar had put him in a bad mood. Mel had known him long enough to see it. She playfully swatted his arm with her pad.

"Snap out of it, sir."

Mac grinned, the irresistible rogue's grin. Mel laughed.

"Doesn't work on me, guv."

Mac chuckled. He straightened as Akhtar and Nari joined them from across the dividing aisle. Kai had finished his call and was collecting sheets from the printer. He started to pin them to the boards, which already bore notes and pictures relating to the Zoe Phillips case.

"Victoria McCourt, forty-four. Dead for around three weeks. Died as a result of a stab wound to the heart and was subsequently mutilated by incisions..."

Mac's mind had switched from his annoyance at Akhtar's office politics to sharp and analytical.

"Incisions? Whose word is that?" Mac asked.

"Mine. The pathologist used the term wounds," Kai responded. "I felt incisions was more accurate. It looks frenzied, but none of these cuts appears to intersect another."

"Placing was deliberate. Surgical," Mac said. "Good spot, Kai."

Now that Kai had pointed it out, it was stark. The images of Vicky McCourt were hard to decipher due to the corruption of her flesh. But on Zoe Phillips, it was clearer. He stood, hands thrust into trouser pockets and walked to the board, looking closely at the images. Kai stood next to him but was unfazed, turning slightly to continue including Mac in the presentation.

"Tox screen came back clean. Vicky was a registered methadone user and, she'd been attending Narcotics Anonymous. Nothing else in her system. Hard to tell if she'd been assaulted prior to being stabbed. Decomposition was too advanced to retain bruising. No broken bones though."

"Maybe she was drugged. No sign of a struggle with Zoe Phillips, either. Something that would render her unconscious but clear itself from her system," Mac said, stepping back from the boards, trying to take them in as a totality.

"Rohypnol, for example," Kai suggested.

Mac turned to Akhtar suddenly. "You've interviewed Fenton?"

"I have. He revealed that he hated her and was motivated by revenge," Akhtar said.

"Revealed? He was hardly trying to conceal the fact. Couldn't wait to tell us all about it," Kai said.

Akhtar gave him a long, considered look, one dark eyebrow raised. Kai cleared his throat, looking at his notes. Mac stepped into her eye line as he turned back to the evidence board.

"Anything else, Kai?" he said.

"Only other wound on the body was a torn ear lobe. Left. There was an ear-ring in the right ear. No sign of the one from the left. I would say it was ripped free."

"Which would indicate a struggle."

"Or a trophy," Mel put in.

"Which fits with the stated motive of revenge," Akhtar said in a voice that spoke of infinite tolerance and patience. Her eyes locked onto Mac with anything but.

"Thank you, DC Stuart," she continued. "I see nothing in the post-mortem to change our strategy. It seems likely that Ashleigh Fenton murdered his ex-girlfriend and then Zoe Phillips. Revenge for one killing and...who knows for the other?"

"That doesn't bother you, ma'am?" Mel asked, looking earnest.

Mac nodded slowly, returning to his seat, giving Kai a wink. The DC suppressed a smile and shuffled together his notes, returning to his own desk. Mac felt a flash of pride at the insights which Kai had pulled from the evidence. Mel's question was one that had been at the forefront of his own mind and he liked that she had raised it.

"What bothers me, DI Barland..." Akhtar began. Then with a glance at Mac she smiled. "Can I call you Mel?"

"Of course, ma'am," Mel replied blandly.

"Mel, our priority is that we have our perpetrator and can reassure the public that the case is closed. A swift resolution will improve the SCU's standing within the force and Police Scotland's reputation as a whole. Everyone wins."

"Except Zoe Phillip's friends and family who have no idea why she was killed," Mac said.

Akhtar shot a razored glance at him before a smile that was very forced took off the edge.

"It's just awfully convenient," Mac continued.

"A confession usually is," Akhtar replied. "You don't want to close this case?"

"No, no. I think we've got him," Mac replied. "I just worry about loose ends. But it won't hold up a conviction. Go ahead."

Akhtar nodded. "I'll act as liaison with the Procurator Fiscal's office, as I've seen the case over the line. I've also taken the liberty of having Meredith Blakeley's office arrange a press conference. I take it you have no objections?"

Mac shook his head. Meredith was head of Police Scotland PR and overly fond of putting him in front of the cameras. He was more than happy for another DCI to do it.

"Well then. If you'll excuse me," Akhtar went back towards her own desk.

"Nari, could I have a word…"

"Sir?" Nari asked.

Mac stood and gave her a smile that he hoped was reassuring.

"Good work on this Nari," he saw the anxiety slip from her features and realised something more was needed. "I'm sure DCI Akhtar appreciates you as much as I do. Take what time you need."

That got a grateful smile, even the traces of a blush. Mac thought about what Mel had said. He hadn't been able to credit it, but could see the evidence in Nari's response. She hurried over to Akhtar and Kai leaned forward, whispering.

"She's had work done."

Mac frowned, "Nari? Surely not,"

"Akhtar. Face lift. She's older than she looks, eh?"

"I think that's why she's so driven. She's got ten years on you, guv, but you've jumped ranks a lot faster than her," Mel said, her back to Akhtar and Nari, also whispering.

"I'll leave the two of you to your gossip. Just give me the final score, eh?" he said.

That got a laugh. As Mac picked up his jacket, though, he

stopped. Staring at the pictures of Zoe and Vicky, he saw what it was that had been bothering him.

"Plastic surgery," he said.

Kai frowned, following his gaze. So did Mel. Mac dropped his jacket back on the chair and hurried to the boards, not caring if Akhtar was watching. He pointed to the straight cuts made on Zoe Phillips' face.

"I knew it reminded me of something. It's like the lines plastic surgeons draw on the face to show where they're going to cut."

"Had much work done yourself, guv?" Kai said.

"Seen it on TV somewhere," Mac admitted, though he couldn't quite place where. He was sure he was right though.

"It does look a bit like that," Mel said, dubiously.

Mac was thinking of the cut under Vicky McCourt's chin. She was an older woman, maybe had some loose skin under there. Then he shrugged, turning away. It was academic. No more evidence was needed. This was intellectual vanity and likely to be wrong anyway. Chances were it was a coincidental resemblance because there was no reason for Ashleigh Fenton to be referencing plastic surgery. He was an animal. Still, there was some small satisfaction that he had chased down the niggling thought that had been bothering him since his first sight of Zoe Phillips' wounds. The rest of the afternoon passed in the mundane of police work. Cases put on hold by a higher priority investigation had to be resumed, briefings held with his team, singly or together. Reports reviewed. Mac tried to resolve himself to the fact that Ashleigh Fenton was going down for a double murder, that justice would be served. But he couldn't escape the urgent need for completeness. It wasn't enough to satisfy the public, the press and the Procurator Fiscal. He wanted to know why Fenton had done it.

A sharp rap at the door announced Reid shortly before he pushed the door open, letting it swing enthusiastically from his hand to bang into the wall. Mac looked up, sat back. Reid leaned into the doorway, looked at the door he'd allowed to slam open, and shrugged.

"Sorry, son. Don't know my own strength sometimes."

"That right, aye?" Mac said with a raised eyebrow.

"Can you spare a minute for a late lunch? I've a hankering for the burger van at the end of the road."

"I'm kind of snowed under here, guv," Mac said.

"Did I misspeak, son?" Reid said pleasantly. "I meant to say come with me now to the burger van at the end of the road, Detective Chief Inspector."

"Yes, sir," Mac said with a wry smile.

Reid turned away and stomped down the aisle towards the door. Mac exchanged a grin with Mel, both knowing their boss's temperament and not taking it seriously. Mac found him waiting by the lift.

"Nice job on the Zoe Phillips case, by the way," Reid said.

"Not much in it for me, sir. Akhtar saw it over the line," Mac replied, watching the floor indicator above the lift.

"I had to give it to her, son. You were out of the picture. Couldn't let a high-profile murder case be put on hold when I have a capable DCI available."

"You've got the argument to yourself, sir," Mac said.

"Aye, that's why I always win," Reid replied as the doors opened.

They left the headquarters building and walked along

Brunswick Street. Calton Hill, with its incongruous mock-Greek ruins rose behind them. Ahead the gabble of traffic on Leith Walk reached for them with increasing volume. Mac felt a moment of reassurance as he walked on wet tarmac past tall tenements. The tan sandstone was stained black by the traffic. A delivery cyclist whizzed past on an electric bike, weaving among traffic. Yellow and brown leaves formed a slick, slimy carpet. Dumpster style bins were out for collection, emitting a noisome odor of rot and decay. It was all the embrace of the city. A hard, concrete and stone embrace but an embrace nonetheless. He relished the anonymity it gave. Being one of millions. Knowing that every face he saw was probably new and would never be seen again, to be replaced tomorrow by another set of fresh faces.

CHAPTER FIFTEEN

"SO, HOW ARE YOU? How's the head?" Reid asked after a moment of silent stomping.

"HR make you ask?" Mac replied sardonically.

"Watch it, son," Reid snapped back.

He walked with hands in the pocket of his overcoat, collar turned up and shoulders hunched. Mac strode straight backed, hands in trouser pockets and overcoat open. There was no malice in his jibe and no real teeth to Reid's reply. They had been through too much together for rank to be a barrier between them.

"My head's fine. I probably rushed it yesterday. My bad," Mac said.

"Glad you admit it," Reid replied.

"Only to you. I'll deny it if you repeat it," Mac said.

"Aye, so you will," Reid chuckled deep in his throat, a bass rumble.

"Lunch is on you?" Mac asked.

"Aye. We need to talk."

"Somewhere away from HQ," Mac stated.

"Yes, Detective. Away from prying ears," Reid growled.

"AC?" Mac asked.

Reid had been the subject of an abortive Anti-Corruption unit investigation which he had dodged by deft use of his own political connections. They had both worked in an AC unit themselves, Mac being recruited to the job by Reid. His performance there had led to a rapid rise through the CID ranks.

"No, if only. That I can handle," Reid said.

They'd reached the end of Brunswick Street, where it joined the wider thoroughfare of Leith Walk. The burger van was actually a pop up sandwich kiosk situated on a wide section of pavement. There were road works on Leith Walk and a group of hi-vis jacket wearing men clustered around with steaming paper cups, munching on rolls and square sausage. Reid ordered two rolls with sausage and bacon and squirted a generous helping of ketchup on his. Mac took his own as it came. Reid jerked his head, and they moved away from the other diners.

"You know who John Lowe is?" Reid asked.

"I do," Mac replied.

"A bad man," Reid commented.

"Drug dealer, loan shark, pimp. Ticks all the boxes," Mac replied.

"Well, I'm in hock to the guy," Reid said as though commenting on the weather.

Mac paused in mid-bite, turned, and looked at his boss. He didn't waste time asking him to repeat what he'd just said, or asking if he was serious. Reid wouldn't have said it if he didn't mean it.

"How?" was all Mac said.

"How? Well, not knowingly, obviously." Reid barked, then he swore as though Mac was being dense.

"Reasonable question. I assumed you wouldn't have done it knowingly," Mac kept his cool.

They were sauntering along Leith Walk now. The Old Town, Waverley, and the Castle all behind them, lost to sight behind the tall buildings, corroded sandstone next to modern structures that mimicked the colour and shape of the original architecture. The contrast was jarring. Reid was determinedly munching on his roll and watching the street from beneath lowered brows. Mac took the occasional bite.

"A wee while ago, I was offered an investment opportunity by an acquaintance. An ex-copper. Property. Seemed a good prospect, and I had a bit of cash on the hip after Marie and I split and sold the house. I jumped at it. It was a gamble but seemed like a good one."

"And you lost," Mac stated.

"Aye, I lost. Then I was offered a way out, a way of recouping my losses. Get back the money I'd put in. I had no choice. Turns out it was a front for a money laundering operation. And now my name's right in the middle of it and it's John Lowe who's standing behind it all."

"Jesus," Mac said, tossing the remains of his roll into a litter bin. "How could you be so bloody stupid?"

"Enough of the lectures, son. I've always been a gambler. The property was legit, I'm sure of it. It was just bad luck."

"Or it was a honey trap. Lure in investors and then offer a

way out when they lose their shirts. A way out that puts them under the control of a man like Lowe," Mac said, coldly and brutally.

"I told you I don't need lectures," Reid snapped.

He tossed his roll aside. A man jogging in the opposite direction did a double take and paused, pulling down headphones.

"Excuse me, you know that's littering, don't you?" he said. "That's an offence."

Reid reached into his coat and took out his warrant card, holding it in the man's face.

"Polis, pal. Now, do one."

He jerked his thumb over his shoulder. The man looked startled, glanced at Mac, who jerked his head in the same direction, silently willing the man not to provoke Reid's temper any further. The man jogged on. Mac glanced back and saw him turning as he ran to snap a picture with his phone. Reid didn't see it.

"What do you need?" Mac asked.

"Thanks for not making me ask," Reid replied, gratitude seeping into his voice through the usual gruffness. "Money doesn't help now. Lowe's not interested in repayment of any debts I've incurred from him. He wants a copper in his pocket."

Mac was silent for a long moment. Finally, Reid glanced across at him.

"I need your help, son," he said.

Gruffness, gone. The world has spilled his pint, gone. Mac saw the plaintive look in Reid's eyes. He remembered his first meeting with, the then, DCI Kenny Reid of the Anti-Corruption Unit. Mac was a PC, driving for DCI Laird Strachan, a bent copper though Mac couldn't see it. He'd been frostily compliant with the investigation into Strack, paying all due respect to Reid's superior rank and giving him nothing. After the interview, Reid had taken him aside, off the record.

"You remember what you said to me the first time we met? After the interview, I mean," Mac said now.

"No," Reid muttered. "I say a lot of things."

"You said there's nothing worse than a bent copper no matter what way they're bending. Strack was a vigilante, he wasn't taking backhanders, and he wasn't in the pay of a gangster. But he was still bent, and it was too late for him. But not for me."

"Did I? Wise words," Reid commented. "I do remember that it was me that stopped you bleeding out when DCI Strachan got shot at with you caught in the cross-fire."

The memory flashed back into Mac's mind, sharp and real in a visceral way. The tang of cordite burning his nose from the gun fired into the close confines of the car he'd been driving. Only the fact that he'd slammed on the brakes when the bike came alongside saved Strachan's life. But it put Mac in the firing line. No pain. A punch in the side like he'd been hit by Mike Tyson. Breathless. Then cold all over except spots on his right and left side where the bullet had gone in and then out before shattering the vehicle's handbrake and embedding itself in the seat that DCI Strachan was sitting in. The pain had hit Mac then. And the realisation that he was alone, bleeding out with Strachan out of the car and running.

"I was lucky you had Strack under surveillance," Mac said.

"Aye, you were. If I hadn't been two cars behind, you wouldn't be here."

"So, what? You're calling in the debt?" Mac said, harshly.

"I'm asking for your help. Like I helped you that day. Like I helped you into AC. I...I'm desperate," Reid said.

Mac knew he should walk away. As a police officer, he should report the disclosure that had been made to him. He already had one bent copper to find. Someone had sold crime scene photos in the Celtic Killer case to a reporter. Said reporter was now sectioned under the mental health act and couldn't be questioned, so Mac still had no idea who he was looking for. Obviously Reid was compromised and even if no crime had been committed, he couldn't be allowed to remain in his post. But Kenny Reid had caught a lot of bent cops. He'd taken pity on a mixed up young PC and helped him realise his potential. Without Reid, Mac would be dead. And the path he'd been on prior to that point? Led only to disgrace and jail, assuming he lived long enough. Mac was obligated. He had a duty which went beyond his duty as a police officer. Then again, knowing he was putting his head in a noose that could break his neck at any moment. He swore.

"Who else knows?" he asked.

"No-one, other than anyone else in Lowe's pocket."

"Lowe's a thug, but he's not corporate enough to infiltrate the police. Not yet. He's no Hance Allen," Mac said.

"Agreed. He doesn't have the structure yet. Just the streets," Reid said. "Which will make it easier to pin something on him."

Mac didn't react to the statement. Not because he was OK with it. Just because he couldn't think of another way to get Reid out of the trap he'd fallen into. A gangster like Lowe made sure he was well insulated from his criminal businesses.

It was hard to get the evidence to legitimately convict him. Fitting him up on the other hand...He didn't like it. It was the kind of thing he'd done for Strack before he'd been left for dead in the car. Fitting up people who deserved it but who were protected behind lawyers and money.

"What in particular?" Mac asked.

"I don't know yet. That's where I need your help, son," Reid said. "I can make it worth your while."

Mac snorted a laugh. "How? You've got no money, by your own admission. Not that I want or need it. What do you think you can offer me?"

"I can recommend you for DCS when I retire. Which, if I get out of this jam I will be doing with full pension, right? Akhtar will be going for it too, and she'll get it unless I spike her guns. She's not as good a detective as you, but she's a political silverback who can kick your backside from here to Glasgow in that arena. You might not want the promotion, but I don't think you want to work for her."

Mac shook his head, running a hand through his hair. A young woman with dark hair framing a pretty, heart-shaped face was hurrying along the street towards him. She was wrapped up in overcoat and scarf, eyes down and collar up. As she passed him, she happened to look up and met Mac's eyes. He caught the ghost of a smile as the connection sparked between them, the hint of a head beginning to turn before she stopped herself. Mac realised he was glowering, but it didn't seem to have put her off. His lips quirked and he let his eyes slide after her.

"Do I have your attention, son?" Reid demanded, looking back at the woman. "Or would you rather be chasing..."

"You're not exactly the easiest boss to work for. Akhtar would be unpleasant, but I could cope," Mac said.

"Aye, you could. You're a big lad, you're not going to let her bully you. But one of the remits coming into my office in the next twelve months is a new cold case unit. I've had a quick look at some of the cases being lined up. They cover the whole of Scotland. Big nationwide initiative. Iona is in there, Mac."

Mac's head whipped round, and he saw that Reid had stopped, was watching him with the cold stare of a crow.

"You want to solve that case. This is your chance. Solve it or maybe bury it."

Mac wanted to grab the wily old stoat by his collar and shake him. He actually took a step, but Reid didn't need height or muscle to stand up to Mac. He just needed the stare he'd practiced through thirty years of facing down the hardest men in Scotland. Bury it? Mac had never mentioned Mark Souter to anyone. Not what he believed Souter had done. Not what Mac had tried to do to him.

"Can of worms and all that, eh?" Reid said with a nasty smile.

Mac could have killed him at that moment. He'd been ready to help from a sense of duty and honour. But Reid couldn't take the chance. He'd laid the groundwork for something not far from blackmail. The old bastard trusted no-one. Looked out for himself. But what choice did Mac have? He swallowed his rising temper and nodded abruptly.

"Alright, I'm in," he said.

He saw a cab coming up from the harbour and hailed it, getting in and leaving Reid to walk back alone.

CHAPTER SIXTEEN

Mac let the vicious, saw-toothed guitars of Swedish death metal flood the car and assault his ears. His insurer had delivered a courtesy car to Brunswick Road, supposedly like for like. It was Korean hatchback that struggled with minor inclines and wasn't, by any stretch of the imagination, a replacement for a two-litre diesel Audi. The sound system was woeful; no amount of tweaking could entirely rid it of a sound that was too bright, bass and drums muddied together. He tried to put it out of his mind as his insides resonated to the riffs and his fingers drummed on the steering wheel. Winter had rolled up the day early, and he drove in the dark, heater turned off so that the sound of the fan didn't take away from the music. Better to be cold than diffuse the almost pure sounds coming from the speakers with the zombie roar of white noise. He was heading west from his apartment, moving towards the leafy idylls of Corstorphine. He'd been seeing Maia and Clio on weekends until now, not every weekend but more frequently as the deadline for their move approached.

He was a pair of hands to pack and stack boxes. A friendly face to take Maia's mind off school and a shoulder for Clio to lean on. For Mac, it was an escape. From dreams and from the cut-throat politics of work. If he could only deal with brutal murders every day, alone, without having to deal with superiors or inferiors. Without wondering who was trying to stab him in the back or what his crooked boss would try and drag him into. He had never acknowledged that he needed anyone. Still couldn't easily. But even Mac had to acknowledge the relief he felt when he stepped through Clio's front door, knowing that work talk was forbidden. He was beginning to think that the counselling session he had arranged for the next day, Talvir Sidhu clearing his diary to fit Mac in and what exactly did that say for his opinion of Mac's mental health, would actually be beneficial. Not just lip service to a HR requirement, and they had a lot of them. Mac had rarely paid too much attention. The entrance to the zoo rolled past, and he made a mental note, becoming more alert to landmarks.

He turned off Glasgow Road at a roundabout before a Chinese takeaway he recognised and onto Drum Brae South. Bungalows with neat gardens and clean, sandblasted exteriors passed in uniform ranks. Windows were lit warmly and occasionally curtains left open to provide tantalising glimpses of families sitting in their front rooms. TVs on the walls throwing out glaring blue light. Dog walkers on the pavement, wrapped up against the cold. Hedges separated gardens where chain-link fencing was used in less affluent areas. Like West Pilton, not far away but enough that the residents of Corstorphine didn't have to think too much about them. Besides which, the Tories they voted for would come down like a ton of bricks on any have-nots who showed their faces in pleasant middle-class communities like this. Cynical thoughts were chased from his head by sonic bombardment as he reached Queensferry road and the street signs told him he was now in Cramond and please drive carefully.

Mac found himself murmuring along to the riffs, nodding his head. Work was slipping away from him. It fell from his shoulders like a discarded coat. Akhtar would take the glory for the Zoe Phillips and Vicky McCourt murders. Who cared? He would make sure his team got the credit they deserved. Reid would have his back. And now he and Reid were diving into an illegal morass in order to pull the teeth of a gangster. It was a concern for another day. The Mac that would go into the office tomorrow would be tough, snappy, and glowering. That man would be up to the task of trawling unsolved cases for a fit up. This Mac was looking forward to an evening of video games with Maia and a glass of wine with Clio. The thought occurred that one of these days he might discover Clio was dating. She'd never mentioned a man other than the ex-husband who had deserted her not long after she discovered she was pregnant. There was a man crying out to be fitted up with something nasty. But Clio was very attractive. She was intelligent and funny, good company and easy going. Her interests in paganism were not quite to Mac's tastes. Her habit of cleansing her home using herbs and a spell was, frankly, ludicrous. He said nothing. It was her business and seemed to give her comfort.

It was better than booze or anti-depressants. Better than

bottling it all up until you started to have panic attacks in the shower or while driving through a busy city with one of your team in the passenger seat. Clio's house appeared on the right and he closed a partition of his mind in which the subject of mental health was firmly locked. That wasn't for tonight's Mac. Maybe for tomorrow Mac. Or the day after. Or the week. Maia's face appeared between the curtains of the living room window. She grinned and waved. Mac gave her a salute with two fingers touched to his forehead. Cringe, as Maia would say. She mimicked with a lop-sided smile that Mac couldn't keep from his own face. He crunched up the red gravel of the driveway and was reaching for the doorbell when Maia flung the door wide. He grinned, best rogue's smile.

"Hey, Maia. I've come to take you out to the library for a few hours quiet study," Mac said.

Dad joke. Not even funny. But Maia laughed, which was why he did it. She stepped back from the door and Mac allowed her an arm about the neck hug.

"Mum, Callum's here!" Maia bellowed through to the kitchen.

"The whole street knows I'm here," Mac winced.

Another dad joke. He took off his jacket and Maia diligently took it from him. She hung it from a hook as Mac kicked off the budget trainers he wore when the uniform of a detective wasn't appropriate.

"You need some better footwear," Maia observed, wrinkling her nose. "How much were they?"

"Tenner," Mac said, deadpan. "They keep the rain out. That's all I care about. I've got other things to spend money on."

"Like what?" Maia asked, leading him through the house to the open-plan kitchen lounge.

"Music mostly."

"Oh yeah, I tried one of those bands you told me about the other week," Maia said.

"Great, which one?"

"Venom," Maia replied.

"Awesome. How do you like them?" Mac said.

"I wasn't too keen," Clio said as they entered the kitchen. "Not sure about Satanism for a teenager."

She was moving between steaming pans, tasting, stirring.

"It's all for show. They never meant any of it. And it'll give Maia street cred," Mac said, taking a seat on an armchair.

"When all her friends are into K-pop or Taylor Swift?" Clio suggested, raising an eyebrow.

"I have literally no idea who they are," Mac responded blandly.

"Well, I like Venom and I don't care what the…" Maia swallowed what was obviously intended to be a swear word. "…others say. I also started listening to Bathory and Celtic Frost."

Mac nodded in approval. "Very discerning. Like it."

"I'm not even going to ask. I'm an historian, so I can guess what the inspiration for the name Bathory was."

"She was the world's earliest recorded serial killer…" Maia began.

Clio held up a hand. "Mac isn't permitted to talk about serial killers in this house, so you certainly aren't. We're having spag bol, Mac. OK with you?"

"Sounds great."

"Maia, could you ask Mac what he would like to drink? And then pour me a red."

Maia vaulted the sofa which she had been perched on, all gangly legs, knees, and elbows. Mac ordered a beer, knowing that Clio kept some for him. Maia busied herself with the task of being a hostess, clearly enjoying being treated as one of the adults. Clio had something banal and easy on the ear, playing through a smart speaker. Clio's tastes were rooted in the sixties and featured acoustic guitars and winsomely sung story-telling lyrics. He let it wash over him, all part of being in the Wray household.

"How many days 'til D-day?" he asked.

"Nine. The new landlord is happy to give us the keys two days before the moving date so we can take the weekend to move. You still OK to help us?"

"As long as no-one in Edinburgh kills anyone else that weekend. I'm on call," Mac said as Maia handed him a bottle of beer.

He chinked it against her glass of Coke with a wink.

"If they do, I'll kill them," Clio said, distractedly, tasting a spoonful of mince.

"So, you want to tell me more about Maia getting suspended?" Mac asked.

Dinner was over; the dishes stacked either side of the cooker and in the sink. Maia had been banished to her bedroom when Clio realised it was close to midnight. They'd played Uno and then a few board games Maia still owned and secretly loved, though being a teenager precluded her from openly admitting that. Cluedo remained on top of her wardrobe since Mac had won hands down the first time he'd been invited to Clio's. First guess. Clio rolled her eyes, pouring herself a glass from the second bottle she'd opened. Mac held out his own glass, having switched to wine when he saw how hard Clio had been hitting the first bottle.

"She wasn't entirely blameless. She shouldn't have done what she did. But it was a reaction, and she got caught. The act she was reacting to wasn't seen and so the troublemaker got away with it. The school just refuses point blank to accept that Maia's ADHN means she is impulsive. The other kids know more about it than the teachers. They provoke her deliberately. And Maia's the one who ends up in trouble."

"You mentioned picking my brains," Mac said.

Clio shook her head silently, sipping from the glass and staring into space. Mac watched her silently. There were tears just behind the surface. Behind the mask. How long had she been bottling it up? No-one to talk to except him. She'd never mentioned other friends. Only colleagues she was friendly with. It had been Clio and Maia against the world for so long that Mac didn't think Clio particularly cared. But that was his view of the world, not hers. He would gladly have spent his life as a hermit. Clio wouldn't.

"She's been getting bullied online. I wanted to know if any laws had been broken and if..."

She blinked back tears, putting a hand to her mouth. "If... I don't know what. It's not like they can prosecute thirteen-year-old girls, is it? I just want them to give her a break."

"If you show me the messages, I can check with some of

my colleagues in child protection. See what can be done. Maybe scare the perpetrators."

Clio nodded and glanced towards the door that led to the stairs. "Just don't let on to Maia that you know. She'd be mortified if she knew you'd seen them."

Mac nodded, sipping his own wine. It made his mouth feel dry, and he didn't like the taste, but it cut down the amount Clio could drink.

"There's something else isn't there," he said, after she'd been quiet for a moment.

She looked up, surprise on her face. Maybe she'd forgotten what she'd intimated in her text to him.

"I'm a detective," Mac said, spreading his hands in innocence.

"You're supposed to be autistic too. Not able to read people well," Clio pointed out.

Mac shrugged. "I'm still learning how to be autistic. Haven't got it quite right yet."

His deadpan expression as he spoke seemed to do the trick. Clio burst out laughing. She put a hand on Mac's arm briefly, squeezing.

"I've been an idiot," she said.

It was easily spoken and with a smile, but Mac could see the worry behind her eyes. Whatever it was, it couldn't be brushed off so easily. At least Clio didn't think so. He waited.

"There's one particular teacher. Michael Gaines. Maia's head of year. He's been particularly difficult and I've…lit into him on some of his social media posts. Gave him a no holds barred piece of my mind."

"Ah," Mac replied.

"Yeah," Clio said.

"How big a piece?"

"I'd had a couple of glasses of wine and my inhibitions weren't as controlled as they should have been. I was furious."

"Are we talking threats?" Mac asked.

Clio looked away and Mac sighed. That brought her head up, eyes bright.

"Sorry," Mac said, raising his hands in placation. "But you never put something in writing that you wouldn't say face to face. I mean, it could cost you your job if he makes a complaint," Mac pointed out, not wanting to hurt her but believing she needed the stark truth.

"In my defence, I'm not the only parent he's clashed with. I found out today that he'd resigned, though on his social media he's making out that it's about how little pay teachers get and how much work they have to do..." Clio swore.

"So, that's a good thing. He's out of Maia's life. So you can just delete whatever you said," Mac said reasonably.

"He was vile about Maia. Called her a troublemaker and said she shouldn't be in mainstream education because of the disruption she causes. Can you believe that?"

"But he's gone now, Clio," Mac persisted, leaning close, putting a hand on her shoulder.

Clio's eyes were afire. It was an attractive look. Mac had to stop and think about how much he'd had to drink. At the same time, the thought popped into his head about whether this friendship was just that. Or was it the beginning of something more? No. He valued his friendship with Clio. It was probably the first such platonic relationship that he could honestly say he valued.

"Show me this threat that you made," Mac ordered

Reluctantly, she took out her phone, woke the screen and navigated to a social media app before handing it to him. He read through a conversation alive with invective and anger.

"Both sides got a bit heated."

"He didn't threaten me," Clio pointed out.

"No," Mac said.

He took out his own phone and took pictures of the conversation.

"Doesn't hurt to have a backup. Is this a private chat?"

"Yes," Clio said.

"Well, the fact it wasn't out in the open is a positive, but who knows how many of his friends he's shared this with? It's pretty tame, relatively speaking. I wouldn't worry too much about it. With the prosecution backlog in the Procurator Fiscal's office, they're not going to waste time prosecuting this."

Clio looked relieved, tears making her eyes gleam for a moment. Then, lurching impulsively, she hugged Mac. For a moment, he froze. Then he put his arms around her and returned the hug.

CHAPTER SEVENTEEN

He lay on the single bed, the only furniture in the room. A thudding, monotonous bass line was seeping through the wall behind his head, but he wore earplugs to shut it out. If he hadn't, he didn't think he could stop himself from knocking on the door. There was no guarantee what would happen then. It might satisfy him in the moment, but it would upset the project in the long term. He couldn't afford to be impulsive, not when everything was going to plan. Boxes filled most of the floor space. Stacks of empty petri dishes took up more. Sealed dishes protected by ziplock bags, the rest. The room was dark except for the blue-white light from the screen of his phone. He held it in both hands and it lit up his smooth, hairless skin. Eyes so dark they appeared black were fixed on the conversation he was engaged in, thumbs moving dexterously over the screen. Bald brows drawn in. An expression of intensity that had made more than one person look at him askance. A smile worked wonders. His smile lit up his face, transformed him. Layered him in a veneer of trust and innocence.

It did so now. Metal_Kitten2010 had just replied to his message with an emoji, kissing face and a heart. She had some kind of manga image as her profile picture, but he'd already won her trust enough for her to disclose her real name. His own profile pic was at the top of the screen. A girl of twelve to fourteen years old with long, silky auburn hair and brown eyes. She was pouting at the camera, holding up two fingers in what used to be a peace sign. He suspected it meant something different now, but wasn't sure what. It didn't matter. He had a collection of pictures from the girl. He'd already forgotten her name and where she was from. It served as the perfect fake profile to befriend a lonely, mixed up thirteen-year-old. She'd revealed a lot of what was troubling her to the friend she'd met online a month ago. A friend who understood her so well. Shared interests with her. Listened.

Now, she was ranting about a teacher at her school. She thought her mum was in trouble for laying into him online. Mental note to check if that had been made public anywhere. The teacher was already on the radar. Parent groups online had mentioned his name. Very direct. Rude according to the yummy mummies. Gay, some of them didn't like that. Or the fact that he was very vocal in support of drag queen story telling time at the local library. He chuckled at the banality of it. But it all fuelled the fire. Unfortunately, his chosen victim seemed more tolerant and accepting. She just seemed to hate him because of how he had treated her daughter. Clio was very protective of Maia. He wondered how far she would actually go in defense of her daughter. From what Maia was saying to him —correction, what she was saying to the person she thought was named Gabby from Chelsea —Clio had quite the temper. He smiled as Maia sent another message, to which he/Gabby replied with just the right words.

He flipped between apps until he found the picture of Clio Wray he'd discovered then copied from the University website. Using a drawing app, he'd expertly added a handful of lines to it. Pin back the ears, just a little. Slight bend to the nose, correct that. Otherwise a very pretty woman. Almost perfect. No-one was perfect. At least not until he had his hands on them. Another app and he tapped a few notes, recording a few choice pieces of information that Maia had just provided him with. That information was the final piece of this particular puzzle. He felt a satisfaction that briefly eclipsed the sense of injustice at his surroundings. At his circumstances. That injustice was his primary emotion. Anger and the desire for revenge. Now, though, he basked in the anticipation of the next masterpiece. The work to come. Two lives ended. One with finality. The other ended in its present form. Diverted onto a path of his choosing. The need for gratification was intense, almost sexual. All the pieces were in place. It was simply a matter of time.

Closing the social media app and cutting off Maia Wray, he skimmed through his notes on Michael Grainger. Habits. Routines. Schedules. Pictures. A life in his hands.

CHAPTER EIGHTEEN

"So, a good place to start would be to set expectations. What would you like to get out of today?" Tal Sidhu asked.

He was about Mac's age, maybe a year or two older, closer to fifty. His neatly trimmed beard was as grey as his hair. His eyes were deep set, and he had a nose slightly too large for his face. His accent held a hint of the Midlands. Mac kept himself still, resisting the urge to shift in his seat. The appointment had been rescheduled twice. Once from Friday morning to Monday. Then from Monday to Tuesday. Then something had come up on Tuesday. According to Mac, at least. Finally, Dr. Sidhu had volunteered to come to Brunswick Road. They sat facing each other in an interview room. Cameras off, no recording device and the adjacent viewing room locked by Mac and the key secreted in his pocket.

Mac sat in the chair he would typically use in this room. Sidhu sat opposite, one leg crossed over the other. A pad rested on his thigh and he held a pen in his right hand. He wore tweeds, slightly creased and a crooked tie. Mac's initial response was that he wanted to get out of today full stop, pure and simple. Instead, he frowned as though thinking.

"I want to be signed off as A1 and get back to work."

Sidhu looked back without expression or words, waiting. It was a basic interview technique, one Mac had deployed more times than he could count. He stared back, at first determined not to blink. Then he remembered the power dynamic between the two of them. The dynamic that Sidhu had never forgotten. Mac needed him more than he needed Mac. With a sigh, Mac sat forward, forearms resting on the interview table. How many times had he sat back, suppressing a smile of satisfaction when he saw this posture of defeat in a suspect?

"I am looking...for help with. Stress."

It felt like he was pulling his own teeth out.

"OK. You've been under stress. How has that manifested?"

Mac's eyes narrowed. "How do you think?"

Again the level, patient look and Mac closed his mouth. Play the game. Play the game. But he daren't be too honest. Would confessing a panic attack leave him suspended? How honest could he be while ensuring he stayed on the job? Sidhu beat him to the punch.

"You're trying to figure out how much to tell me. Which reveals one thing. The stress is manifesting in such a way that you think I won't sign you off as fit to work if you share the details."

There was a kind smile on Sidhu's face and a friendly twinkle in his eye. Mac felt as though his mind was being read. Was this how suspects felt when he talked them into a corner, drawing a confession from their lies and evasions? It was intensely uncomfortable being on this side of the table.

"I've had a...panic attack," Mac said.

He watched Sidhu's reaction. There wasn't one. Sidhu merely watched him. Mac decided that he wasn't going to look away first.

"Felt sick to my stomach and my heart was racing."

"How many times?"

"Just the once."

An eyebrow was raised, but Mac wasn't surrendering anymore. He stared back as though daring the psychologist to challenge him. Sidhu gave the ghost of a smile and wrote something down. Mac couldn't see the pad which was hidden by the psychiatrist's knee. But he made out the shape of the first letter. It was a t. There was another at the end of the word. Mac could tell because there was then a gap. A lower case i came next. Mac saw the dot. As he watched, he thought about the words that could be so spelled. Trust issues came to mind, and Mac smiled.

"What?" Sidhu said, also smiling.

"Nothing," Mac said, shaking his head.

"Where did it happen?" Sidhu asked.

"At home."

"Has it ever happened at work?"

"No."

"Driving?"

"No."

Mac's tone didn't change as he answered. Nothing to give away if one of those nos wasn't emphasised more than another.

"Where in the home were you?"

"In the shower," Mac replied.

"What triggered it?" Sidhu asked.

"How the hell should I know?" Mac said, his reserve cracking.

Sidhu hadn't shown any lack of patience. He didn't seem even close to breaking a sweat.

"Well, what were you thinking about when you became aware of the symptoms?"

Mac sat back, folding his arms, then realised how defensive that looked. He resisted the urge to wipe sweaty palms on his trousers. He felt guilty and then felt angry at feeling guilty. Mac glared at Sidhu, but it bounced off the psychiatrist.

"I was thinking about my sister. She died when I was younger. There was something about rain. The shower made me think of it."

"Rain?" Sidhu asked.

"I don't remember. Maybe it was raining on the day of her funeral. I don't know. But suddenly I was thinking about her and..."

He tailed off, feeling as though what he was saying was unbelievable. Weak. But Sidhu was nodding, making more notes.

"How did she die? If you don't mind me asking," Sidhu asked, his voice dropping a notch.

"She was murdered," Mac replied, finality in his voice. He wouldn't besmirch his sister's memory by lying about that.

"I'm sorry," Sidhu said, genuine sympathy in his voice. "Have you ever had any grief counselling?"

"No. I was seventeen. My dad was drinking himself to death and finished the job later that year. But it's never been an issue before."

"Trauma doesn't necessarily manifest its effects immediately. The mind has a lot of different ways to protect itself in the moment. I understand you went through a traumatic episode last year in the line of duty?"

"Yes. Again, I didn't go to pieces immediately after."

"As I said. But, it might be the cumulative effect. Or some change in your life. It could be anything, quite frankly. It might not be connected in any way. But something happens and all that pressure that you didn't know you were carrying suddenly becomes too much."

"I can't think of anything," Mac said.

"It doesn't matter. There's significant trauma in your past that you've never resolved. Never dealt with. And it's been lying dormant in your sub conscious. Or perhaps you've had issues with anger in the past? Or addiction maybe?"

Mac didn't have to think hard to answer yes to both those questions. He'd been an addict when he'd left home, with cash in his pocket from the sale of the farm. Then when he'd joined the force, there had been alcohol and tobacco. Anger? Mac smiled to himself. It was on his record from the early days. A bit too much of a hothead when a drunk threw a punch on a Saturday night. Or on Derby day when the Hibs and Hearts fans went at it.

Sidhu was a police psychiatrist, so he'd be privy to Mac's record. No sense in denying it.

"Yes. As you know," Mac replied.

"It's textbook. The pressure bubbling to the surface. I've done it myself."

Mac would have looked surprised except he'd been waiting

for it. Bonding over a shared experience. He'd been through hostage negotiation training. This was textbook too.

"I mean it. I'm not just trying to build rapport. When my dad got cancer, I was too wrapped up in my career to give him the time he needed. Then it was too late. I never got a chance to say goodbye, and that experience profoundly affected me. I'm in AA now. No reason not to talk about it. There's nothing to be ashamed of."

Despite himself, Mac was beginning to warm to the man. His openness was refreshing. It reminded him of Clio. There wasn't enough of that in his life. He was always being lied to or trying to avoid knives in the back. He ran a hand through his hair, sitting forward again.

"I'm not ashamed," he began. "I just haven't...talked to anyone about what happened to Iona. My sister. I buried it. Police work is good for that. It's all consuming, so it's a useful job when you have a lot you want consumed."

Sidhu spread his arms. "I'm in the same boat there, Mac. Being a clinical psychiatrist is a good way of avoiding dealing with your own issues. You just focus on everyone else's."

Mac smiled and for the first time since he had sat down with Sidhu that the expression was genuine. Sidhu chuckled.

"Cut from a similar cloth, aren't we?" he laughed.

"That's some good rapport you're building there," Mac said.

"I'll use whatever I can to achieve a break through," Sidhu said. "I can be ruthless like that."

"Something else we have in common then," Mac replied.

"These issues aren't going to go away, Mac. Trauma has to be healed and, just like a physical wound, you can't do that by ignoring it. Think of these panic attacks as an infection setting into a wound that you've left untended."

"I get it, doctor. I really do get it. I need to talk about my feelings regarding what happened to my sister. I do know about trauma. When you have a dead body that someone has carved up in frenzy, you look for the reason for that frenzy. And it's always there. The killer might seem just plain bad, pure evil. But there is always something in their past that turned them into murderer. A catalyst."

"Good. That's a good start. So let's talk about your sister."

"Now?" Mac said.

Sidhu raised his eyebrow again, tapping his pen against the top of the pad.

"Why am I thinking that you're telling me what I want to hear but have no intention of actually doing the work?"

"No, I want to do the...work. But it just feels like there isn't a lot of time left to get into that," Mac replied.

"We've got another half hour. Plenty of time to make a good start, as far as I'm concerned," Sidhu said reasonably.

Mac felt as though he was squirming. The conversation had become easier as it progressed. Sidhu seemed more and more like a human being as the conversation had gone on, easier to relate to. But the idea of talking about Iona with anyone was impossible. The idea of thinking about Iona was impossible. His chest felt tight suddenly and all Mac could think of was the need to hide it from the man sitting opposite him. The man whose dark eyes missed nothing. The man who had the power to stop him from working. Stop him doing the one thing that stopped him from thinking about her.

"I'd rather discuss it in the next session," Mac said, pushing his chair back.

"Why?" Sidhu asked.

"I'd like to prepare myself," Mac shot back.

"It won't make it any easier. It's like pulling off a plaster. Just one tug." Sidhu came back just as quick.

Mac was beginning to feel trapped. He avoided licking his lips, even though his mouth felt dry as sandpaper. He resisted the need to get to his feet and pace the room. Staying still with monumental effort, he watched Sidhu watching him. He willed the other man to look away, to open his diary and book another session. Just give him some breathing space. Just let him out of this room. Sidhu didn't move, but Mac's jacket pocket buzzed. His phone.

He tried not to sound relieved when he answered it. Tried not to look triumphant as he met Sidhu's intractable eyes.

"Guv," Mac said to Reid.

"Got one for you, Mac. Wait, was this your counselling session?"

"Just finished, guv. Perfect timing."

Mac stood, holding up a brief hand in goodbye. Sidhu smiled fatalistically and wrote something on his pad. Mac turned his back to stop himself from trying to read it upside down.

"'Cause I could give it to Akhtar. Give you a chance to really get into it, the counselling, I mean."

Mac swore once he was through the door, and Reid chuckled.

"You've gone to the appointment. That should satisfy HR and you don't have to see the guy again. Get back to work, case file's in your inbox," Reid said and was gone.

CHAPTER NINETEEN

Got one was what Reid had said. Got one. He didn't need to explain what he'd got. There was only one kind of crime to which Mac would be assigned that required no description or explanation. It was a dead body. Mac knew that he was Reid's first choice as DCI. Above Akhtar. He took a measure of pride in that. Akhtar might be able to climb the ranks politically, but she couldn't match Mac as a detective. Once more, he was heading west into the affluent suburb of Corstorphine.

It reminded him of the evening he had spent with Clio and Maia. He had drunk more than he had intended, all with the intention of leaving less for Clio to drink. In the end, he'd been drunk and Clio had been...not so drunk. He remembered laughter and music, Maia sleepily coming down the stairs to protest at the noise in a bizarre reversal of roles. Then waking up on Clio's sofa, top to tail with her, Maia curled up in an armchair. They'd been watching movies; he vaguely remembered insisting on Spinal Tap. Their reaction brought a smile to his face.

"Share the joke, guv?" Nari asked.

She was in the passenger seat of Mac's courtesy car, reviewing the case file on her phone. Mac had absorbed the salient facts from the files emailed to him from Reid's office. They'd become burned into his brain, a trick he'd learned over the years.

"No joke. Just...remembering something. Ignore me. Remind me where we're headed."

He knew exactly where they were headed, had looked it up online and memorised the route. But it gave him something to distract Nari. Hopefully forget seeing him go all sentimental. Mac straightened his mouth and gritted his teeth behind his lips, not allowing himself another sign of weakness.

"It's a recycling depot just outside of town, right next to the airport. Workers found a car abandoned and a body inside. We follow this road, then head onto the Turnhouse Road until we see the signs."

"Right."

"Guv, can I ask you a question?" Nari asked in a loaded voice.

"Sure," Mac replied, focusing on the road.

They passed the roundabout that would lead to Drum Brae Drive and, eventually, Clio's place. The houses to either side were either one storey or one and a half, looking like bungalows, but with windows set into the roof line giving away the fact there was an upper floor. The car had been found less than a mile from this cosy suburb. Mac found it jarring that violent crime would exist in a place like this. He knew that was prejudice. There was no reason why people in Corstorphine wouldn't be just as capable of violence as people in Craigmillar.

But it seemed to fit into the latter. In places like this, with pensioners walking dogs and gardens well-kept, expensive German SUVs in the driveways and solar panels on the roofs, it seemed out of place. It was a mindset he tried to push away, not wanting it to cloud his judgement. He was glad to be back to work, doing what he knew he did best. But there was a pressure that he hadn't felt before and it came from the proximity of a rival. Nari had been working closely with that rival. He wondered for how long. They shared an office, after all. They were both from immigrant families.

"Would it be a problem for you if I did more work with DCI Akhtar?"

Mac nodded slowly, eyes not leaving the road where traffic was building.

"Of course not. We're all colleagues. All the same team," Mac said.

"We know it's not that simple though, don't we, sir?" Nari said.

Mac glanced in the rear-view mirror, caught sight of the car driven by Kai. He was alone. Mac frowned; Mel should be with him. A SOCO van was behind them. The team had been at HQ finishing up reports from their last case. The entire convoy was headed to the new murder scene.

"Do we?" Mac said, playing for time.

"I think so. You don't get on with Akhtar. That much is obvious. But, she has experience in an area I'd like to explore as part of my development. And she's offered to help. But I don't want to do that at the cost of our working relationship."

Nari sounded sincere. Mac glanced at her and found her looking at him. Concern creased her face. Worry clear in her eyes. Mac's initial reaction was to shut down the conversation. It made him uncomfortable. But he couldn't afford to be dismissive to the feelings of his team. He was their boss and supporting them personally as well as professionally was within his remit, whether he liked it or not. He thought of his conversations with Clio, even his session with Talvir Sidhu. At one point he had wondered if Nari was interested in him, had tried to avoid thinking about it. That was a complication he didn't need.

"I can take or leave her, but she seems to be...combative when it comes to me. Not sure what I've done in the past to put her nose out of joint, but there it is. We're both professionals though. I have no issue with you working more closely with her if it helps your career. It won't harm our relationship."

Nari grinned, looking relieved. Mac wondered just how combative he and Akhtar appeared if it caused a member of his team so much stress. Then he pushed the thought aside. That was low down on the priority list. Top of it was a dead body in a car near the airport.

"Good, 'cos I really value being on your team. You have a reputation in Serious Crimes, you know? As a detective. A lot of officers would love to be on your team."

"Right," Mac said, biting back a smile.

"Right," Nari replied, openly smiling. "Don't pretend that doesn't appeal to your ego, sir."

Mac smiled. "Don't push it, Nari. Akhtar wouldn't let you get away with speaking to her like that."

"I wouldn't speak to her like that. She's a dragon," Nari said with a wry expression.

"No arguments from me on that score."

The city released them, the houses falling away to be replaced by fields. Bare earth and grass alike were dusted in frost under a steel sky. The airport was a looming presence in the near distance. Planes coming in and landing every few minutes. For a place where millions of people passed through every year, it felt lonely and empty. The recycling depot was a fenced off collection of low buildings with the look of portacabins. Larger warehouse type constructions were behind, around a large, open yard, bounded by coils of razor wire. A road led to a gated entrance and a track led from the road between mounds of gorse, around a frozen hill.

A police car was parked beside the beginning of the track. A PC got out as Mac's car approached. Mac wound down the window.

"Up the lane over there, guv," the PC said. "Just around the bend."

Mac pulled the car in that direction, bumping over frozen ruts. The scene wasn't hard to find. Around a bend there was a line of police tape, secured against two trees either side of the lane. Beyond that was a Honda hatchback. He got out and went to the boot of his car, where he'd stowed a bag of forensic clothes. He and Nari put on the required paper suits, shoes, and gloves. Mac glanced at the number plate of the car; Nari was already on the phone getting the plate run through the Automatic Number Plate Recognition database. While she waited on a name and address, Mac slowly approached the vehicle, looking at the ground. It was hard as stone, waves of mud and broken earth frozen as though set in concrete. Nothing soft enough to take the imprint of a tyre or a foot. He glanced up at the car, at the crime scene awaiting him.

The windows were completely frosted over, opaque. That told him the engine had been off for a few hours overnight. Long enough for dew to form and then freeze. The doors were closed, but the file said a member of staff had walked up here for a fag, had looked into the car, and tried the door. So the car was unlocked. His gaze returned to the ground as he made a slow, awkward circuit of the vehicle.

"Belongs to a Mr. Michael Gaines, sir," Nari called over. "3 Craigmount Wynd, The Gyle. We probably drove past it on the way here."

Mac looked around sharply and Nari frowned. "You know him, guv?"

Sharp shake of the head and eyes back to the ground. "I know of a man with that name. Doesn't sound unique. Probably coincidence."

Mac felt a hollow thump in his chest. A Michael Gaines taught at Cramond Secondary School. Not far from the Gyle. Easy commute. Has to be a coincidence. Mac went to run a hand through his hair and then remembered the glove he wore. He stopped, keeping his hands away from his sides and any possible contamination. Walking around the car, he noticed damage to the rear bumper on the driver's side.

Something had collided with the car there, breaking the plastic of the bumper and the carbon-fibre of the bodywork. He crouched beside the damage, seeing something. There were flecks of white paint on the damaged section, but the

Honda was dark blue. Possibly paint from whatever or whoever had hit it.

His attention was drawn to the ground just beside the rear driver's side wheel. Something amid the white sparkling frost. It caught the light with a dull glint. He carefully walked over to it. It was a silver ring, ten yards from the car. A narrow band which widened to house a circular face with what appeared to be a stags head and the word 'bydand,' a Scots term meaning steadfast. He picked it up and fished a clear plastic bag from his pocket, putting it inside and sealing it. The metal lacked any tarnish or scratches. Only recently abandoned then. Finally, he went to the rear passenger door and opened it.

The handle pulled out but the door stuck for a moment, frost holding it shut. Then the metal pulled free. Inside was dark. A naked man sat on the rear seat, driver's side. Mac took out a pen torch and twisted the head to its brightest setting, shining it inside. The man was staring straight ahead, eyes open. His torso was covered in stab wounds, some crossing each other. Blood had been cleaned away, leaving the wounds as clean cuts. He leaned in, detecting no smell of putrefaction, and shone the torch to the left side of the man's chest. The wound he was looking for was there. In just the right place for a blow angled slightly upward to hit the heart. Nari opened the door opposite, also leaning in with her own torch. She held it in her mouth, holding an evidence bag and her phone in one hand, supporting herself against the door frame with the other.

"I think we'll find that was the killing blow and the rest all happened post-mortem," Mac said.

"Looks familiar," Nari pointed out.

"Doesn't it just. But our perpetrator for Zoe Phillips and Vicky McCourt is locked up."

"So, either this killing pre-dates those..." Nari speculated aloud.

"Which it doesn't. The body's in too good a condition."

"A copycat?"

Mac shrugged. "A duo maybe. Copycats tend to copy famous killings, ones that have had plenty of press. We've kept quiet about the details of the killings we've arrested Ash Fenton for. So, it could be that there were two of them involved."

"Or we got the wrong man," Nari said.

Mac nodded slowly, still looking up and down the body that could belong to Michael Gaines. Who might be Maia's teacher and the man Clio had threatened. He slammed a partition into place in his mind, pushing thoughts of Clio and Maia aside. He saw the body and nothing else. Similar MO. Body dumped somewhere other than where he was killed. The lack of blood on the body or in the car told him that. A thought occurred to him and he shone the torch into the man's face. There was a small, neat red spot high on his right cheek. It looked as though something had been cut away. Very precisely. Surgically. Mac sat back on his haunches, looking at the face thoughtfully. Zoe Phillips' face had been marked and so had Vicky McCourt's. All with cuts displaying control and precision. What the hell did it mean?

A crunch of frozen earth underfoot announced the arrival of Mac's convoy. Kai was walking up the track from his car. A forensics team was carrying bags of equipment with them. Derek Stringer appeared around the bend in the track, unable to drive his vehicle as far up as Mac had due to the narrow road. He was puffing, head down. Mac stepped away from the motor, leaving the door open. Nari was making notes on her phone, taking pictures.

"Kai, I see security cameras down there in the yard. Find out if they can access the footage and see what they picked up. Someone drove the car up here and then left. Either in a vehicle or on foot. Nari talk to whoever found the body. Get them to go over everything again with you. Where's Mel?"

"She decided to go home, guv. Hoped you wouldn't mind. Whiplash from the accident, remember? It's playing up a bit," Kai said.

In the excitement of a new case, Mac had completely forgotten about the accident. He waved it away, feeling guilty. Made a mental note to call and check in on Mel as soon as he could

"Sure, no problem. Ok, get on it, Kai, eh?"

Kai nodded, peering from the roadside down the short slope of stiff, scrubby grass to the fenced off yard. Men and vehicles were moving about down there. The sound of heavy machinery reaching them on the frigid air.

"What about the..." Nari began.

Mac stopped her with a raised hand and a glare. He knew what she was going to say. Kai had been about to begin trudging down to the yard. He stopped, an interested look on his face.

"Just focus on your actions," Mac said, leaving no room for discussion. He wanted to keep the similarities to the Phillips and McCourt cases to himself for the moment. He didn't want the team to be prejudiced by assumptions. Although Nari had obviously picked up on it immediately, she knew better than to let it cloud her judgement. It was better to treat it as a standalone crime, work the evidence.

"I'm going to check the home address of the car's owner. See if we can confirm the identity of the body, whether it's him or not. Anyone have questions?"

Nobody did.

CHAPTER TWENTY

MAC DROVE AS RAIN BEGAN TO PATTER on the windscreen. After Reid had told him about the new case, his mind had been focused on the facts that were known. Now, his musings ran to something more personal. The panic attacks. He thought about the smash that had led to Mel taking time off work. Guilt coursed through him like fire. He hit the windscreen wiper, but the rain just came harder, barely cleared before it washed down again. Mac fought to keep his mind focused. He was having difficulty breathing. Chest rising and falling as though he'd been running. Hands on the wheel were damp with sweat. He forced an image of the dead body in the car into his mind. Visualised it in as much detail as he could. Cuts all over the torso. One solitary wound on the cheek. Naked. Middle-aged, pale with dark hair on chest and lower arms. No tattoos. A ring on the ground outside the car.

The road was quiet. This was a b-road heading out of Edinburgh into the countryside. It skirted the airport but wasn't a major route from anywhere to anywhere. Headlights swept passed. His own had come on automatically in the gloom that had descended with the rain. Iona. The case being reopened. If he was DCI, he could oversee it. Prove Mark Souter was the killer. Unless Souter knew who had almost killed him that night. Unless he had seen something. Maybe when Mac was running away, looking back over his shoulder to where Souter lay beside the concrete bus shelter. His face lit up in a flash of lightning. Mark had looked right at him towards the end, but his eyes had been glassy, perhaps through an alcohol or drug induced haze? Maybe he hadn't recognised him? Nothing had come of it and Mac had been waiting for the hand on his shoulder for years. If Mark really knew who'd nearly killed him that night, he wouldn't have hesitated to report him. Would he? Was the wee scrote playing games? After all these years? But maybe Mark hadn't trusted his own memory? He knew what that felt like. Mac's heart was hammering in his chest and a terror gripped him that this was the beginning of a heart attack. Or a stroke. He gripped the wheel hard and slowed down. Headlights were suddenly dazzling in his rearview mirror. They flashed even brighter as the driver became irate. Another car went by in the opposite direction. A horn sounded and Mac jumped, slowing even further.

He stopped. At first Mac didn't know he'd done it. One moment he was crawling along, scared of blacking out, driving the car off the road. Then he was stationary, across two lanes and the driver behind hammering on his horn. Mac's teeth were bared as he heard a car door open and close. The body he was investigating was gone. There was only the sight of Mark Souter on the ground, cowering but still being beaten. Terrified for his life, but still being kicked and stamped on.

"Hey! Idiot! What the hell are you doing?" was accompanied by a sharp rap on the window.

Mac opened the car door and got out. The man was wearing a fleece and a baseball cap. His car had two mountain bikes mounted on the roof rack and there was a woman in the passenger seat, watching with a pale face and wide eyes. Mac swung and caught the man on the jaw. The man hit the ground, his hat flew off and came to rest on the other side of the road. He looked up at Mac with wide eyes, rubbing his jaw. Those eyes got bigger as Mac reached down and grabbed him by the front of his fleece, hauling him back up, turning and slamming him into the side of the car. The rush of air leaving the stranger's lungs was audible. Mac hit him in the stomach. The cardiac arrest was coming. His heart a runaway engine, the pulse was in his throat, wildly erratic. Vision narrowing to a pin point. Head spinning. The grip on the man's fleece was the only thing anchoring him to reality. The rain on his face and the cold air numbing his bare hands all took him back to Skye. To the night he had failed to avenge Iona. The night he'd decided to leave. To run. But he'd never managed to outrun those demons. They were on his back constantly, hunting him down.

Then he was staggering back, releasing the man. His victim sagged, fell to one knee, and then half ran, half fell back to his car. Tires screeched, and the engine whined madly as he reversed at speed. Mac put a hand to the roof of his own car, doubling up and vomiting. He was barely aware of the man tearing past in his own car, mounting the grass verge on the side of the road, and almost scraping the side of Mac's car. He looked up to watch the rear lights disappear around a bend, saw a set of white lights coming towards him. Moving slowly, he got in and started the engine, pulling over to his own side. Then he rested his head on his hands, upon the wheel. That man had done nothing except get rightfully angry. But Mac had been ready to kill him. The face of the other man was already lost in his mind. He couldn't have picked the guy out of a line up. The only faces Mac could recall were those of the dead body and Mark Souter. What was happening to him? And why now? Memories were being triggered that were completely debilitating him. He lived in Scotland for god's sake, you couldn't avoid the rain. Mac found himself bringing up Sidhu's number, hitting dial before he could think twice. A cold sweat soaked him.

The call went to voicemail.

"Dr. Sidhu. It's Mac, DCI McNeill, I'd like to make another appointment. I think...I think you're right. I...I need help. I...don't know what or...but just now...something happened...I..."

Mac's words failed him. He growled in his throat and hung up. Then he thought about ways he could delete a voicemail made to a civilian phone. What good would it do? To talk about the past. Talk about his feelings. It would change nothing about who he was or how he'd got there. A man was dead. Mac was suddenly hammering his fists into the steering wheel, catching the horn in the embossed centre. He screamed, his rage being vented into the pummeling. Anger vomited from his body, flowing through his fists. The world was blurred by the rain on the windscreen. Or was it his eyes that were blurred with tears? Frustration stoked the anger. Impotence. Iona was dead. Some scumbag had snuffed her out and then gone on with his life. Another scumbag was slaughtering innocent people. Killing and then marking them. Dancing rings around the police. This wasn't a lowlife ned like Ash Fenton. This was someone calculating and intelligent. Someone way ahead by several steps. Another one who thought he could get away with it.

"Not from me. You won't get away from me!" Mac screamed.

The engine was still running. He put the car in gear and moved back onto the road. A car that had been coming up from behind, preparing to overtake, sounded his horn as Mac put his foot down. He raised an apologetic hand to the rear window. It took less than half an hour to find the address for Michael Gaines. Craigs Wynd was a collection of new builds. At least they would have been around twenty years ago. Stock three and four-bed semis, all pressed from the same mould. No character to speak of. A ring of trees separated the Wynd from the school, Craigmount Secondary. A soulless corporate structure of concrete with an additional annex of bright cladding, at least a decade younger than the parent building. A clamour rose from the school, kids expending their energy in the grounds. They'd also been thronging Glasgow Road, queuing outside shops that only allowed two in at a time. Filling up Tesco Metros or Sainsbury's Locals, watched by security in Hi-Viz. Number two was the first house on the left after turning into the cul-de-sac that was the Wynd.

It had a monobloc driveway with an oil stain at the top. A

closed garage and no sign of a car. No lights on in the house. There was a gate to the side of the garage, six foot high and painted matt black. Mac pulled into the drive and went to the front door, up six stone steps. He pressed the doorbell. No answer. He rapped sharply on the glass of the front door. No answer and no sign of movement inside. A sound came from his right, next to the gate. An old man appeared with an elderly, shaggy golden retriever on a lead. He was pulling down a flat cap against the rain, which had now turned to drizzle, and caught Mac's eye as he looked up.

"Is Mr. Gaines in, do you know?" Mac asked, fishing in his jacket pocket for his warrant card.

"At work, I expect. Saw him leave early this morning when I took the dog out. He's a teacher, eh?" the man said.

Mac crossed the drive to him, holding up his ID.

"DCI McNeill, Police Scotland. Do you know Michael Gaines well?"

"Aye, he's bought number two about the same time my wife and I bought ours. He was a big help to me when she passed on last year. Very kind he was."

"Don't suppose you have a spare key?"

"Aye. But not sure I should be handing it out."

"I'm police," Mac said, holding up the ID again.

The man scrutinised it. "I don't know what a police badge looks like, eh?"

"Would it help if I got a patrol car out here and some uniformed officers?" Mac said, an edge creeping into his voice. He tried to stamp it down. This was an elderly man he was speaking to, not a criminal. He needed to get control of his anger before he did something he would truly regret.

The man licked his lips, eyes darting about the street as though looking for help.

"Look, I tell you what," Mac said, his tone softer. "Go inside and call the local station. Tell them to send someone as there's a man claiming to be from Police Scotland Serious Crimes Unit. Detective Chief Inspector Callum McNeill." He was trying for patience in his voice but not confident he was succeeding.

"No, no. I'm sure you're on the level. You've got a badge, after all." The man said. "I'll get the key, eh? Just you wait here."

Mac turned away, heading to the side gate, and tried it. Locked. He walked across the front of the house, squelching across sodden grass, and peered into a bay window. A living room was revealed with a TV on the wall and a mug on a small glass table beside an armchair facing it. A single armchair and the only furniture arranged to face the TV. Had the hallmarks of a single man's house. Big for a single man, though. Maybe he hadn't been single when he bought it. Then why keep it? Unless the separation had been recent. Further past the bay window was another expanse of lawn and a fence. The house on the other side was attached. Mac's phone rang. He fished it from his pocket.

"McNeill."

"This is Sergeant Foster at St John's Road station, sir. Just checking on your whereabouts? Had a call from a Mr. Benson..."

"Saying I want his neighbour's keys? Yes, Sarge, it's me."

"Very good, sir. Sorry to disturb."

Moments later, the old man came back out with a key. Mac smiled as he took it.

"Thanks, Mr. Benson. You did the right thing."

"No offense," Benson said.

He hung about on the drive as Mac pulled on a pair of gloves and opened the door, closing it behind him, forgetting the old man's presence as soon as he was inside. A staircase was directly in front. A door to the left was ajar and led into the living room. A hallway went past the stairs and another door on the left. He could see a kitchen at the far end. Keeping his gloved hands in his trouser pockets, he cautiously stepped into the middle of the hall, not allowing himself to brush against the walls or the stair's balustrade. A few steps in and he saw the blood. A smear against the white painted wood of the staircase. A smear on the laminate wood floor. Excitement rose in Mac, sharing emotional space with dread. He had been almost certain of it before, but there was no question now. The blood didn't look more than a few hours old. If this was where Michael Gaines had been killed, then Ash Fenton couldn't be responsible. Either he had an accomplice or they'd got the wrong man.

CHAPTER TWENTY-ONE

MAC STEPPED AROUND THE BLOOD CAREFULLY, following the trail into the kitchen. There he saw a congealing pool of it on the floor in front of the oven. Smears and streaks were all over the cupboards on either side of the cooker. Looking closely he could see hairs trapped in it. Finger prints were discernible in one of the streaks to the left, on the handle of a cupboard and the door itself. Mac turned his back, putting his own hand out to hover over the blood which held the prints. A man of Michael Gaines build, because in all probability the body in the car was him, sitting on the floor with his back to the oven door could cause those blood smears. And his head would rest against the handle of the grill, above the main oven, where a cluster of dark hairs was pinned in place by a sticky residue. The head must have been bounced back. There'd been no sign on Michael Gaines' face that he'd been struck. So, the killing blow was struck in here. The killer had shoved him in the face, possibly with the heel of a hand against his forehead. That had sent Gaines staggering back to crash into the oven, slamming his head backwards against the metal handle.

Then he'd died. Arms outstretched sideways, maybe, in the last moments of his life, scrabbling for a handhold to pull himself back up. Mac had noticed another streaked print on the other side. Sitting with arms outstretched like Christ on the cross. An idle thought went through his mind that it might have been deliberate. Ash Fenton was connected with an organisation of god-botherers, wasn't he? The New Covenant.

"Ash Fenton didn't do this. He was locked up. So, maybe he didn't kill the other two either? Or perhaps he only killed one, the ex-girlfriend, Vicky McCourt, admitted that murder because...because he's a born again Christian and the charity that got him out of prison asked him to. But why admit to one and not the other? The MOs are practically the same in all three cases," he muttered to himself, vocalising his thought process. "But he couldn't have killed Michael Gaines."

It all seemed far-fetched, with no obvious motives or answers. The hypothesis was mentally filed, pushed back to make more room at the front of his awareness for additional data. He glanced around the kitchen, seeing limited signs of a struggle except for the blood. A mug had been knocked off a dining table next to the door leading out into the hallway. The fact that the blood started out there suggested Gaines had been answering the door. Letting his killer into the house. He was stabbed. Then stabbed a lot more times after he'd collapsed in the kitchen. Someone he knew then. Someone he would let into his house in the middle of the night. There were no security cameras on the house or garage and no video doorbell either. What a fantastic invention that was. As a detective Mac thought whoever first invented those things should be knighted for services to crime prevention. He wondered if the neighbour had one. On the kitchen table was a laptop lying open. Mac hit a key at random to wake it and was confronted with a login screen. There were papers on the table next to it.

Mac flicked through them, handling them by the corner and trying not to disturb how they were lying too much. Handwritten paragraphs, most with a grade written at the top and notes written in red ink in the margin. Some kind of creative writing exercise. Mac frowned. This was obviously student work, but according to Clio, Michael Gaines had resigned, so why did he have this stuff at home still? From what he'd understood from Clio, Gaines' resignation was sudden, so could be he hadn't had time to return it. Mac filed away the information and moved on. At the other side of the laptop was a pile of papers which were sprawled towards the edge of the table. As though someone had run their hand over the pile, brushing it from the table top to the floor. More marking but some had smears of dried blood on them. A scene appeared in Mac's mind. Gaines backing away, maybe being stabbed as he did so. One hand reaching out, sweeping the papers but not knocking them all the way off. He crouched and looked under the table. A couple of sheets were crumpled at the far end, under a dining chair. Straightening, he walked around and picked up the first, pulling it by a corner to expand the crumpled mass but taking care not to tear it. He stopped when he saw the name. Maia Wray. Mac frowned, imagining Gaines staggering and grabbing blindly, scrunching the paper that came into his grip as he fell to the floor.

But that would place the scrunched paper at the other end of the table, the end closest to the kitchen door. A man who had been struck close to the heart, a man moments from death, wouldn't waste seconds throwing a balled up piece of paper the length of a six foot dining table. Not by accident? But if the action was deliberate then what was its motive? Why isolate those two pieces of paper from the rest? A man mortally wounded didn't have a lot of time. But if he had presence of mind he might want to point a finger at his attacker. Seeing a piece of paper and the name on it. Grabbing that paper and trying to put it as far from sight as his spasming, weakened muscles allowed. Christ, no. It was a ploy straight out of a bad seventies detective show. Things like that didn't happen in real life. But the paper had been thrown. Or kicked. Some force had moved it to where Mac now saw it. He was looking at the effect and knew there was a cause.

Cautiously, he unrolled another one of the pieces of paper. He saw the same name at the top. Maia Wray. It gave Mac a sick, cold feeling in his stomach. This was nothing that the Procurator Fiscal could use in their case. You couldn't convict someone based on a balled up bit of paper. But it struck a chord with Mac, it was the kind of thing that sparked a hunch. He dropped the paper back where it had been. Moving swiftly but carefully, he left the kitchen and made his way back along the hall.

A glance into the living room didn't reveal anything out of the ordinary. He went up the stairs, taking out his phone as he did.

"Nari. I'm at Michael Gaines' address. Looks like this was the murder scene. Get a SOCO team down here ASAP. I'm at the address and I'll be here when they arrive."

"Ok, guv. Want me and Kai down there with you?"

"No, stick with your actions. I need to hear from anyone who might have seen or heard anything unusual last night. It's a twenty-four seven site, so we've got a good chance of there being someone who saw the car drive in. Or the killer leaving. Track down everyone working in the window of time the body was there for. Did Stringer give a time of death?"

"He did. The cold makes things challenging, but he's estimated a three hour window from midnight on."

Mac swore. He was on the upstairs landing, looking into a master bedroom. But something the neighbour had told him had come back to him.

"What is it, guv?" Nari asked.

"The neighbour, a Mr. Benson, said Michael Gaines left for work this morning. From his house. He saw him while he was walking his dog. But it couldn't have been Michael Gaines."

"Our killer? How did Benson mix his neighbour up with a stranger?"

"It would have been dark. This time of year, early morning. I'll need to check the time, but if it was dark then the neighbour would only have seen a car with headlights on and a silhouette behind them. Obviously assumed he was seeing Gaines."

"But Gaines was actually in the back, already dead?"

"Right."

Mac's mind was racing now, pursuing and discarding multiple avenues.

"Get on it, Nari. I'll hold down this end."

Mac hung up. A brazen killer, going to his victim's house at night, committing murder, then driving the body away in the morning, several hours later, knowing there was a chance of being seen. But with the presence of mind to know that in the dark and against the glare of full beam headlights, no-one would make out their face. Someone who was confident and clear-headed. Prepared. But why wait? Unless it was important that someone witnessed Michael Gaines' leaving for work. He went into the largest bedroom. Probably neat for most people. Mac noticed the pile of clean washing left on the bed, which hadn't been made up. The curtains were drawn. A hairdryer and straighteners sat on one side of the bed, plugged in. He checked the wall socket, seeing it was off. Surely, Michael Gaines didn't have enough hair to need a blow-dryer or straighteners. A female friend? Mac noticed that both gadgets were Dyson. He didn't know much about hair products but he knew that Dyson were expensive. A casual visitor wouldn't leave such valuable items around. They must belong to someone who was either living with Gaines or visiting regularly. He hadn't noticed any pictures anywhere in the house, of Gaines or anyone else, just some artwork in frames.

Mac slid open a mirrored wardrobe, seeing jeans, shirts, and jackets on hangers. A shelf held folded t-shirts and sweaters. He pushed the sliding door further aside and then understood. The other half of the wardrobe contained dresses hanging in transparent plastic bags. Through the plastic he could see the garments were gaudily decorated, heavy with sequins and in bright, vibrant colours. Shoes were lined up on the wardrobe floor. High heels. Knee high boots. All sparkly.

The topmost shelf held a selection of wig stands, all in use. This wasn't the day to day wardrobe of a woman. This gear belonged to a drag queen. No-one else dressed in such exaggerated bling. Either Gaines was living with a man who was a drag entertainer or...he *was* the entertainer. Mac filed the information away, sliding the wardrobe closed again. Could be important. Needn't be though. Plenty of people out there with unreasonable hatred of anyone who was different. But, it was a potential motive. He considered the other two victims. They just didn't fit. An addict and a student. Now a teacher who was also a drag queen.

At the bottom of the wardrobe was a shoe box. Mac lifted the lid, seeing pictures. All of a man in drag. Some were old-fashioned polaroids. Others larger and looking more professional. He recognised Gaines beneath the heavy make-up. In one, a close up selfie, Mac noticed a small blemish on his right cheek. It was the same colour as the rest of his skin but looked like it could be a mole, under a lot of concealer. It only stood out to Mac because of the small wound he had seen on Gaines' face in the car. It was in the same place as this blemish. The killer had removed a mole after killing his victim. Odd.

Standing at the bedroom window and opening the curtains, he saw Mr. Benson at the window of a conservatory that jutted from the back of his house. He was looking up at his neighbour's window and saw Mac looking down. Mac completed a cursory inspection of the rest of the house. Nothing in the other bedroom or the small box room stood out to him. No evidence of another person living here. He went out of the front door and crossed to Mr. Benson's house. Benson had a video doorbell. When the old man answered, Mac held up his warrant card again.

"You believe me this time?" he asked.

"Aye, I do. Had to be sure."

"'Course. Can I come in?"

Benson shuffled aside and Mac stepped into a house laid out identically to Gaines' place. Except the orientation was all reversed.

"Is that video doorbell working?" Mac asked.

"Aye, it is."

"You have access to old videos? Say from the last week?"

The dog was sniffing at Mac's legs and he casually ruffled its shaggy fur. It sat back, lifting his head for more strokes. The man took out a phone from his trouser pocket and began swiping and pressing.

"Aye, I think so. Shouldn't you have a warrant, though? Am I not supposed to ask for one?"

"Why? You're not a suspect," Mac told him. "But seeing the comings and goings from next door might be important. It looks to me like your camera would catch someone at the bottom of next door's drive, just about."

He turned himself so that he could look over Benson's shoulder at the screen of the phone. The app was showing a history screen. Benson scrolled through a list of thumbnail images each with a date and time stamp. Mac held out his hand.

"May I?" he said, beginning to feel his patience wearing a bit thin. Kai was much better at dealing with the public. In five minutes, he'd have had Mr. Benson's life story out of him.

Mac saw videos of Mr. Benson leaving his house, the dog going before him. Coming back home. Several walks a day. A milkman leaving a delivery on the doorstep. Mr. Benson opening the door to take it in. A postman. A delivery driver in polo shirt and baseball cap, a box under his arm. Mac was about to swipe away when something on the edge of the frame caught his eye. He scrolled to the feed and noted something white, a car or van parked in front of Gaines' house, its rear end just visible to Benson's camera. Mac tried to zoom but couldn't see more than a bumper and a section of rear door. It looked tall. When he zoomed he saw some discolouration, three snaking lines of dark. There had been a white van connected to the Zoe Phillips case, seen in the vicinity. Now another. Were those dark pixels damage? Was he seeing an impact that had cracked the paint and broken the bodywork on that corner?

Michael Gaines' car had been damaged too. A fender bender on the rear driver side bumper.

"Would you like a cuppa, Detective?" Benson offered.

Mac realised he had been utterly engrossed and had forgotten the old man was even there. He weighed the phone in his hand. This was evidence, but to an old man living on his own, the phone was a lifeline.

"I'm going to download this same app you have. Then I'd like you to share your sign in details. My team will need to review these videos, Mr. Benson," Mac told him.

The old man looked utterly bewildered. "What is this all about? Why do you need to look at my camera? What is it you think I've done?"

He looked scared and Mac realised that he'd had tunnel vision focus on the evidence to the exclusion of everything else.

"Sorry, Mr. Benson. Don't worry, you've done nothing wrong. Come and sit down," Mac said gently, ushering Benson towards his living room. "This is going to be a shock for you..."

CHAPTER TWENTY-TWO

MAC WAS BACK ON THE PHONE as he got into his car. Looking around the cul-de-sac, he could see several other video door-bells. He tried to triangulate the angles the lenses were pointed in, trying to figure out which ones would give a view of Gaines' drive.

"Guv," Nari answered.

"Nari, I'm still at Michael Gaines' house. Get over here as soon as you can. I've got log in details for a Ring doorbell account belonging to his neighbour. And I need you to go door-to-door round the others in the street who have similar and see if their cameras picked up any useful footage. I'm interested in any comings or goings prior to the estimated time of death. He was killed here, as I said earlier."

"Right, guv. Not much to report here. Apparently, that road has a bit of a rep for dogging, y'know? So, when they're taking a break, quite a few of the lads down here have a wee nosie to see if they can see anything. But, no-one saw anything until the guy who reported the car. Didn't see Gaines' car driving in or anyone leaving in another vehicle or on foot. Surveillance cameras in the yard are all pointing the wrong way. Even the ones on the side of the yard facing the hill are angled downwards."

Mac felt mildly disappointed. But then the killer had to have a reason for dumping the body where they did. Maybe they'd used the site for the purpose it was known for. Maybe they'd looked for a site like that because it would be secluded and not observed, though they would run the risk of being seen by doggers in that case. He shook his head.

"Doesn't matter. We've got plenty of forensics here. And the Ring account I'm sending you the details of has footage of a white van and a delivery driver. Might be nothing, but remember we identified a white van in the vicinity of Zoe Phillips? Could be something or nothing."

"Zoe Phillips? But, guv. We got someone for that. Got a confession too," Nari sounded confused.

Mac swore. "Confession? You mean Fenton confessed to killing Zoe? When the hell was this and why wasn't I informed?"

"I'm sorry, guv, I thought you knew. DCI Akhtar interviewed him and he admitted killing Zoe. It was in her report."

"I'll call you back," Mac said and hung up.

He signed in to the team inbox and scrolled through until he found the email from DCI Akhtar, and there it was in black and white. Ashleigh Fenton had confessed to the murder of Zoe Phillips, using the same method as he had with his ex-girlfriend. When pushed on the reason why he just said he saw her and something came over him. He felt a need to kill her, couldn't help himself. There was no mention of the odd cuts on either woman's faces, and Akhtar hadn't asked. As far as she was concerned, she had her man. Case closed.

Mac signed out and stared out of the windscreen, brooding. He should have known about the confession and was pissed off with himself that he hadn't checked the reports. But by the same token, it was no longer his case. While he'd been having his head examined both literally and figuratively by the hospital and Sidhu, Hafsa Akhtar had taken over and seen the case over the line. It was only because of this new murder, Michael Gaines, that Mac was involved again.

He called Nari back.

"Don't mention Zoe Phillips to anyone."

"OK, guv," Nari still sounded unsure.

"Nari, we're going to pursue this case as a standalone, ok? Follow the evidence. But, the similarities between the cases mean we have to consider a link. Or that we got the wrong man. Better to find that out now than after Fenton's been sentenced and has done time, right?"

"Yes, guv. I get it. Just seems tenuous to me and the evidence on Fenton is strong. DNA tying him to the scene."

Mac paused, looking out of the windscreen. He wondered why he was in a debate with his DS. Why was Nari not simply accepting his orders and his judgement? Unless she was questioning his judgement. Maybe someone else had put it into her mind that Mac's calls were questionable.

"Nari, do we have a problem here?" he asked quietly.

"Problem, guv? No, of course not," Nari replied, too quickly.

"If you have something you want to say, then now's the

time. When we get into this investigation, I want my team united behind me, eh?"

Pause. He could hear the wind gusting across the mic.

"I'll take the silence as a reply. I'm thinking about what you asked me. About transferring? Is that what this is about?"

"No...guv, the Zoe Phillips and Vicky McCourt cases. They were completed by DCI Akhtar. She...she said you'd probably look for any way of...well, that you might not be best pleased at her seeing the cases over the line. It's not like she was taking them away from you. You were out of action. It was proper to reassign the cases and..."

"DCI Akhtar is capable of looking after herself," Mac interrupted, feeling a flash of anger. "You don't need to fight her battles. I can see where this is going. Did she tell you I might try and unstitch those cases? Sabotage the prosecution?"

Silence. He could almost see Nari's pretty features creased in consternation.

"I didn't say that."

"You didn't have to, Nari," Mac said. "Look, I need you. You've got a sharp brain and you're a natural detective. I've been in this job a long time. I've cut a lot of corners in my time. Maybe Akhtar knows I haven't always been whiter than white. But, I'm not a bent copper, Nari. And I wouldn't jeopardise a conviction for the sake of advancing my own career. I don't need to."

He felt like he was having to justify himself to his junior officer. It felt wrong and he fought to keep the anger out of his voice. Because at the same time he did not want to lose his young sergeant to another DCI. He valued the members of his team. Kai's energy and technical ability. Nari's brain and her thoroughness. Mel's organisation and planning.

"It just seems like you're trying to drum up a case for Fenton being innocent. Even though we have DNA and a confession. There's a lot of stabbings happening. If Gaines' was killed with a similar blade...well, it might just be that it's easy to get hold of."

Mac ground his teeth in frustration. Nari had been talking to Akhtar already. This wasn't coming from her. She'd seen the body and called Akhtar to warn her the Fenton case might be shaky. And Akhtar was running scared. Her promotion hopes were based on her name attached to the solving of a double murder. If that conviction was unsound, then the promotion board would consider it a black mark. Mac may not have been the political player that Akhtar was, but he understood enough about the game to know that. He could ask for Nari to be transferred. If he couldn't trust her, then she couldn't remain on the team. But that would be a sledgehammer tactic. He knew it. It would alienate at least one, possibly two members of the team, both Mel and Kai liked Nari, viewing her as a daughter / niece figure and a potential date, respectively.

"I just need you to carry out my orders," Mac finally said. "We can talk again once we know more."

"Right, guv. Kai and I will get on it."

There was a note of relief in her voice. A lightening of tone towards the end. Like she was glad Mac had made this purely professional, not dragging out the difficult part of the conversation. Mac hung up and started the engine. Nari did have a point. There was a chance, albeit a slim one, this case wasn't related. Vicky McCourt was a revenge killing by Ash Fenton because she had reported his assault on her, got him sent down. Zoe Phillips could have been a random attack or another outburst of rage from Fenton, possibly at being rejected by her. If that had happened. Michael Gaines might be gay. Did you have to be gay to be a drag queen? Mac wasn't sure these days. But if he was, there were plenty of nut jobs out there who took a dislike to those they viewed as an abomination. Especially if they were religious. Could even be a clever psycho looking to hide behind Ash Fenton's notoriety. But none of that felt right to Mac. There was nothing concrete he could point to. A hunch only. It took another ten minutes for a SOCO team to arrive. Mac got out to greet them, briefing the team leader and giving directions to the sealing of the crime scene.

Nari and Kai turned up as the SOCO team was going into the house. Nari met his eyes boldly, as though daring herself not to act in any way guilty. Kai seemed oblivious.

"Where will you be, guv?" Kai asked as he and Nari began walking towards the nearest house with a video doorbell.

"I'm going to talk to the school Gaines' worked at. Cramond Secondary." Mac said.

Nari paused. "That was quick work, guv," she said. "How did you know that?"

Mac smiled tightly, concealing gritted teeth. It was starting to feel like an interrogation every time he spoke to Nari. Like she was a spy. If she'd thought about it for a minute, she'd realise there were several simple ways of obtaining that information. The neighbour, Mr. Benson, for one.

"I'm a bloody detective, right?" he snapped.

177

Kai was looking from one to the other, not failing this time to notice the atmosphere. Mac was glaring at Nari, pausing in the act of getting into his car. She wasn't quite glaring back but she refused to look away. Refused to be bullied. Mac wasn't bullying her. He just felt under attack. Sidhu was intent on diving into his psyche. Reid was on his case, looking to engineer a fit up. Now Akhtar was undermining his own team. And a murder to solve on top of that. Not to mention the flashbacks, panic attacks and barely concealed anger bubbling just below the surface constantly. He hardly recognised himself, and what he did he didn't like. What the hell was happening to him? He got into the car, breaking the staring contest, and not looking back at Nari. As he started the engine it occurred to him there was someone who should know about Michael Gaines' death. Before she heard it from someone else. The school would tell Mac who Gaines' next of kin was and he would get them to make a formal ID of the body. But Clio would want to know. His mind went back to the messages he'd seen her exchange with Gaines. The vitriol. He thought of the wine she'd consumed the last time he had stayed over. Remembered waking on the sofa, Clio's fluffy socked feet across his legs, his feet up on the coffee table.

"You're an idiot," he said to himself as he turned the car and left Craig Wynd. "Clio isn't capable of it."

He called her as he drove away, switching the phone to speaker and dropping it onto the seat next to him. It rang out for a long time. Then Clio's voice, thick with sleep.

"Mac?"

"Jeez, Clio. You sound like you've only just got up. It's midday." Mac said.

"Yeah. I know. Maia had a sleepover and I had a few drinks with a friend of mine. I'm working from home while Maia's suspended. Maia's still in her bed, too, I think. She didn't sleep at all at her friend's house. Neither of them did. Wait, let me check…"

Mac heard Clio calling Maia's name. Then again.

"No, she's asleep. I think her friend's mum was none too pleased. Her daughter still had to go to school."

"Are you compos mentis, Clio?"

A yawn. "Yes, yes. I'm up. I'm up. Oh my head!"

"It was a school night for you too, remember?" Mac pointed out.

"We went home at about ten last night. I stopped at an off license for a bottle of wine." Clio explained.

"You were drinking alone then," Mac said.

"Yes, but don't say it like that. I've been under a lot of pressure lately," Clio replied. ""With the new job, getting ready to move, Maia being suspended and trying to get her some support. I've emailed my MSP about the line the school is taking. It's discrimination, pure and simple and that snake, Michael Gaines, is responsible."

"That's why I'm calling," Mac said.

He was heading approximately north, orientating himself based on the hill that rose up from the Glasgow Road through Corstorphine. Cramond was beyond that, so heading uphill was roughly the right direction.

"Oh?" Clio asked.

"There's no easy way to say this, so I'll just come out with it. Michael Gaines is dead."

Silence from Clio. The sound of her breathing.

"Say that again," she almost whispered.

"I've just come from his house. He was murdered there and his body was dumped outside of town."

No answer. Just breathing.

"Do I need a solicitor?" Clio asked finally.

"We're going to have to talk to you formally. Take a statement. Because of the social media chat. If I could hide it, I would. But the victim's social media is one of the first things we look at in a case. And there's no way of knowing who else he showed those messages to. You were pretty angry in them."

"I couldn't actually kill someone! Mac, how could you think that?" Clio said, distress in her voice.

"I don't. I know you didn't do this, Clio. It's routine. Nothing more. OK?" Mac tried to soothe her. "I'll ask you where you were last night, about midnight...."

He waited, wanting to hear Clio's alibi. She wasn't capable of it, but Akhtar would be out for blood to protect her double murder case closure. She would be pushing for the case and wanting to pin it on the first person who looked like they could get her across the evidential threshold.

"Come on, Clio. You and your friend parted about ten and you...what? Got an Uber? Flagged down a cab?" Mac prompted.

"It was an Uber. He stopped at the nearest offie for me."

"Good, so we'll have the driver's details on the app and the time and date on his records. No problem."

"I was home by midnight. But, Mac, I was alone," Clio said.

CHAPTER TWENTY-THREE

CLIO WAS WELL AWAKE NOW. Her eyes were wide as she scanned Michael Gaines' social media posts. He was a serial poster, from serious items to frivolous. She'd blocked him after her tirade, now she unblocked and saw with a suddenly dry mouth that his last post was the previous night. Mac had been asking about her whereabouts. He'd been asking for an alibi! An icy fist clutched at her heart. Her stomach clenched and, she suddenly felt nauseous. Getting up she began to run to the bathroom but realised halfway that she wasn't going to make it. She did make it to the kitchen sink. Why had she indulged her anger? Why had she let him get under her skin? The horror of the situation made her heave, even when her stomach was empty. The sound of it echoed off the metal sides of the sink. Clio was wracked with guilt. Maia deserved better. She deserved a mother who could rise above men like Michael Gaines, who could protect her. Clio couldn't protect her daughter from a prison cell.

She reached for the tap and turned it on, turning her head to rinse out her mouth. Then letting the cold jet of water clear the sink. Her phone was still clutched in her hand. Mac had been quiet for a moment after she had told him there was no alibi for her for the time he was interested in. That quiet had filled her with dread, tearing away the last vestiges of sleepiness. She had wanted him to say that everything was going to be alright. That she had nothing to worry about because they both knew she was innocent. He'd tried. But Clio knew him well enough to know when he was telling her what she wanted to hear. She straightened, but her legs buckled, knees going weak. Instead she slid to the kitchen floor, knocking over the empty bottle of wine she'd drunk after getting home. It rolled away to clink against the kitchen island. Clio put her hands through her hair, raking them backward and forward. She had done nothing wrong. This was a horrible co-incidence. Michael Gaines was outspoken on social media on the subject of disruptive children and discipline in schools. He'd also voiced his skepticism on the subject of ADHD and other neurotypes that led to issues in school.

From other parents, she had a feeling this outspoken-ness had led to him being forced to resign from Cramond Secondary. There was even talk of a tribunal for unfair dismissal. He wasn't the kind to let the matter of being cancelled go. That's how she was sure he would see it. That's the kind of man he was. At their first meeting she had thought he was gay. None of her business and she didn't care if he was, but if he was it made his stance all the more jarring with his narrow minded views. Clio shook her head, clambering to her feet as she heard Maia upstairs. Should she tell her? Maia would almost certainly find out soon. That kind of event was hard to keep out of the ears of complete strangers a hundred miles away, let alone a student who'd come into regular conflict with him. And with a parent who'd threatened him in writing. Maia was coming downstairs, her footsteps slow and dragging. Clio tried to arrange her face in a normal welcoming smile as Maia appeared in the kitchen door, wearing a fluffy onesie and oversized slippers, barely picking up her feet as she walked. Her hair was a haystack and she was rubbing her eyes with one hand, her phone was in the other.

"Mum? Claire has just told me that something's happened to Mr. Gaines," Maia said.

"Happened?" Clio said, making the decision not to tell her what she knew.

She went over to her daughter, reaching for her phone. Maia stepped back, holding it away from her. Suddenly, her daughter looked alert and awake, seeing the unusual behaviour in her mother.

"Mum? What's going on? Why do you want my phone?"

"I just want to see what people are saying," Clio protested.

"About what?" Maia backed away.

"Mr. Gaines, of course. Isn't that what you just asked me?"

"No, I said Claire told me. What do you know? What's happened?" Maia demanded, alarm rising in her voice.

"You know as much as me. I'm just curious to know what people are saying," Clio said.

Maia was shaking her head. "They're saying there's police at his house. Claire knows a boy at St Johns, which is around the corner from where Mr. Gaines lives."

"Maybe he's had a break-in," Clio suggested.

"He says the house is sealed off. There's a SOCO van and a forensics tent and everything," Maia said.

Clio rubbed at her eyes, wishing her brain would work faster. Maia had taken in everything Mac had ever said about his job and added to it with true crime documentaries and podcasts, wanting to be able to sit and talk to Mac about police work. She hadn't thought that Maia would know people outside her own school, which was stupid. Of course she did. Kids were connected across the world these days. It wasn't the eighties anymore. A school half a mile away was a foreign country when Clio had been Maia's age. Strange and exotic.

"Mum, just tell me. I heard you on the phone. Right before you threw up. Was it Callum? What did he say? Is he investigating? Is Mr. Gaines dead?"

It came out in a rush, firing at Clio faster than she could process. She stepped forward, taking Maia by the upper arms and pulling her close. The edge of hysteria was in Maia's voice and her eyes were wide, getting wider. Clio instinctively pulled her close, hugging her and realising she had no choice but to tell the truth.

"Mr. Gaines has been...killed sweetie. I'm sorry. Mac is investigating and that's all I know," she said in as calm and gentle a voice as she could manage.

"That's not all, though. I can tell. Is it to do with Mr. Gaines?" Maia demanded.

Now there was naked fear in her voice. She pushed away from Clio in order to look her mum in the eye. Clio saw the fear there, but also resolve. Maia was bracing herself to push back against any false placation. She wasn't about to be fobbed off, treated like a child. Clio saw a scared little girl but also a determined young woman. Very young. Too young to face the fears that Clio was harbouring. Especially as she knew those fears might be completely groundless. She was innocent and one of her closest friends was...no, her closest friend, was the investigating officer. Mac was good. He would find the killer.

"I had a bit too much to drink when I was out with Cindy last night and feel a bit rubbish this morning. That's all. With the stress of everything lately, I just wanted a break. That's why I had more than I should. OK? It's got nothing to do with..."

"I saw some of your comments online. You were really angry, mum." It was true. The main message, the one she'd shown Mac was private, but she had commented on some of Gaines' posts as well. Not threatening, but she had been angry at what he was saying. "And you were really rude to him at the last parent's evening," Maia continued. "And when you came to pick me up the other day. What if...?"

Maia, for all her attempts to be an adult, couldn't keep the panic from rising. It came bubbling out of her, and Clio hugged her close again. Maia didn't resist and Clio stroked her hair, holding onto her tightly.

"Things like that just don't happen, ok? Those were just words, and Mr. Gaines probably laughed at me with his friends over them. He'd already left the school at that point. I just couldn't let his bigoted and narrow minded comments go without saying something."

"They might think that you did it. That you had a reason to," Maia said, her voice muffled by Clio's shoulder.

She had both arms about her mum's waist, holding on

tightly, no longer able to maintain the facade of the cool, independent teenager.

"They won't. It was just an argument. Mr. Gaines probably had a lot of them. From what I've heard, he was asked to leave. So, I won't have been the only person he fell out with. Please don't worry, Maia. It's so far from being possible, it's unreal."

Maia nodded, releasing her hold. Clio brushed hair from her daughter's face and then kissed her on the forehead.

"It was Callum on the phone?" Maia asked.

The debate in Clio's mind was done in a flash, the need not to frighten her daughter further making her think fast.

"It was. He just wanted to tell me about Mr. Gaines' death. He didn't tell me anything else. Mac is the SIO," Maia knew enough jargon to know the acronym was for Senior Investigating Officer.

"I suppose if he thought there was any evidence against you, he wouldn't have called," Maia said, surprising Clio with her level-headed perceptiveness at that moment.

"No, he wouldn't. As SIO he couldn't do that. It would be against the rules."

"And Callum always goes by the book," Maia said with the same certainty she would have used to state the sky was blue.

"Always," Clio smiled around the lie.

She'd talked to Mac about his job enough to know that, while he was honest, he was also brutally pragmatic. Rules could be bent and Mac's connections meant he knew when he could push the boundaries. Maia was idealistic though and Mac was her hero. Maia smiled, nodding.

"Sorry, mum. I was being silly," she said, sniffing.

"No, you weren't, Maia. It was a big shock. I didn't like the man, but I wouldn't wish death on him," Clio said gruffly, accepting another hug from Maia.

That Maia would volunteer it told Clio just how shaken she still was. As a tween, Maia had started to move away from the very tactile little girl she'd once been. That had been a form of loss for Clio, even resulting in a period of something almost grief like, while she came to terms with Maia establishing her own personal space, pushing her mother back. Now, she took any opportunity for a cuddle.

"I don't know about you, but I'm starving. Let's go and get a McD's."

"Mum, we're in our PJs," Maia said skeptically.

"So? It's a drive through. I'll put on my onesie and my crocks and no-one will know."

"What if I see my friends?" Maia asked.

"Your friends are in school, remember?" Clio replied.

"Oh yeah," Maia said with a grin.

"Where you'll be again from tomorrow. Come on."

She went to the sofa where she had discarded her fluffy onesie, matching Maia's. Then she grabbed her coat from the hallway and handed Maia hers. Something caught her eye through the glass of the front door. Or rather, something didn't. She couldn't see the shape of her car. A slow, crawling feeling of dread began to seep through her. She opened the front door and stood for a moment, gaping. The car was gone. She had left it at home before her night out, the previous evening. Left and returned the back way and hadn't looked out of the front window since. She turned to Maia who was frowning, trying to see past her mother.

"Mum, where's the car?" she asked.

"I don't know. I think it's been stolen," Clio answered.

She hurriedly closed the front door and went back through the kitchen until she remembered that she'd put her phone into the pocket of her onesie. Fishing it out, she hovered with her finger over Mac's name. No, he was knee deep in a murder investigation. She couldn't bother him now. Not with this. A DCI wouldn't deal with a car theft. But, coming so close after the death of Michael Gaines...It had to be co-incidence. She'd never experienced a break in, stolen car or even vandalism since moving to Cramond. It was a quiet little village and her street had more than its fair share of pensioner residents. Crime was something that happened to other people and her car wasn't particularly valuable. Nor was it particularly new. It didn't have keyless entry; an old fashioned lock opened the door. Clio knew that made it more vulnerable than modern cars with their key fobs linked to an immobilizer. An enthusiastic colleague had mansplained it to her once in the staff canteen when she'd made the mistake of telling him she was shopping around for a car.

For Maia's sake, Clio smiled. Smiled to hide the dread that was turning her insides to ice.

"Don't worry. We'll order it in. And I'll call the police to report the theft. We're insured, so we'll let the insurance sort it out."

Maia nodded uncertainly. She didn't look like she believed it was a random theft any more than Clio did.

CHAPTER TWENTY-FOUR

ELEVEN DAYS SINCE THE BODY of Zoe Phillips had been found. It felt like eleven months. Mac had swiped into the headquarters lobby and was walking through the private area behind towards the lifts.

"Coffee, guv?" Kai asked from somewhere behind.

He turned to see him holding a cardboard tray of coffee cups and smiled, waiting for him to catch up.

"Good night, guv?" Kai made the ritual greeting.

"Same as all the others since Gaines turned up dead," Mac said, smiling to soften the remark. "Working late. But I don't tend to notice when I'm on a case."

Kai turned the cardboard tray he held, offering him one in particular. Mac took it and raised it in salute as thanks.

"Me either. Stayed as late as I could but had to get away for Chloe. It was her birthday."

They walked towards the lifts where three other people were already waiting.

"How old is she?" Mac asked.

"Four. Going to school next year. Her mum's been difficult. Don't know what her problem is, but when she gives me a chance to see her on her birthday...you know. There's always words."

Kai was normally brashly confident, always with a quip and always immaculate in his appearance. Today he looked a little harassed. His tie was crooked. When Mac's eyes strayed to it, Kai touched it self-consciously, and straightened it.

"Don't worry about it, Kai." Mac said. "You have to spend time with your kid."

"Kids. There's two others. Their mums aren't any better."

"Different mums?" Mac asked.

Kai shrugged and Mac got a taste of the rogue's grin that he deployed himself from time to time.

"What can I say...I'm an idiot," Kai said sheepishly. "Doesn't make things easy, though. Keeping track of three different visitation arrangements and maintenance payments. After Jack was born, I honestly thought it would be a breeze because I was going to be a footballer like my dad. Quids in. My knee saw to that."

"I didn't know your dad was a footballer. Professional?" Mac asked.

He didn't know the first thing about sport, any sport really. But he knew the question was expected. He stepped into the lift, the doors closing. It was only the two of them, the other three were deep in conversation. Mac leaned back against the wall, hands in trouser pockets. Kai seemed blithely unaware of any social awkwardness. Mac was only too aware.

"Cowdenbeath for fifteen years. Bit of a local legend. I never really matched up to him on the pitch."

Mac shrugged. "My dad was a farmer. And none of his kids ever did anything that was good enough for him."

"Yeah? Farmed round here?" Kai asked.

The lift chimed, and the doors opened.

"Out west," Mac said, noncommittally.

He stepped out, but Kai caught his arm before he could cross the hall to the double doors that led into the open plan office.

"Guv, I wanted to catch you for a minute. If that's OK?"

Mac stopped. "Sure."

Kai licked his lips, glanced towards the doors. "I heard a whisper that...Nari might be moving on? And if she is, then I wondered if I'd be able to have a crack at her job. You'd need a sergeant, eh?"

Mac nodded. "I haven't been told anything about Nari leaving. Where'd you hear that?"

"Just around. She's been seeing a PC from downstairs and he and I go back to Tulliallan."

"She told him she was leaving?" Mac asked.

"No, just talked about going for the DI exam and how there might be an opening at that rank under another DCI. I know that Duncan in DCI Akhtar's team is on long-term sick."

Mac gave his best rogue's grin. "Kai, you're better informed than I am. Look, if Nari goes for Inspector and gets it then I would want a sergeant. If you want to go for it, there's nothing stopping you."

"Do you think I'm ready, guv? I've been a DC for two

years now but since Abby came along the DC pay doesn't go very far, eh? Not for three kids. It's either that or...some of the guys I was on the beat with have moved to work for private security firms. The pay's much better than at my rank. But if you think I've got a shot, eh?"

Mac thought that Kai didn't have much experience in a leadership role. A DS would be expected to manage any DC in the team and if a cold case unit was opening up under Reid's remit, then more officers would be recruited. Kai might end up in charge of two or three. He wasn't sure he could see it in him. But he smiled and clapped Kai on the shoulder.

"You've got a shot. Maybe pick up the phone to Mel and have a chat with her about running a team. I can spare you sometime next week maybe, when we've chased down some of the Gaines' evidence."

Mac wanted to bail on the conversation. He had always felt uncomfortable with personal conversations, and Kai had unloaded a truckful in the space of a few minutes. He would always support his people to develop and move up the ranks, but Mel had always been so much better at it than him. He wondered when she was due back to work. He'd phoned to check in and she assured him she was improving daily and it wouldn't be long before she was back, but couldn't give a date as the pain came and went. His question was answered when he pushed through the doors and saw her setting up the evidence boards down at his team's cluster of desks.

"About that guv," Kai said, as they moved into the room. "Got the image from Joe Benson's video doorbell enhanced. You know, Gaines' neighbour. Nice guy, used to be groundsman at Celtic Park. Anyway, I'd say definitely a van. High-sided. Transit. And what you thought was damage was mud or something. The enhancement software shows it up."

"What about the damage I saw on Michael Gaines' car?" Mac asked.

"We found white paint in the dent. But even if we had the white van, all we could do is match it to a van with that paint. Which is pretty standard across dozens of commercial vehicle makes. We couldn't link it to a specific vehicle. But I did find some clearer images of the van in question on two of the neighbour's cameras. It's been driven into the street on four different occasions in the last month. Always delivering or picking up from Michael Gaines house."

"In his spare bedroom I found flat packed cardboard boxes," Nari put in from her desk.

"And his laptop shows he's been active buying and selling online," Kai finished.

He cleared his throat as he handed out the coffees. "Particularly seems to be fond of female clothes, you know?"

"Any reason why he shouldn't be?" Mel asked levelly.

"No, no. Takes all sorts but, he was into some, like pantomime dame stuff," Kai said.

Mel covered her face with her hands. Nari shook her head.

"What?" Kai said.

"Like you said, Kai, takes all sorts. So, he's been getting deliveries and pickups from a courier. Always the same vehicle, so we assume the same driver."

"That would make him a sub-contractor, guv," Kai said. "If it was a big company, it would likely be different drivers every time, right? Probably, this smaller site offers courier delivery and has sub-contractors working in each location."

Mac perched on Kai's desk. He was hanging his coat from the back and looking slightly chagrined. He glanced at Mac, who gave him a wink. Being insensitive, or more likely in his case naive, to gender issues wouldn't cost him the sergeant's exam. Plenty of other traits in Kai's arsenal might. But it was Mac's job to encourage him to move up and give him the support he needed to do so.

"Do we have a reg on this van?" Mac asked.

"Not yet. Angle's wrong. We could stake out the street, see if he goes back?" Kai suggested.

"But if it's always been Gaines he was delivering to, he might never go back," Mel said.

"Kai, get onto the website Gaines was shopping on and find out what you can about how they get their goods delivered. Nari, ask everyone in that street and surrounding area about couriers in white vans. Mel, welcome back and can you start trawling the wider net of CCTV to see if we can pick up this van anywhere else and get a Reg?" Mac said.

"Will do. And I'm glad to be back, guv," Mel said, putting a hand to her neck. "And good to be out of that collar."

"Sorry about that," Mac said, guiltily.

Mel waved away the apology. "It's not you we'll be suing, sir. Just Police Scotland," she said with a laugh that Mac returned.

"What else do we know today that we didn't yesterday?"

"DNA found at the scene and on the body. Which didn't belong to Michael Gaines, any of the neighbours or workers at the depot," Mel said, looking pleased.

"Well done, Mel," Mac said, knowing chasing that lot down would have taken a monumental effort.

Mac was looking over the evidence boards, particularly at the pictures of the body. The more he looked at the wounds and how they had been inflicted, the more he was certain that Ash Fenton wasn't the man they were looking for. But he'd kept that out of his reports to Reid and, so far, no connection had been made by the media. Mac had kept the precise nature of the wounds out of the press. But it was only a matter of time. The fact that Fenton was on remand, waiting on a court hearing to decide how long he was going to prison for, made Mac uncomfortable. Someone else was out there. And there was no reason to believe they were done yet.

CHAPTER TWENTY-FIVE

"MICHAEL GAINES, OUR VICTIM. 46. Secondary school teacher. Gay, though private about it. We know this from his social media but not all of his colleagues were aware. His...hobby was performing in drag."

Mac was standing in front of his team, leaning against a desk, hands in trouser pockets. It was just after ten am, twelve days after the discovery of Zoe Phillips. Pictures of Gaines body were behind him as well as others gleaned from his social media posts to give an idea of his personal life.

"According to his colleagues, he was outspoken on certain topics and got himself into trouble more than once with his inability to back down, particularly on social media. Vocal in support of trans-rights. Has been at the heart of a blazing row last year after a student used a homophobic slur in his hearing. He believed it was directed at him and he posted about it, omitting the child's name. Lot of people divided about his actions."

"How did he keep his job after that?" Nari asked.

"By the skin of his teeth, eh?" Kai put in.

"Maybe not even that much," Mac said. "Less than a year later and he's no longer teaching at Cramond Secondary after seven years working there. So, maybe that was the last straw."

"Where did he go to?" Mel asked.

"No record of him taking another teaching job, so we don't know."

"Social media chats and DMs on his phone don't shed too much light. He was cagey about what he was going to do next," Kai said. "I've got a list of his most frequent contacts and the social accounts that he was most chatty with online."

"According to Cramond's head teacher, there was more than one parent who was aware of his online profile and disliked it. The school, like any other, has a cyber-bullying problem and it was felt that a teacher getting into that many arguments might be sending the wrong message," Mac said.

"I've put up the list of people he'd had the biggest rows with. Omitting those who are resident in another country. Six names keep coming up who are UK residents and three of those are parents at Cramond Secondary," Kai said, pointing with his pen.

Mac didn't look where he was pointing, having spotted the list as soon as it went up. The three names were circled, and Clio was one of them. The team would all have clocked it. He wondered if they knew of the relationship he had with Clio. It wasn't something he made public knowledge, preferring to keep his private life exactly that. If Nari or Kai made the connection they would query why he didn't recuse himself from the investigation. That was the ethical thing to do.

But, his reluctance to do so wasn't just about his need and having the ability to reassure Clio. He just couldn't hand over a case that he had begun. Mel did know to some extent already but was thankfully keeping quiet. For now. However Clio had posted images of the two of them and Maia walking recently on social media. It was only a matter of time.

"So, we look at those three people. Establish where they were at the time of death and check their DNA against the foreign DNA found on the body."

"Already underway, guv," Nari said. "I collected samples yesterday afternoon and this morning. I also have statements from each giving their whereabouts. Two don't have any kind of strong alibi. Natalie McKinley and Clio Wray. Both parents at the school and both have clashed with Gaines over his treatment of their children. Natalie McKinley tried to get him fired through her role as PTA chair. Clio Wray had some very heated exchanges online."

"That name sounds familiar," Kai said. "I can't place it."

"Dr. Wray acted as a consultant for us. The so-called Celtic Killer," Mac said, blandly.

"Oh yeah, I remember. Wow, she just can't stay away," Kai remarked.

Nari looked at Mac and he looked back, seeing something in her glance and challenging her to speak her mind.

"According to Gaines' next-door neighbour, he drove to work at the same time he usually does," Mac said. "Kai, did he have any more to say on that?"

"Yeah. He admits it was pitch black at that time and the car had its headlights on. All he actually saw was a silhouette. A man, he insists. Wearing a hat or a hood."

"It was a cold night, so that wouldn't be unusual," Mac said. "But he feels sure it was Michael Gaines he saw?"

"Yes. But he obviously saw what he wanted to see. Michael Gaines was already dead by that time, which was about six thirty in the morning."

"Right. So, he actually saw the killer driving Michael Gaines' body out to the place where he dumped it," Nari said. "Having already killed him in the house. Not one of the neighbors saw anyone carrying something large, man-sized out of the house and putting it into the car."

"Could have been done any time after midnight. So, what we do know is that Michael Gaines was caught on a few doorbell videos leaving his address the day before he died," Mac began.

"That's right, guv. I found three different sightings. Him in his car, and when we isolate the frames and enhance the image, you can see it's him in the driver's seat," Kai said.

"Good. On the night of his death, he went out for drinks with a few friends but was back home by nine. We have statements from the people he was with?"

"We do, guv. And DNA samples," Nari said.

"He gets home and his neighbour's doorbell shows a white van at the bottom of his drive." Mac said. "We don't see another vehicle after nine, but that doesn't mean his killer didn't just walk in. How much coverage of the street do the neighborhood doorbell cams give us, Kai?" Mac asked.

"Not great. Everyone has their doorstep and driveway covered, but there's a dozen blind spots. You could walk in and out without being seen quite easily, eh?"

Mac grimaced. That would have made the case so easy. If

this wasn't an isolated crime, but instead linked to Zoe Phillips and Vicky McCourt, then it could be a crime of passion. Someone with a grudge against Gaines for his outspoken attitude. Someone angry enough to do something bad on the spur of the moment. But, clever enough when calm to hide the killing. Or with the help of someone else clever enough. Nari was still watching him, looking shrewd. A thought floated through his mind at that point about Vicky McCourt. Not exactly outspoken as such. But she'd certainly been outspoken on the subject of her abusive partner. Enough to ensure he went to jail. Zoe Phillips? He didn't know, but her relationship with her on and off boyfriend was volatile. It was a connection. Tenuous but something about it felt promising. It set off a resonance within him that he recognised. The kind of gut feeling he got when he knew instinctively that he was onto a winner.

"So, we wait for those DNA samples and eliminate the people who gave them. Then we look to establish comings and goings from his house. Talk to the neighbours again, get everything they can remember. Talk to posties. Delivery drivers. Taxis. Bus drivers. There's a bus stop a few hundred yards away on Glasgow Road. Find his vehicle on city CCTV. Piece his movements together."

"Mac, a word please," Reid suddenly called out from the main door.

Mac nodded and stood.

"Mel, assign some actions and track them. Good luck everyone. Next briefing end of shift at 5," Mac said as he strode to the exit.

Reid had already disappeared. When Mac pushed

through the double doors, the hallway was empty. He walked past the lifts to a door at the far end, flanked by two tall pot plants. It bore a plaque with the name DCS Kenneth Reid engraved on it. Mac knocked once and opened it. Reid sat behind his desk. A man in a crisp uniform and the pips of a Deputy Chief Constable sat in one chair, holding his cap on his knee. His hair was the colour of iron and his features were fine-boned. Grey eyes bored into Mac's from the moment he stepped through the door, with as much warmth in them as a shark's.

"You know Deputy Chief Constable Mayhew?" Reid asked.

"We've never met, but he can count the pips," Mayhew said, standing and offering a slim, pale hand.

Mac shook it, surprised at the strength of the grip. Mayhew sat first, never taking his eyes from Mac.

"I can. What can I do for you?" Mac asked, sitting slowly.

Mayhew looked to Reid, then back to Mac.

"A little birdie tells me that you're looking to reopen the Ashleigh Fenton case, son," Reid said, lacing his fingers together in front of him on the desk.

"There is some evidence that we got that case wrong," Mac said, levelly.

"That DCI Akhtar got it wrong," Mayhew corrected.

"Yes," Mac said, bluntly. "She was given the case and handed it to the Procurator Fiscal."

"You see. I'm a little concerned about the optics of this," Mayhew said. "We have a case successfully concluded by a female DCI from an ethnic minority. And a white male officer trying to unstitch it. It doesn't look good for us at all."

Mac frowned, 'optics?' was this on the level? He glanced at Reid, who was keeping his face morose.

"With respect, sir, if the case is unsound, *optics* won't matter. We'll look a helluva lot worse if Fenton is found to be innocent because other killings come to light while he's been locked up."

"He confessed, didn't he? Kenny, am I missing something? We did get a confession?" Mayhew said with a look of exaggerated puzzlement on his face.

"We did, sir," Reid admitted.

"And DNA evidence?" Mayhew demanded, pushing the incredulity in his voice even more.

"Yes," Reid replied.

"But no motive for the killing of Zoe Phillips. Only for Vicky McCourt. He wanted revenge on her for getting him sent down," Mac said.

"Do we need a motive?" Mayhew asked. "As well as the fact he confessed, we have this man Fenton's DNA on the body. If he didn't kill her, then how did it get there?"

"Who knows?" Mac was getting angry. "Maybe he met her in a night club and got close to her. Maybe they knew each other."

"And is there any evidence of a relationship between them?" Mayhew said.

"Not that we've found, but we can keep looking..." Mac began, urgently.

Mayhew put up a hand, smiling patiently. "I appreciate your efforts, DCI McNeill, but it concerns me greatly that this just looks like sour grapes. You lost the biggest murder case of the year so you're trying to undermine your female colleague."

"What?" Mac protested, turning to Reid. "Guv, surely you don't believe this nonsense?"

Reid spread his hands and looked to Mayhew from beneath his usual lowered brows. "Sir, I can't go along with that interpretation. Mac is my best DCI. He's the best DCI in the country as far as I'm concerned..."

Mayhew held up a hand and sat forward in his seat, looking conspiratorial. "Look. You and I know that it probably isn't quite like that, but the Chief Constable has to keep an eye on how this will be perceived outside this station and, for that matter, outside of Police Scotland. How certain people with less knowledge and experience will view it. Which means I have to keep an eye on the situation, which therefore means so do you, Kenny. From a PR perspective, this is a hornet's nest I don't intend to poke. And we haven't even started on the fact that your fine detective here is in a relationship with one of the chief suspects? Is that right?"

Those shark's eyes latched onto Mac and he saw straight through the false camaraderie. Mayhew had scented blood in the water. Mac sat back, sharing his stare between his two bosses.

"Not in the way you're suggesting. We are just friends."

"Mac!" Reid exploded. "Jesus Christ man!"

"Frankly, it doesn't matter if you're sleeping with her or not. It's all the same to the press and to AC. Not to mention the Chief Constable and the Police and Crime Commissioner. It looks very much as though you're trying to undermine a successful case just to protect your...friend," Mayhew said. "All fake friendliness sloughing away. The smile he had worn throughout vanished.

"Guv, this is BS. This is Akhtar conspiring against me," Mac said.

"This information didn't come from DCI Akhtar, Mc-Neill, but from one of your own team," Mayhew said quietly. "They were concerned about your impartiality."

Mac's head swung to him slowly and something in his face made the DCC sit back and lick his lips. Reid was also glaring at him.

"You didn't tell me that...sir," Reid grated.

"Didn't I? It hardly matters, does it?"

"It matters that there's a bloody grass in my team, going above the chain of command," Reid spluttered.

"Oh, come off it, Kenny! That doesn't mean anything these days. We have to be transparent with each other so we can control the stories that go public. Otherwise, the bloody Justice Secretary and the Home Secretary will engineer things so that everything is transparent and then where would we be? You want everything aired in public, Kenny? You, of all people!"

A redness had crept into Mayhew features and he was stabbing Reid's desk with his finger as he spoke.

"Who was it?" Mac asked.

"You're such a fine detective, I'm sure you can work it out," Mayhew said, tugging his jacket straight. "As of now, you are off this case. I am reassigning you."

CHAPTER TWENTY-SIX

MAC STALKED BACK DOWN THE HALLWAY. He almost stopped at the lifts, but then kept going. Reassigned a second time in favour of DCI Hafsa Akhtar. Last time it had been necessary. He was out of the picture with a concussion. Reid had no choice. This time it was done for political reasons. The Chief Constable wanted to protect the optics, avoid being accused of misogyny and racism. The fact that the majority of senior officers in Police Scotland were still white men just made that worse. But it infuriated Mac, just as Akhtar's incessant scheming irritated him. The doors to the open plan office housing his and Akhtar's teams flew open from the palms of his hands. Akhtar was in front of both teams. Nari was next to her. There was the grass. Nari had gone to Akhtar and then the DCI had gone above Reid's head to the DCC. Akhtar saw him as he strode up the centre aisle but continued speaking.

"Therefore, she has just become our number one suspect. Nari, could you escort DCI McNeill from the room please?"

Mac stopped, hands in trouser pockets, dark glare going from Nari to Akhtar and back.

"And who's that?" he asked pleasantly.

"I'm not at liberty to disclose to you the next steps in this investigation," Akhtar said.

"Guv, come on," Nari said at the same time, stepping forward.

Mac looked straight through her and returned his attention to Akhtar. "You're really going to treat this as career advancement instead of catching a killer?"

Akhtar faced him. "I'm well aware of how much a man like you feels threatened by a woman doing his job better than him. You've been itching to find fault in the Ash Fenton prosecution."

"You're welcome to your promotion, Hafsa. You can keep it. I don't care. What I do care about is stitching up an innocent man just so you can get a pat on the back and an extra badge on your jacket."

"I care about the killer not getting away with it," Akhtar spat back.

"Then step aside," Mac snarled, trying to step around Nari.

But she stepped in front of him, looking away but pointedly not allowing him to go further.

"Step aside, Detective Sergeant," Mac ordered.

"I can't, guv. You can't be in here," Nari said quietly.

"Why? This is still my office. I've been reassigned. Not suspended."

"Because you're compromised, guv," Nari said.

Now she looked up, looking him in the eyes and searching them. Mac stared back, disbelieving.

"You should have recused yourself when Clio's name came up. At least disclosed that you knew her," Nari said.

"She didn't do this."

"Her DNA was found on the body. We got the match back in the last few minutes," Kai said. "Then DCI Akhtar marched in and Nari went to her as though she'd been whistled over."

Nari shot him a look, but Kai stared back stolidly. His face said that he supported his guvnor and didn't agree with the way Nari had gone about it. Mel had got up, picking up her coat from the back of her chair.

"Come on, guv. We'll get a coffee downstairs."

"You have actions, DI Barland," Akhtar told her, sternly. "DCI McNeill, if you do not remove yourself from this office, I will have you removed."

"Was it worth it, Nari?" McNeill whispered.

Nari's face looked stricken and Mac instantly regretted the barb. He hadn't wanted to hurt her. And if he was being honest with himself, she was right; he should have been open with his team about knowing Clio. But she should have been honest too, come to him face-to-face rather than behind his back. "Be careful, Nari," he said quietly. "Akhtar isn't a team player. Watch your back, eh?'

"And if you decide to tip off our suspect, then you will be facing suspension, pending criminal prosecution," Akhtar said to Mac. "And believe me, I will find out if you do."

Mac gave the rogue's grin, but it was forced. More an attempt to show how unconcerned he was about Akhtar's power move. As he turned away, he caught Mel's eye and glanced quickly towards the exit and back. Mel looked away, suddenly scrutinising something on her computer screen and nodding to herself as she did so. Mac walked away. As he neared the doors he saw Reid waiting. Mayhew didn't meet Mac's eye as he walked past and through the double doors. Mac heard him greet Akhtar effusively and by her first name. He put it from his mind, walking to the lifts.

"Mac, I'm sorry, son. My hands are well and truly tied." Mac frowned, that sounded suspiciously like Mayhew had Reid over a barrel about something. Reid continued, "Mayhew's got a bee in his bonnet. He's linked to those two cases. He did some press conferences praising Akhtar and the Serious Crimes Unit in general. I think he's got a stake in it staying solved."

Mac stabbed the down button. "Understood, sir. It's hard to find a suitable case for now when I'm banned from working with my own team."

"I don't think so. This might be just what you need. A break from casework and a chance to focus on my little problem. Our little problem, don't forget, son," Reid whispered while looking over Mac's shoulder to check no-one could overhear.

He turned away, heading for the double doors to the main office. Mac looked at the lift indicator, seeing Mel heading out of the office as Reid went in. She didn't look at him as she walked towards the ladies, phone in hand. As the doors closed, Mac followed her. Mel didn't glance around until she reached the door of the ladies' toilets, around a corner of the corridor. She looked at Mac anxiously.

"What the hell is going on here, guv?" she whispered.

"I'm being screwed over and Clio is being lined up for a

quick conviction just like Ash Fenton," Mac said, putting his head close to Mel's.

"He confessed."

"Aye, but Clio did not, *could not* have killed anyone. Certainly not by a method that matches two previous murders. We haven't made the method public. I haven't seen it reported anywhere. How the hell would she know?"

"Because you told her," Mel said, looking straight at him.

"Jesus! Is that what Akhtar is saying?"

"It's what she's intimating. Clio is the killer and trying to disguise a revenge killing under a previous crime with your help," Mel said.

Mac felt a chill. He felt cornered, outplayed in a contest he hadn't even realised he was in. Now, not only was he stripped of the Michael Gaines case, but was facing an attempt to fit him up. Akhtar was going for the jugular. Was she bent? Was this a criminal conspiracy? You could never tell. A colleague you had trained with could turn out to be corrupt, whether that was taking money from the press for information or being in the pocket of a gangster. Akhtar knew that too. She had to be thinking that he was bent. He would in her place. The fact that he hadn't recused himself from the case. That he had a relationship with a suspect and that he knew details of the previous killings that no-one outside of the investigation knew. And therefore the only source for Clio to discover it.

"There's something else going on here. Mayhew was in Reid's office. He wants any talk of wrongful arrest shut down. He wants Ash Fenton to go down, and this case separated from those. It's political."

"I get it. And you've played right into their hands, you

fool," Mel said, poking him in the chest. "You should have come right out and disclosed your relationship with Clio from the beginning. So should I. As soon as her name went up on the board, I recognised it and I said nothing."

"Keep it that way. If Akhtar finds out, you'll be in the same boiling pot as me."

"I intend to. What do you need?"

Mac smiled bleakly. Even with the risk to herself, Mel's first instinct was to help. They had come up together through Tulliallan. Mac had once had a crush on her, had even pursued her. Until she'd told him he was barking up the wrong type of tree. She hadn't wanted the other cadets to know. There was too much prejudice against being gay in the police, even for a woman. Mac had kept the secret and she'd become one of his few friends. Their careers had gone in different directions after graduation. Mac had hit the beat hard in some of the most deprived areas of Edinburgh. Mel had gone into family liaison, courses, and education, earning promotion rapidly. Mac's time in AC under Kenny Reid had accelerated his own promotions until he had eclipsed her. Breaking the case that the press had dubbed The Angel Killer had been a big help, catapulting him into the media spotlight and that of senior officers.

"They're going to arrest Clio and she'll be remanded. She has no alibi and with the DNA, Akhtar will be able to hold her for the maximum amount of time. She has a thirteen-year-old daughter. There's family in Yorkshire but you know what will happen when Clio's arrested. Maia will be taken into care. Can you and Cazzy take her in?"

"Jesus, guv! You don't ask much, do you?"

"It will help Clio keep it together. She trusts me and knows that I trust you," Mac said urgently.

A peculiar smile twitched Mel's mouth. "Oh yeah? How does she know that then?"

"Because I've told her often enough. I trust you more than anyone. You're the only person I do trust."

"You've never said so."

Mac ran a hand through his hair, stepping away, feeling exasperated. "I don't tend to say anything, do I? Unless it's a safe topic like work. Maybe that's part of being on the spectrum. Will you help me, Mel?"

Mel beamed. "I'm going to get shot if anyone finds out, but yes of course I'll help. No question. Autistic, eh? I always wondered. It was either that or you were just a tosser most of the time."

"Probably a bit of both," Mac grinned. "We don't have much time. I have to get to Clio before the heavy squad does. Maia's at school. Cramond Secondary. Can you get to her? Get her out and take her home to yours. I'll tell Clio."

From around the corner came the sound of the double doors opening and multiple footsteps. Akhtar could be heard barking out orders. Mac and Mel exchanged looks and then ran for the stairs, located beyond the ladies and gents' toilets at the end of the corridor. Mac took the concrete staircase two at a time, Mel hurrying after him. Mac typed in a code on his phone which would disguise his number for the recipient of his call. He didn't want anything showing up on Clio's call history from him. Akhtar would check and a private number could be explained away as spam. He was at the bottom of the stairs, having vaulted the metal handrail at the end, and hauling open the door opposite which led out to the car park at the rear of the HQ building. Clio hadn't picked up and Mac left a breathless voicemail then redialed.

He was in the car, watching Mel run past to her own vehicle, and on his third attempt to get through to Clio when she finally picked up.

"Mac? What's happening? Is Maia OK?" Clio sounded as harassed as Mac felt.

He stabbed the speaker button and tossed the phone to the seat beside him, pulling out of the space and heading for the car park barrier.

"I don't have much time, Clio. Just listen and don't interrupt. Your DNA was found on Michael Gaines' body. I don't know how it got there yet, but I'm going to assume you haven't been in physical contact with him since midnight on Monday."

"No, of course not. The last time I saw him was at school when Maia was suspended and I didn't touch him."

"Well then, something funny is going on but it doesn't matter. I'm off the case. DCI Akhtar is coming for you. She'll probably head to the university and send some other officers to your home. This is strong enough evidence for her to arrest and hold you. It may even be enough for the Procurator Fiscal. I can't stop any of that happening. They may already think you and I are in collusion. Mel Barland is on her way to Maia's school. You need to phone them now and tell them her auntie Mel is coming to collect her. Make up a story. Death in the family or something. Do not identify Mel as a police officer. Got it?"

"Yes, yes. I've got it. I won't let them take Maia away, Mac."

"I know, which is why I've asked Mel and her wife to take her in. As far as the school and eventually the police know, she's staying with her auntie. Message her directly, make sure she gets it. Tell her to expect Mel and then delete the message, make sure Maia deletes it too. I won't let her be taken into care. No way. And I will get you out of this, Clio. I promise."

"Oh god, I'm scared, Mac. How did my DNA end up on Michael Gaines' body? Someone must have done it deliberately, but who and how did they get it? Oh god, why is this happening to me, Mac?"

"I don't the answer to any of the questions right now, Clio. But I'm going to find out."

CHAPTER TWENTY-SEVEN

MAC PARKED IN A LAYBY on Queen's Drive. Arthur's Seat loomed to his right. To his left was the Dynamic Earth attraction with the bizarrely shaped Parliament building just beyond. He had just sent a text to Kai, trusting in the loyalty of his DC. The text had simply read:

ETA to uni?

Kai might not be on the team heading for Clio's most likely location at this time of day. It was a gamble for Mac to go. He had to avoid walking into the building on Canongate and straight into Akhtar. The reply had come back as he was striding away from his car, clicking the keys in his pocket to lock it. He glanced at the notification.

A has just left HQ. A 2 U. N also. Me Cram.

Akhtar had only just made it off site. That meant she was twenty minutes away. Nari was along with her. Kai had been sent to Clio's house in Cramond. Mac was five minutes away from Clio's office on foot. He'd asked her to stay put, but half expected her to bolt. Being told you were about to be arrested for murder would be enough to make anyone panic. But if she ran it would be worse for her. And it would throw suspicion on Mac. He vaulted a car park barrier at the rear of the Holyrood Hotel, walking past the kitchens which were belching steam from extractor fans, circling a cluster of industrial sized wheeled bins, then between a public library and a primary school before emerging onto Canongate. He jogged the remaining hundred yards to the main entrance, hitting the entry buzzer for Clio's office.

Moments later, he was in Clio's new office. It was up the stairs from the old cubby hole, where he had first met her. This one overlooked parliament and was spacious enough for a breakout area comprising three examples of Swedish furniture design in vibrant, primary colours. Clio was standing in front of her desk when he walked in and she ran to him. Mac hugged her, Clio's face pressed to his chest. She was trembling. He didn't say anything for a count of sixty, another part of his mind counting the time it would take Akhtar to get here. Then he gently took Clio by the forearm and held her at arm's length. There were tears in her eyes but her jaw was set. There was anger and resolution there.

"I won't lose her, Mac. They won't pin this on me and take my daughter away."

"You're right," Mac said, holding her gaze. "You're being stitched up by someone. It can only be out of revenge. Nobody would do something this elaborate for the sake of a random victim. We don't have much time. Give me your phone. If Akhtar asks about it, you lost it."

"I'll say it was in my car," Clio said, taking her phone from a pocket of her jeans.

"Your car?" Mac asked.

"It was stolen. Couple of days ago. I didn't want to bother you with it. I reported it to the local station though."

Mac frowned, compiling that fact along with the others at his disposal. Clio was out on the night Michael Gaines was killed. Drinking alone at the end of the night. Not as sharp as she might otherwise have been. Opportunistic thief? Too much of a coincidence. Then he remembered the damage to Michael Gaines' car. White paint in the dent.

"Your car's white?"

Clio nodded, holding out the phone.

"But, when we met, you had a mini, a blue one."

"Yeah, I traded it in for a Polo just before my landlord told me he wanted to sell the house. Why?"

Mac shook his head, looking for the SIM tray on her phone. She held up the card, smiling shakily. "Way ahead of you, detective."

He took the SIM and added it to his trouser pocket. "Thanks. I'll go through your phone at home. See what I can find. Anything that might tell me who is targeting you. I'll dispose of the SIM so Akhtar can't have it traced."

"What's going to happen to me, Mac?" Clio said, her voice brittle.

"Akhtar or one of her team will tell you what you are suspected of and read you your rights. Do you have a solicitor?"

"Not on retainer. The only one I know is the guy who handled my divorce."

216

"Give them his name when they ask and follow his advice. You've got nothing to hide. Be honest with them."

She squeezed his forearms, biting her lip. "Maia is going to be so scared."

"Mel and Cazzy will take good care of her. She'll love them. Mel is always trying to mother me and Cazzy is even worse on the occasions I've met her. They'll take Maia under their wings. And Mel worked for years as a family liaison officer. She knows exactly how to explain things to Maia. I trust Mel with my life."

Clio nodded, breathing in shuddering gasps. Mac checked the time on his phone. Akhtar would be here in about ten minutes. Or maybe right now if she had patrol cars with her and they lit up the roof.

"My only lead so far is a white van. Kai caught one near the scene of Zoe Phillips body and there's one linked to the man who was arrested for that. There was a white van at Michael Gaines' house. A delivery driver. Have you seen any white vans recently? Probably a transit. The tall type."

Clio's brow furrowed. She brought her hands together over her mouth and Mac saw them shaking. She folded her arms across her chest, shaking her head frantically. The trembling was spreading and, she was white as a sheet.

"I...I don't know. Oh god, Mac! What's going to happen to Maia? I didn't do anything!"

The hysteria in her voice was ramping up, tears filling her eyes. Mac needed as much as he could get from her before Akhtar arrived to nick her. He couldn't allow hysteria to waste the precious time they had. A second of clear thinking could be all that was needed. Mac stepped close, gently taking

Clio's face in his hands, and lowered his head to kiss her. She stopped breathing. Stopped trembling. Time stretched. When Mac broke away he couldn't say if the kiss had lasted a second or a minute. His heart was racing. Clio's eyes stayed closed.

"Have you noticed a white van recently?" Mac asked softly.

"Yes. I've been selling stuff on a website. The guy who comes to collect the parcels drives a white van," Clio replied in a voice calm and steady.

Mac smiled and for a moment, they were looking into each other's eyes. Then Clio slapped him across the face. It staggered him but didn't shift the rogue's grin.

"Sorry, but I couldn't spare the time for you to calm down. You were getting hysterical. And you've just given me something I can work with."

"You...I...really?" Clio stammered.

The intercom on her desk buzzed. Clio jumped, looking around wildly as though fearing the kiss had been observed by someone. Mac went to the desk and pressed the receive button.

"DCI Akhtar, Police Scotland, Serious Crimes Unit. I need to speak to Dr. Clio Wray," Akhtar's clipped voice.

Clio stared in horror until Mac gestured for her to speak.

"Uh, yes, I'm here. I'll buzz you in. I'm on the fourth floor. East wing."

When she went to press the door release button, Mac took her hand.

"Give me a minute to get to the fire escape. Then let them in."

Clio nodded and Mac hurried back around her desk towards the door. As he passed her, she seized the lapel of his suit jacket and hauled him towards her. She pressed her lips to his fiercely and for longer than he had. Then she breathlessly broke away.

"Now, we're even," she gasped. "Go!"

As he dashed out through the office door and followed signs for the fire exit, he heard the buzzer sounding again. He was clattering down the external fire escape steps less than a minute later, while Akhtar must have been climbing the internal staircase. He hurried away along Canongate, slipping into the first side-street he came across and navigating his way through alleys and car parks towards Holyrood Gait and back to his car. The white van had to be significant but the question remained how to find it. With a team behind him he would have them trawling the database of traffic cameras, capturing the registration plates of any white van and then chasing down the owners. Painstaking and time consuming for a team of four. Impossible for one man. He needed to narrow down the field. Kai had already told him the video doorbells of Craig Wynd didn't give a clear look at the van which had been seen there. That left the footage Kai had found overlooking the New Covenant retreat out at Loanhead.

A white van had been seen driving up to the retreat, then away again. They'd assumed this was Ashleigh Fenton on his way into town to kill Zoe Phillips. Whether it was premeditated or not. But, that meant he had an accomplice. One who might now be proceeding with the murders. A scenario just as unlikely for Akhtar or Mayhew to accept given they would have to climb down over their public assertion that the killer of Zoe Phillips had been caught. A murderous accomplice at large would be unacceptable to the public and, most importantly for those two, the press. Mac looked up the New Covenant website. A few minutes of searching brought him the address of their Loanhead retreat. It was an area on the southern borders of the city, just off the bypass that ringed Edinburgh's south side from west to east and then joined the A1. A suburban area but one of the furthest out from the city with the Pentland hills not far beyond. Secluded but not so much that it would be an inconvenience for anyone needing to get into the city.

The phone rang as he put the address into the sat nav.

"Kai," he answered.

"Guv. Akhtar has picked up Clio Wray and is heading back to Brunswick Road with her. Press were there when she arrived."

Mac swore. "What's your take on it?" he asked.

"Akhtar acted like she was annoyed but didn't try and have them moved on before she brought Clio out. She had enough uniform bodies to do it. I'd bet the leak came from her. Or Nari."

"She's gone well and truly to the dark side, has she?"

Kai swore. "She's gone all feminist militant, guv. I asked her about it and she just kept going on about how Akhtar deserved a chance to prove she was right. I don't know her anymore."

"Forget it, Kai. Do what you can to make sure Clio's okay. Akhtar has got this badly wrong and I'm going to prove it. I'm heading to that New Covenant retreat, remember? Out at Loanhead."

"Yeah, I remember. You need some backup, eh?"

"No, you can't afford to lose your job, and you don't have

the flak jacket of a few high profile cases to protect you. Don't stick your head above the parapet, Kai."

"It's not right, guv. What they're doing. I'm going to speak to DCS Reid."

"Really?" Mac said.

Silence. "No," Kai grunted. "I'm basically a coward, eh?"

Mac barked a laugh. "I need you inside the enemy camp feeding me info every now and then. You're in the best position where you are."

"Right, right," Kai sounded frustrated. He was a good lad, not very subtle, naïve and still with a lot to learn, but his heart was in the right place, and Mac knew he had his loyalty. "What do you want me to do though?"

"I want to explore the possibility of there being an accomplice. Someone who was driving that van the night we think Fenton left the retreat and killed Zoe Phillips. The van didn't drive itself there and back and if his pal Kirk was telling the truth, Fenton was back there for morning prayer. Let's start with who he was in prison with. Get onto Saughton. Who shared a cell with him? Which screws knew him and what can they tell you about who he hung around with. Let's see if anyone got released around the same time as he did. I'll grill the God-botherers. Just keep a low profile, Kai, eh? Maybe find yourself a quiet room somewhere to make the calls."

"Guv, I'm on it. Anything to get away from the two witches. Hubble bubble toil and trouble and all that, eh?"

"Kai, you never cease to surprise me. I wouldn't have expected Shakespearean references from you."

"Eh? Shakespeare? I thought it was Harry Potter, guv."

Mac laughed, genuinely.

CHAPTER TWENTY-EIGHT

Mac took a minute to connect his phone to the car's Bluetooth, then headed south along Queen's Drive, navigating without looking at the map. He knew the city well enough to choose the best route. The actual location of the New Covenant retreat was the small village of Bilston, just outside the larger suburb of Loanhead. To clear his mind he selected a Swedish black-thrash crossover. Dissonant but rhythmic pulsing riffs filled the small space, almost eliminating the sounds outside the car and even those of the engine. Snarling, throat ripping vocals occasionally veered into intelligible words. He knew the lyrics anyway. Depictions of bleak forests, dark and cold. It suited his mood. He needed to drive thoughts of Clio from his mind. Maia too. It was difficult. The idea of Clio locked in a cell. Or of Maia with strangers, wanting to know what was happening to her mum. She would be scared. But now was the time he needed to be focused solely on the case. It was Clio's only chance.

It took the best part of an hour to reach his destination. For the most part, he used his knowledge of the city to find his way. Then he followed the instructions of the satnav to reach the retreat itself. The Pentlands were visible in the distance to the right, a dark shape on the horizon. He passed retail parks and industrial estates, following a busy dual carriageway. He tried to still the voice telling him he was clutching at straws. Rationally there was little he could expect from anyone currently at the New Covenant retreat. Even if he found people who'd been there the night Zoe Phillips was killed, what could he learn from them? Instinct was a smaller voice. It whispered insistently. There was something about this white van. Something significant. He couldn't put it before Reid as justification for reopening the investigation. Certainly couldn't be put before a judge. But he had learned to trust the tiny whispering voice. Mac didn't know what was going to happen next. All he knew was he had the longest of long shots to chase up.

The retreat had the look of a farm. A collection of single-storey buildings, painted white with tiled roofs, were clustered together at the end of a lane. The lane ended at a gate with an open-sided barn in front of it. Another gate to the side led to the buildings. Behind them was an assortment of agricultural style outbuildings. The fields around the retreat were wild, overgrown with grass. There was no sign of livestock. Mac stopped at the gate leading to the barn. For a moment he sat looking out of the windscreen. Then he got out, phone in hand. There was a white van parked in the shelter of the barn's corrugated iron roof. Three cars were parked next to it, all fairly ordinary looking. The usual collection of hatchbacks and SUVs that occupied the average driveway in Scotland.

Mac noticed the gate was secured by a simple loop of rope. He lifted it and opened the gate just wide enough to squeeze through. Hinges groaned. The ground was wet, a mixture of gravel and mud.

Approaching the barn, he began to take pictures, first of the van, then the other vehicles. The van was a tall-sided transit. He made sure the registration plate was captured. There was no sign of damage. Fresh mud splatters sprayed back from the wheel arches but otherwise it looked in good condition. Standing on the front tire he looked inside, turning on the torch of his phone against the gloom of the barn. The interior was immaculate. It was a contrast to what he expected from a commercial vehicle. No takeaway wrappers or disposable coffee cups. No discarded dockets or invoices. Apart from the mud splashes, which probably happened when the vehicle was driven up here, it could have been brand new.

"Can I help you, friend?"

Mac hopped down. A man was standing at the entrance to the barn, watching him with a quizzical smile on his face. He wore a baseball cap which shadowed his eyes. Brown hair stuck out beneath the brim and at the back. He wore cargo pants and boots, a woollen jumper that had the look of a homemade Christmas present. Mac produced his warrant card, walking towards the man.

"Detective Chief Inspector McNeill, Police Scotland Serious Crimes Unit. And you are?"

"Brad," the man said with a smile, offering his hand and not looking at the ID.

Mac shook the offered hand, which had a strong, dry grip. He was met with a confident smile and eyes so dark they almost looked black. Mac noticed that the man had no eye-brows. A quick glance to the hair showing under his cap and Mac had the distinct impression it was a wig. Those black eyes gave him an alien appearance.

"You're interested in my van?" Brad said.

"Yes. What do you use it for?"

"I'm a delivery driver."

"You're making a delivery to this place?"

"No. I'm here on my own time. I'm part of the New Covenant," Brad replied, smile not slipping.

His eyes hadn't slipped either. This man had no discomfort in making or holding eye contact. Or at least he masked it well. Mac glanced at the buildings where another man had appeared at a window.

"So, how can I help?" Brad asked, mildly.

"How long have you had the van?"

"About eighteen months. New Covenant arranged it for me, to help me get back on my feet. They helped set me up as a delivery driver."

His accent had tinges of the north, Aberdeen way. But it was muted, the Scottishness repressed. Mac had heard it before. A classic example was the so-called Glasgow Uni accent, a hybrid of English, American and Scottish. Posh. Privately educated then. Now a delivery driver.

"Back on your feet? You were inside?"

The smile broadened, but didn't reach those unblinking eyes. "Yes. I did time. Now, I've found Jesus. He saved me."

"Good for you," Mac said, walking past him and breaking the eye contact.

"Have I done something wrong? The tax is paid up and,

it's just been MOT'd. I know I don't have any tickets. I use a speed limiter and I don't drive in bus lanes. So..."

Brad had turned, arms out from his sides, as though to indicate how harmless he was. Another man was emerging from the nearest building. He wore jeans and boots with untied laces, like he'd just stepped into them. He also wore a woollen sweater, similar design to Brad's but different colours. Maybe everyone at New Covenant got one for Christmas. He had brown hair, swept back from his temples and receding. His face was long and thin, chin raised. He looked like Richard E. Grant a little and that told Mac who it was.

"Michael Fielding?" he said.

Fielding stopped what had been a purposeful stride. Then he wagged a finger and smiled.

"Police. In fact, you would be DCI McNeill. The man who arrested Brother Ashleigh," Fielding replied in an educated Southern English accent.

"I took him in for questioning. It was my colleague DCI Akhtar who formally charged him. I was indisposed," Mac replied, thrusting hands into his trouser pockets.

"Well, we will get him out. He's innocent. I'm convinced of it and our lawyers are hard at work proving it."

"I'll help in any way I can. I also believe he's innocent," Mac said.

Fielding had been walking towards Brad. Mac noticed Brad's gaze shift to the other man. Then he squeezed Fielding's shoulder, mouth quirking into a half smile. It was a man in authority giving reassurance to a subordinate. If anything, Mac would have expected the relationship to be the other way around. At Mac's words, both men looked at him.

Fielding's mouth was open. Brad's brows drew down tightly, mouth firming. The intensity of his stare was dramatic. Almost too intense. There was charisma there, natural leadership.

"You do? And why are you here?" Fielding asked.

Mac gave an exaggerated shiver, hunching his shoulders. "Maybe we could talk about it inside? Over a cup of tea?"

"Of course! Where are my manners? Please come in!" Fielding said, indicating with a wave of his arm the door he had stepped out of.

"I'm going to hit the road…" Brad started to say.

"If we're going to talk about Ashleigh, then shouldn't you stay? You were cell mates after all and became good friends," Fielding said.

The look that came from Brad was enough to make Fielding clear his throat and look down. Mac saw anger in Brad's face, just a flash, gone in an instant. But in that moment, Brad had been enraged.

"Yeah, so we were. Well, if DCI McNeill thinks I should stay…" Brad began.

"Yes. I do," Mac replied and began walking towards the house.

Inside was a long room with shoe racks against one wall and hooks holding coats against the other. A door led through to a tiled hallway with white painted walls. A variety of religious paraphernalia hung from the walls, ranging from crosses to posters and framed paintings. In one direction Mac could see a sink through an open door. The other way led to a series of closed doors. A woman appeared in front of the open door to the kitchen. She had hair tied back in a ponytail and a round face with blue eyes. She held a dishcloth and was drying a ceramic bowl.

"Hello. Nice to see a new face," she said, coming towards him. "I'm Annie Sullivan. And you are?"

"DCI McNeill," Mac said.

She stopped halfway along the hall, still with her hand outstretched. Her smile faltered.

"DCI McNeill is here to help us prove Ashleigh's innocence, Annie," Fielding said, following Mac into the hall.

Annie's smile returned with gusto. "Oh wow! That's fantastic! Thank you! Come in. I'll put the kettle on."

Her outpouring of enthusiasm had the feel of innocence. A person showing their genuine emotions, unfiltered. As Mac followed, he saw her gaze slip past him. The smile faltered again, and she looked away hurriedly. Mac glanced over his shoulder and saw Brad standing in the doorway, looking intently after Annie. When he noticed Mac watching he smiled. It transformed his face. He glowed when smiling, appearing genuinely joyful. But, before that he had been anything but. Mac looked away and entered the kitchen. It was dominated by a large, white painted wooden table. An old fashioned range occupied one wall. A cabinet holding china plates stood opposite. The epitome of a farmhouse kitchen. Fielding pulled out a chair for Mac while Annie busied herself with mugs and milk from a fridge standing in the corner, incongruous in its sleek modernity.

"I'll help Annie," Brad said.

He stood close to her and Mac saw her shy away. A small action, but he spotted it. When Brad made a move past her to place a cast iron kettle on the range, she shrank away again.

"So, what can we do to help?" Fielding asked eagerly, sitting himself opposite Mac and leaning forward, hands clasped in front of him.

On impulse Mac, putting his hand into his jacket pocket, took out the evidence bag containing the ring he'd just found near Michael Gaines' car. He pushed it across the table to Fielding.

"I think this belongs to Ashleigh," Mac said, lying but for a reason.

Fielding frowned, picking up the bag and peering at the ring within.

"I never saw him wearing a ring. Especially not a signet ring. Did you, Annie?"

Annie narrowed her eyes as though racking her memory.

"Not that I can recall."

"Brad, you knew Ash better than we did. Is this his?" Fielding held the back towards Brad.

Mac was watching for a reaction. It was the reason for this whole pantomime. Brad had come forward quickly enough and had Mac not been watching him closely, he would have missed the reaction. Dark eyes widened slightly, there was an exaggerated blink and the merest suggestion of a hesitation before he took the bag.

"Nope. Never saw him wearing anything like this. What is it?"

"It's a clan ring," Annie said. "The Gordon clan. My family are Gordons. My dad has the motto on his wall. A stag and the word 'bydand'."

Brad shrugged, turning away as though it was irrelevant, tossing the bag onto the table. Mac reached for it, also shrugging. He'd gotten what he wanted out of the interaction. He immediately began talking.

"Well, the first thing is to look at Ashleigh's alibi. He claimed to have been here...at your retreat on the night that Zoe Phillips was killed. He wasn't believed because his DNA was found on her body. But we know that a white van arrived here at about 11.30 that evening. Pulled in, then straight back out again. Returning later that night. The SIO, sorry that's Senior Investigating Officer, argued that Ashleigh was picked up, taken into town where he committed murder before being given a lift back here. All without anyone else who was staying here at the time being any the wiser. Gary Kirk was willing to testify that Ashleigh had been here all night."

Mac had put the bag with the signet ring into his jacket pocket before slipping the jacket off and hanging it on the back of his chair. He clasped his hands together on the table as though making himself comfortable for a long conversation. Brad was watching him and then seemed engrossed in the contents of the fridge before moving around the room until he was lost to sight behind Mac.

"Yes, and Gary is a very honest man. I have known him for ten years and never known him to lie," Fielding said.

"He may not have known that Ashleigh snuck out," Mac said.

"I thought you were here to help prove Ash innocent," Brad put in, from over Mac's shoulder.

"I am."

"Then why are you questioning his alibi?" It wasn't really phrased as a question. More a statement that he was daring Mac to challenge.

"Why are you questioning my question?" Mac said with equal aggression in his voice.

Brad scoffed and walked back to where he had been standing, in front of the range. As he did, he brushed Mac's jacket and it fell to the floor.

"Brad, let's just hear the officer out," Fielding interjected, raising his hands in a conciliatory manner.

Mac had already got the picture, though. Whoever Brad was, he was the alpha of the two. Despite Michael Fielding being the founder and CEO of the charity that presumably had got him out of prison. Annie had gone to the other side of the kitchen. Brad glanced towards her and she turned her back when she noticed. There was an uncomfortable dynamic there. Maybe Brad had come onto her and she wasn't comfortable with it. Or they had a history.

"You knew Ashleigh Fenton in prison?" Mac asked Brad.

"Brad referred a lot of his friends to us," Fielding said. "He was one of the first to join when we set up in HMP Edinburgh. And he brought a lot of others with him. It's thanks to him the retreat is so successful, and we secured the funding we needed."

Mac looked at Brad, who hadn't uttered a word in response to Mac's question. A man with significant influence and authority among his fellow inmates. Enough to persuade them to become born-again Christians. That would have to be a man capable of violence. It was the only kind of man who earned respect inside.

"Where do you stay, Brad?" Mac asked, quietly.

"I'm just at the end of my tenancy, actually," Brad replied.

"Really? Why haven't you said anything, Brad?" Fielding's face was a picture of concern.

Brad's intensity melted, and he smiled sheepishly as he looked at Fielding. "Yeah, sorry about that, Mike. I know how busy you are with the programme. I didn't want to bother you but I was hoping I could stay here for a while. I'm just feeling the need to be with my brothers and sisters."

Fielding beamed and clapped his hands. "Of course! We've got plenty of room. Don't we, Annie?"

Annie looked as though she wished she could answer otherwise, but nodded. "Yes, Mike. Plenty of room."

CHAPTER TWENTY-NINE

MAC DRAGGED THE CONVERSATION ON. Fielding had another woman bring in a notepad and pen while asking Annie to prepare some food. Brad excused himself. Mac didn't object and paid him no attention as he left the room. He had no cause to arrest him, only a suspicion based on the odd dynamic between him and the other members of the New Covenant. Annie visibly relaxed when he was absent. Mac went through the motions of gathering evidence that might disprove Fenton's conviction. But it was all to give him a reason to be there until he could talk to Annie alone. She could tell him something about Brad, whose second name was Buchanan, he had discovered. When he got back to the office, he would check Brad's criminal record, though he pretty much knew what he would find. The accent was a Scottish public school boy. The hint that he was able to influence other inmates at HMP Edinburgh, otherwise known as Saughton by most people, told him that he was violent and known for his willingness to be so. Not a white-collar criminal then. He had been put away for assault, probably Actual or Grievous harm. Possibly a sexual offence.

There came a moment approaching four in the afternoon, when Fielding excused himself for a video conference he had to attend. He had been enthusiastic and positive during the conversation over the last few hours. Mac's assessment said he was exactly what he seemed, a man of faith and no little wealth, trying to rehabilitate criminals through Christianity. Mac pretended that he had enough to be going on with and requested a tour of the facility, claiming an interest in New Covenant's work. Fielding had cheerfully volunteered Annie to show him around. When he was out of the room, Mac waited a few seconds and then went to the door. He looked out but could see no sign of Fielding. He looked back at Annie. She looked nervous.

"Annie, I noticed something between you and Brad. I'm interested in finding out more." As he spoke, he casually put a hand into his jacket pocket. The evidence bag and the ring were gone. Mac knew a pick pocket tactic when he saw one. Brad had pulled it off skillfully.

Annie frowned, playing with a tea towel. "I'm not sure I know what you mean."

Mac put his hands in his trouser pockets and watched Annie silently. She glanced up at him from time to time, turning away hurriedly each time.

"Don't stare at me like that. He does that. It creeps me out."

Annie's accent was western Scotland, Kilmarnock or Ayr, something out that way.

"Brad?" Mac asked.

"Aye, Bhradain Kelso Buchanan," Annie said bitterly.

"That's a mouthful," Mac said with a low whistle. "I'm guessing his parents are nationalists."

"Who knows? I don't care to get to know him any better to find out," Annie said.

"Why not?" Mac asked.

"Is it relevant? You're here about Ashleigh, aren't you? What does Brad have to do with that?"

Mac weighed his options. She was scared, that much was obvious. Scared of Brad and scared of talking about him. Which meant she didn't think her fears would be taken seriously. Maybe Brad Buchanan held the real power at this commune.

"I'm investigating a murder. One very similar to the two Ashleigh has been charged with. Now, he openly admitted to one of those killings and apparently has also confessed to being responsible for the second, but I wasn't the one to interview him. I'm concerned he was coerced in some way, even though his DNA was found on the body…"

Annie shook her head, throwing the tea towel down and looking to the ceiling, folding her arms tight about herself. It was a pose of pure frustration. Mac considered his words, trying to identify what had triggered this reaction. Something about Ashleigh confessing to killing his ex-girlfriend he thought.

"Annie, he put his hands up to the killing of his ex. Even told us where to find her…."

"He didn't do it! Ok? He's innocent. When I met Ashleigh, he was a changed man. I know what he went inside for, but as we worked with him in prison, you could see how letting Jesus into his heart was changing him. But he was being pulled in a different direction."

"What direction?" Mac asked, quietly.

"The Alpha Brotherhood," Annie said.

Mac nodded, as though the name meant something to him. He could hazard a guess at what it represented, though. An organisation founded in prison by the inmates and claiming to be a brotherhood. That wouldn't be a male voice choir.

"Some kind of gang centered on toxic masculinity," Mac voiced his educated guess.

"The worst kind of testosterone fuelled misogyny. Brad had been wronged by a woman because that's what he did, assaulted women, and one of them had the guts to speak up. Ashleigh was the same. He went from being in tears and truly remorseful over what he'd done to his ex-girlfriend to blaming her for it. Brad got into his mind. That's what he does. Manipulates and controls."

"You're saying that Ashleigh Fenton confessed to a crime on the orders of Brad Buchanan?" Mac asked, unable to keep the urgency from his voice.

That whispering voice was getting very loud now. The instinct that had made him start his investigation here, against all reason and rational thinking, was now a pulsing thrill. The hairs on his arms were standing up. But Annie had glanced at him with wide eyes, thoroughly spooked. She backed away from him.

"No. I didn't say that. You're putting words in my mouth. He's...disturbing that's all. Now, do you want this tour or not?"

"Yes, please," Mac replied.

He followed Annie through the complex of buildings. He saw a dormitory fitted with three tier bunk beds and evidence that at least a dozen people were living there at the moment. He saw private rooms, looking like student accommodation, single beds, a small desk, and chair. A chapel, plain and un-adorned, plastic chairs laid out in rows in front of an altar comprising a camping table with a bible on it. Makeshift workshops producing a range of craft items, all with religious connotations. Finally, meeting rooms, some occupied with people sitting in a circle of chairs, talking earnestly. There was a large dining hall at the back of the complex, made from three shipping containers lined up. Another container looked as though it contained an office. Annie didn't take him inside, but he saw Fielding striding about, wearing a wireless headset and talking with energy and much hand movement.

The whole place looked the way he'd expected it to look. Space for worship and prayer meetings. Or possibly addiction anonymous meetings. A place to eat and sleep. He was going through the motions, though. Brad was his main interest, and he just wanted more time to talk to Annie about him. But she was going through the motions too, tight-lipped, and thoroughly frightened by all she had said so far. When they returned to the kitchen, Mac decided to try his hand at honesty.

"You're scared of him. That's obvious. Come with me and I can protect you. If he has anything to do with the crimes Ashleigh has been charged with, then he needs to face justice. From what you've said Ashleigh might turn out alright himself, providing he's away from Brad's influence. Here's my number."

Mac pressed a card into her hand, taken from the few he kept in the inside pocket of his jacket. Annie's eyes filled with tears. Mac could see that she was torn by the need to do what was right and pure terror. A man strolled into the kitchen at that moment. Tall with prominent cheek bones and a jutting jaw. He had bushy, dark eyebrows and was frowning.

"Everything OK, Annie? Is this copper upsetting you?"

He didn't wait for an answer, but immediately reached out. Mac didn't move, even when the newcomer gripped his elbow.

"I'd let go if I were you, pal," Mac said.

"Davey, let him go. Don't be an idiot," Annie said.

"Brad told me to look out for you," Davey insisted.

Mac saw it then. This was another member of the Alpha Brotherhood and Brad Buchanan was very firmly at the top of that particular pack.

"I was just leaving," Mac said, pulling his arm free. "Annie, don't get yourself into trouble for his sake. When I come back, I expect answers to my questions. Understood?"

He was staring at her and speaking harshly, the way he would if he were trying to intimidate a recalcitrant witness.

"She won't say anything without a lawyer, mate. Get out," Davey told him, squaring up to him.

Mac hoped his little performance had convinced the man that Annie had told him nothing. If she wouldn't let him help, then he had to do what he could to protect her. He backed away, dividing his glare between her and Davey.

"I'll be back," he said.

"Aye, do one, pal," Davey said.

Mac turned and walked away. As he passed it, he looked into the barn. The van was gone. The ring was gone. If the ring was a trophy, then Brad would have been keen to get it back. So keen he took the insane risk of stealing it from under Mac's nose. It wasn't conclusive evidence. His brief could and would argue that he stole it for the sake of stealing it. Or that he wanted to stitch up a copper. Or just had a fetish for objects related to real crime scenes. But it was evidence enough to make Mac go after him.

When he was back in his own car, turning it to head down the lane, he called Kai. There was no answer. He called the ANPR team and gave them the registration of the van. The address was Southhouse Broadway. He'd passed through Southhouse and its neighbouring sinks, Burdiehouse and Gracemount. All areas with high crime rates, low education and high unemployment. Where better to house an ex-con? He called Brunswick Road, got through to the switchboard, and asked for the custody sergeant. Jim Maxwell was on duty again. Mac explained the special favour he needed. Promised Jim a rare single malt for his trouble. Then told him it would help stitch up Mayhew. There was no love lost between rank-and-file coppers and the current Chief Constable and his deputy. They were deemed as pen pushers and Tories. Not many Tories among the beat coppers of Scotland. That swung it. Mac waited, drumming his fingers on the wheel. Then he heard Clio's voice.

"Mac?" her voice was hesitant, scared.

It was a kick in the guts for Mac. He closed his eyes, hands tightening on the wheel.

"Hey, Clio. How are they treating you?"

"OK, everyone's a bit cold," Clio sniffed. "Trying to hold it together."

"Good. That's all you can do. You've done nothing wrong, Clio. Hang in there."

"My solicitor asked me if I did it. He didn't seem to believe me. Said that if I had anything to do with it, the best strategy would be to cooperate."

"That's what you are doing. Telling the absolute truth."

"Mac, how did my DNA end up on his body? That woman says it can't be there other than through an intimate contact. That's the word she used, intimate. So either I killed him or I was…"

"Well, I'd say he was as gay as it gets, so that rules out the second option," Mac said.

Clio chuckled, which was why he'd said it.

"Clio, I don't know how your DNA ended up on a dead body and I'm out of the official loop at the moment, although trying hard to get back in. Can you remember exactly what she said?" By 'she,' Mac knew Clio meant Akhtar.

"Remember? It's burned into my brain. She said it was stuck in one of his wounds. No chance that I brushed against him at the school or…no chance of anything other than my hair getting caught on a blade and then…"

She cut off, sounding as though she were about to be sick.

"Mac, she told me that just last week she got a conviction on the same evidence. A stabbing and one piece of DNA that tied the suspect to the killing. She told me to come clean now and do myself a favour."

"Clio, listen to me, Akhtar only got that conviction because the suspect confessed. Yeah, the DNA is strong evidence, but I'm onto something here. I don't know what it is, but give me twenty-four hours and…"

"Mac, do I even have twenty-four hours?" Clio said, desperate terror alive in her voice.

"Akhtar can hold you for twenty-four hours before they have to charge or release you. If Akhtar isn't satisfied she's crossed the evidential threshold, she can apply for an extension. Up to 96 hours."

"That's…that's…four days! I can't be in here for four days, Mac!" Hysteria was taking hold now.

"You won't be," Mac promised without any idea how he was going to keep that promise. "I'm onto something and I'm not going to rest until I've chased it down. I'm going to find the evidence. But listen to me. Maia is safe. They can't touch her. You are safe. I know a lot of coppers and I'll make sure they're looking out for you. No-one is going to think you're a criminal. Jim is the custody sergeant just now. He's a good guy. He'll look out for you."

"Mac, I wish you were here," Clio said.

"I'll stop by later on, when it's quieter, I promise. I'll bring you a McD's. You shouldn't have to deal with canteen food on top of everything else. Just stay strong for me, Clio. I'm working on it."

He didn't hear what Clio said next. Maxwell was on the phone.

"Sir, Akhtar wants her back in the interview room."

"OK, Jim. When are you on 'til?"

"Night shift, sir."

"Akhtar's going to try and fit her up. She didn't do this. I'd bet my pension on it. Keep an eye on her, eh?"

"Will do, sir."

Maxwell hung up. Mac thudded his head back into the headrest of his seat. Then he started the engine and headed out for Southhouse Broadway.

CHAPTER THIRTY

WINTER HAD DRAWN THE NIGHT IN. By the time Mac was driving along the curving residential street that was Southhouse Broadway, it was pitch black. The lampposts were stark, rendering everything in orange tinged monochrome. Kids with hoods and masks loitered or roamed. He passed a play-park where a crowd of them were huddled together. Consuming something. The street was lined with houses in dead gray pebble-dash, with white bordered tiled roofs and squares of lawn in front. Grass verges were sloppy with churned, waterlogged grass and the roads gleamed from a downpour that Mac had driven through at a crawl. His jaw ached from gritting his teeth, fighting the anxiety and rising panic that was hitting him at every spit of rain now. He hoped that full disclosure to Talvir Sidhu would cure him. But that would be too easy, and probably a mistake. There were other contributory factors now weighing him down further. Clio and her murder charge. The real killer out there still. Maybe Brad Buchanan.

And the blackmail from Reid. Fit up a gangster, break the law and become a bent copper once again or...

Iona. And Mark Souter. The chains around his neck that he'd carried for so long the weight was part of him, he hardly felt anymore. But he was feeling it now. Ahead, the housing changed to blocks of flats. They were squat and corpse grey, designed in cross shapes. Coincidentally, it was a design favoured in newer prisons, with the wings radiating out from a central hub. And a lot of the residents of this estate probably felt right at home with that architecture. Brad's address was off the main road and up a slight hill, behind two blocks that were on Broadway itself. A row of lockups faced the block and the inevitable No Ball Games sign on the grass that surrounded it. Some young kids were kicking a ball about and turning the air blue with their swearing. Older kids sat on the roof of the lockups, drinking from long cans and smoking.

Mac got out and ignored them all, heading for the main door. Above it windows showed the staircase zig-zagging the height of the building, five floors. Brad was on the second. Mac pressed the button for Brad's flat. No answer. He pressed the neighbour's.

"Yeah?" male voice, annoyed.

"Is Brad in, eh?" Mac exaggerated the accent, laying on Craigmillar thick as tarmac.

"Whit?"

"Brad, is he there or wha'?"

"I don't know any Brad, mate," then a string of expletives.

The intercom went dead. Mac growled and hit the Services button. Surprisingly, the door clicked open. The stairs started to his right, a black rubber covered stair rail and bare concrete steps. A caged light at each landing gave some illumination. As Mac reached the landing halfway between the first and second floors, he slowed. Craning his neck, he looked up. There were voices up there. Movement that echoed down the stairwell. There was no lift in this building, so there was only one way up or down. Maybe a fire escape on one side. Mac turned the final corner and saw the flat he was interested in. The door was open, and a man was coming out carrying an armload of cardboard boxes. All were taped shut and had neatly written labels on the side. Mac caught of glimpse of what seemed to be a list of names and dates, but the carrier had turned the boxes so that he could look down the stairs. He had a shock of greasy dark hair and a lazy mouth, open and shapeless. He wore a tracksuit, blue with white trainers. Dark eyes locked with Mac's.

They were the kind of eyes that had seen so many coppers it didn't matter that Mac wasn't wearing a uniform. Equally, Mac had seen that look so many times that he knew he didn't need to pull out his ID or identify himself. It would be dangerous to get caught with a hand trapped in an inside pocket. And a waste of breath. Mac lunged to one side as the man shoved his boxes forward into the stairwell. Dimly, Mac was aware of a familiar voice screaming in fury. Then the box carrier was on him. A kick caught him on the shoulder and his heel slipped off a stair. Mac tumbled back, conscious of the hard-edged concrete steps. His hand caught the rubber coated railing and slipped down it, slowing him but not stopping the fall. The man above him shoved with both hands and Mac seized his wrists. As he released the only thing holding him up and began to fall, Mac twisted. Dark eyes alive with malice went wide as the man found himself pulled off balance. They went down together; half a dozen steps with Mac's fall broken by his assailant.

A blow landed in Mac's ribs. Then a box hit the side of his face. It made him let go, then he was being shoved onto the concrete landing. A kick landed in his stomach, he grabbed an ankle, holding on for his life. The attacker tried to hop back; one foot caught and fell back against the railings. Two more men were running up the stairs, shouting. Mac released his grip, scrambled back and up, kicking out as his assailant lunged in. Someone came in from the side, one of the two coming up the stairs. Mac lashed out, reacting to the movement alone. Another swing and his arm was caught. The first assailant swung at Mac's stomach and Mac doubled over.

"Hey! Let him go! He's police, you morons! Get out of there, or I'll kill you!"

The voice was Brads. The grip let Mac go and he fell once more to the landing. Looking up, he saw Brad swinging with a bottle that shattered over the head of the box carrier. Then he waved the broken neck of the bottle at one of the other two. The expression on his face was pure savagery. Feral, primal ferocity. His baseball cap was on the ground along with...a wig. Brad was revealed to be completely bald. Clean shaved, no eyebrows and not a hair on his egg like head. Mac hauled himself up by the railings, watching as Brad chased the three men away. He came back up the stairs, gathering the scattered boxes and breathing heavily. Mac met his eyes, and a chill ran down his back. There was nothing in the orbs that looked back at him. It was like Brad observed him through the eyeholes of a mask. His eyes were emotionless, dead. The excitement of the fight never reached them.

"You OK?" he asked Mac

"Yeah. Friends of yours, eh?"

"Yes, actually. Thought they were doing me a favour. I'll speak to them later."

"Doing you a favour?"

"They knew you were polis. They've both done porridge. Instincts kicked in, I think. But they know the rules." The slang words sounded odd, coming in Brad's cultured voice.

He walked up the stairs to the door of his flat, pulling it shut.

"I need to look in there," Mac said.

Brad stood in front of the door. He'd picked up the baseball cap, and he replaced it on his head, watching Mac passively.

"Do you have a search warrant?" he asked.

"No, I don't need one," Mac replied, reaching the landing.

"You do," Brad replied evenly.

He'd stacked the boxes that had been thrown at Mac beside the door. Mac stooped, turning the first until he could see the label. Two names, addresses, and dates.

"What's this?" he asked, reaching for the next one.

"Parcels to be delivered. The depots work 24/7, but I can't deliver 24/7. Can't leave them in the van overnight either. Not around here. So I take them in."

"Your employer know about that?" Mac said.

"I'm a contractor for a lot of different companies and it's common practice," Brad replied patiently. "Why did you come all the way out here? To see me? Why? What have I done that warrants a personal visit from the polis?"

Mac stood, rotating his shoulder and touching his ribs. "I don't know yct," he replied.

"Do I need a solicitor? I can't afford one, but Mike can."

"Innocent people don't need solicitors," Mac said.

Brad laughed. It transformed his face, which became instantly joyous. Mac tried to place his age. Mid-thirties, maybe.

"Try telling that to Ashleigh Fenton," Brad said.

"He innocent?" Mac asked.

"Yeah, he is, actually," Brad replied, stepping forward.

The laughter fell away like a mask, dropped to the floor. What lay beneath was a face carved from stone. The naked brows came down over eyes that seemed to draw the light in, devour it. Devil's eyes.

"If you've got nothing to hide, then why not let me look in your flat?" Mac said, refusing to back down.

Brad was the same height but lacked Mac's width, making him the smaller man.

"It's empty. I'm moving out. This was the last load," he said.

There came the sound of movement behind him. Mac glanced back and saw two men, possibly the same two that Brad had chased away with a broken bottle.

"I told you to get out of here!" Brad roared suddenly. "Move! Now!"

They moved. Mac couldn't help but be impressed.

"Alpha Brotherhood?" he asked.

"Yes. Now, I wonder how you know that, Detective Inspector McNeill? Has someone been telling tales out of school?" Brad said, breathing heavily through his nose and glaring at Mac. Mac's blood ran cold at the thought of the danger Annie could be in, but he kept his face straight.

"You the boss, then?

"What gave it away? It's a fraternity I started in Saughton

248

to help men survive in there. And when your system takes men from those hellholes and makes them live together in a different hellhole, the brotherhood survives."

"Was Ashleigh Fenton in the brotherhood?" Mac asked.

"He was," Brad replied.

"Why do I feel like you're challenging me? Feeding me incriminating information and daring me to do something with it," Mac said softly. He looked down at the boxes. "Or maybe you're just trying to distract me from something right in front of my nose."

Brad didn't react. He didn't look at the boxes. Instead, he sniffed, looked aside, and spat. Then he looked back, fixing Mac with an unblinking stare.

"I don't care if you open every box. I just have to tell my employer I've lost a load and why. Then they sue you. I don't lose out. Go ahead."

The trouble was, he was right. Mac wanted nothing more than to tear into each box. But by the morning he'd be suspended and Clio doomed. Unless the box contained bloody body parts. Which it wouldn't. If this was the killer, he was far too intelligent for that. Mac thrust his hands into his trouser pockets. Grinned a rogue's grin.

"I'm away to secure a search warrant for your flat...Brad," he said.

"It's not my flat anymore. Fill your boots," Brad said.

Mac turned his back on Brad and descended the stairs. On the ground floor he saw the two men, standing back like cowed dogs. Outside, smoking, he saw the man who'd been glassed. Blood ran down the side of his head. As Mac walked back to his car, the man hurried inside. By the time he'd reached his vehicle, Mac could see Brad leaning on the railings of the stairs on the landing, gazing out. The man in the blue tracksuit stood a step below him and as Mac watched, Brad turned and clasped the man's shoulder, smiling. It had the look of a general commending one of his soldiers for courage in the line of duty. As he started the engine, the image stayed with him. Brad was charismatic. Not a man born into menial labour. He spoke with a cultured accent but commanded the obedience of men who thought nothing of the worst kinds of violence, except to enjoy it. How far could that command go? Could he persuade one of his Brotherhood to put his hands up to murder? What about the DNA? Simple. Take a hair from Ashleigh Fenton's head, or get him to pluck one out, and place it on the body. Could he really make someone innocent go down for murder? Using pure charisma and a winning personality?

Mac's ribs hurt, but he didn't think any were cracked or broken. His ear ached and the side of his face was warm. A tooth felt loose. Most of it was from the tumble down the stairs. He'd given as good as he'd got otherwise. Mac drove away, feeling those black eyes on him until the building was lost to sight. Brad was clearing house. That wasn't a coincidence, Mac was sure of it. But he didn't have the evidence to get a search warrant. Brad knew it. Mac didn't know how he'd done it, but he was certain he had killed Michael Gaines and framed Clio.

CHAPTER THIRTY-ONE

MAC SAT ON THE STONE BENCH that served as a bed in the cell. He was eating fries from a box, a vanilla milkshake on the ground next to him. Clio sat by his side, contemplatively sucking on the straw of her Coke. Her feet were tucked underneath her and she leaned into him, eventually resting her head against his shoulder. Jim Maxwell had kept the visit off the books and closed the cell door, trusting Mac's judgement.

"Mac, I don't know how I'm going to survive in here overnight," Clio said.

"I know how scary this is for you, Clio, but you will survive. It's just one night. You can do it." Mac replied. "I'll have you out of here before you have to go to court."

"What if the station has a busy night and I have to share a cell?"

"You won't. We don't do that here, Clio. If the cells are full, Jim will send prisoners to the next nearest station. This isn't America."

"And you think this delivery driver is the killer?"

Mac nodded, reaching down for his milkshake, and suppressing a groan of protest from his sore ribs. "He's far more than a delivery driver. Kai did some research and I've done some of my own. Until August 2019, Brad Buchanan was in Saughton on charges of rape and assault of his ex-girlfriend. He was a successful cosmetic surgeon who forced women to undergo surgery they didn't need."

"Oh, my god."

"I think that's why he marks his victim's faces the way he does. It's the same way a plastic surgeon draws on his patients to mark where they're going to cut. I think he sees it as improving them in some way. A scalpel would fit the profile of the murder weapon."

"But why me? And how? I've wracked my brains trying to think how this happened to me. I still don't know."

"I saw him with boxes. They had names, addresses and dates on them. His job was handling packages to be delivered from one individual to another. It's conceivable that there could be skin cells caught under some packing tape. Or a hair. Saliva even, if you know how to extract it. If you're the courier, you know who the package has come from. You know who the DNA belongs to."

"And I've been sending out a lot of parcels because of the move. I've been selling stuff I don't want to take with us. So, he got my DNA? But why use it? Why does he want to destroy my life? I don't even know him, Mac!"

Mac shrugged. "I don't know yet. That comes down to motive and without questioning him, I can only hazard a guess. Maybe it was purely malice, or simply ego. Surgeons hold your life in their hands perhaps that was his motive; to feel that type of power again. In his old life he had extraordinary wealth and a successful business with clients from all over the world. Brad's business partner was a politician and there was a nasty political scandal. Kai found some older historical stuff along similar lines, but this incident pertained to serious allegations of sexual abuse against interns and a couple of PAs. Then several weeks after the allegations came to light they seemed to fade away, like they were quietly settled out of court and hushed up. Brad was well connected, worked as an advisor to a member of the House of Lords. His father and grandfather were Tory MPs. But his life of privilege ended due to a woman speaking out. It could simply be because you're a woman."

"Stop. I just can't hear it spoken of so matter-of- factly. I can't believe there's a human being so evil that he would randomly destroy someone just for...for..."

"For kicks? For nothing? To regain the power he lost? It could be any of those, but my bet is he needs to feel powerful, particularly over women. He's targeting you, Clio. I think you may be just as much a target as the people he's killed. This way he gets two victims for the price of one."

"Jesus, Mac, this is horrible. How would he even know enough about me to make sure I was without an alibi when I'd need one? Or that I wasn't on holiday or something? Has he been stalking me?"

"I don't know, Clio. Could be any number of ways. Have you made any new friends online recently? Or had a request from an old friend, out of the blue?"

"No. Nothing like that."

"Is Maia online?"

"Well, yes. She's on a few things but..."

"He could have been grooming Maia for information about you. Your movements, your...car."

Mac trailed off, seeing Michael Gaines' car in his mind's eye. And Clio's had been found at the airport in a short-term parking bay. With a dented fender. Parked there after the estimated time of Michael Gaines' death. The driver had been wearing a hood and a mask. Brad would have seen the car after making a pickup or delivery at Clio's house. And found out about the vendetta against Michael Gaines by talking to Maia online.

"He probably set up a fake profile, pretending to be a girl Maia's age. Became friends with her and pumped her for information."

"Oh god, Mac, this is a nightmare. I've tried so hard to keep Maia safe and it's made no difference," Clio cried.

"Of course it has, Clio. Stop blaming yourself. None of this is your fault, okay? I'll check in with Mel and ask her to talk to Maia and have a look at her phone. Is Maia likely to still be up, it's after eleven?"

"She will. Even in normal times it's hard to get her to sleep. It's the ADHD. Sorry, ADHN. Hate the D, it's not a disorder, just how she is."

"I'll find a way to prove all this. I promise. I just need one loose string to pull on and this whole thing will unravel."

"Please hurry, Mac. I'm holding on by my fingernails," Clio said, her voice muffled as she pressed her face against his arm.

Mac lifted his arm and put it around her shoulders. She

snuggled into his embrace. Mac thought of Siobhan. Of the hope she had given him less than a fortnight ago. He should have called her. But life had got in the way. He couldn't think about her now. The observation slot in the door opened and a face appeared. Mac knew what the gossip would be, but found that he didn't care. Weariness swept over him and he put his head back, closing his eyes for just a moment. He would have to leave Clio soon but he would go up to the office and review the files Kai had sent over. Had he ever doubted that Kai could make Sergeant? He'd really stepped up. Mac felt a father's pride at the risks the young man had taken for him. And pulled off. His mind wandered as he presently heard deep, even breathing from Clio. He let his conscious mind off the hook, allowing his sub-conscious to come through. He felt comfortable holding Clio like this, feeling the warmth of her beside him. It was reassuring and relaxing.

He rested his cheek on the top of her head. A name came into his head and it took him a moment to place it. Derek Tonford. That had been the first of the names on the box he had examined, the box belonging to Brad Buchanan. He let it flow through him, not trying to hold on to it but allowing his consciousness to stream. Derek Tonford. Amanda Croker. That had been another name. Victims? No way of knowing. They could just be people who had parcels to be delivered. Or waiting to be received. Amanda Croker. Why did that name suddenly sound familiar. Because he'd just read it on a piece of paper? No, there was another reason. He tasted the name, played with it, letting it tumble about in search of a memory. Clio murmured in her sleep and shifted. Mac realised he had begun to tense and she'd felt it. He forced the muscles of his arm and shoulder to relax. Where did he know Amanda Croker from?

When it came to him he sat up. Clio jolted awake with a small gasp. Mac sat on the edge of the bench, running his hands through his hair, and staring at the floor. But seeing short, cropped, dyed blonde hair. A dark face, hazel eyes. Fierce and lapsing into West Indian vernacular when angry. Amanda Croker was a solicitor. A thorn in Mac's side more than once. A very good solicitor who was often called in when suspects couldn't afford their own legal representation. Outspoken. Independent. Was it that simple? Was Brad targeting women who stood up for themselves publicly? Michael Gaines was gay, a drag queen and outspoken on a number of topics which had brought him into conflict with parents and school governors alike. Zoe Phillips had been active in student politics. Clio had stood up for her daughter online. Vicky McCourt had stood up against her ex-husband.

"It makes no sense. Each death has been a tableau. Public. He'd not made any effort to hide them. Why do that with Vicky McCourt? He left her for two weeks in her flat. Then all of a sudden Fenton confesses. Unless..."

Ashleigh Fenton gives up a strand of hair as DNA evidence. Why? Because his leader asked him to. Could Brad have that much of a hold over members of his Brotherhood? What does Fenton get?

"Fenton wants revenge on his wife. Brad kills her. Tells Fenton to confess only after he's been arrested for Zoe Phillips. Fenton hates his ex so much he agrees. Brad was testing his system!"

Mac stood up, feeling as though a light was suddenly shining on him, shining through him. Brad comes up with the idea of planting DNA evidence. Maybe in prison. Maybe years before. He wants to see if it works. He needs a volunteer. Needs someone to owe him. Ash Fenton.

"Murder my ex and you can have a hair to plant on the body of the girl you want to kill. And when we arrest Ash Fenton, Brad puts his plan into action. He knows his system works. We've proved it for him!"

"Mac, I don't fully understand. I don't know who all these people are but you're obviously excited about something. Have you made a breakthrough?"

Mac turned, beaming. "I'm close. I'm bloody close! I'm getting you out of here, Clio."

He hammered on the door until Jim Maxwell appeared, looking harassed.

"Sorry, Jim. Don't mean to cause a scene. Look after her, eh?"

Then Mac was striding back to his office. It was dark when he went in, the lights responding to movement a moment later. He flung his jacket down over his desk and fired up the laptop. Half eleven at night. He had to risk it. Pulling up the New Covenant website, he scanned the contact details for the Loanhead retreat. Michael Fielding was listed and Mac considered his number briefly. Then he found Annie Sullivan. He put the number into his phone, hoping she would pick up, hoping she had put his number into her own phone from the card he'd given her.

"Hello?" Annie's voice, hushed.

"Annie. Are you alone?" Mac asked urgently.

"Yes. I'm in my room, at the retreat," she replied. "You shouldn't be calling me!"

"I know. But it might just save an innocent woman's life. It's Brad. But to prove it I need access to his stuff. In particular boxes marked with names, addresses and dates. Is he at the retreat?"

"He was here for dinner. But he went out," Annie replied.

"Do you have access to his room?"

"His room?! You're saying he's a killer and you want me to go..."

"Yes. I'm sorry, Annie. By the time I get out there, it might be too late. I need to see those boxes. I need the names. I think they're his planned victims. I have no idea how many there are or in what order he's targeting them so I just need the list and I can do something to protect them. Please, Annie. I wouldn't ask but there's no other way."

Silence. Mac's heart was attacking his ribcage, trying to escape. His breathing was quick and hard.

"OK. I'll go now."

"Call me back on a video call. All you have to do is point your phone at the boxes if they're there," Mac said urgently.

The line went dead. He waited a minute, then two. After five, he was about to call her again when her number appeared on his phone, requesting a video call. He accepted and saw a darkened room, lit by the light from a phone torch. A single bed against the wall. A desk and a flat pack wardrobe were the only other furniture. The bed had three cardboard boxes. Annie went closer until Mac could read the labels. Two were sealed. One was open. And empty. It bore the names of Derek Tonford and Amanda Croker. His online search had not yet yielded any satisfactory matches for Derek Tonford. There was one who was a professor at Stanford University in California. Another was a CEO on LinkedIn. A string of them on Facebook, some with no location given, others a long way from Edinburgh. Amanda Croker was easy to find. She lived in Morningside in a refurbished Victorian villa. Ran her practice from the ground floor along with her numerous campaign and lobby groups. All touched on the LGBTQ+ community in some way.

He didn't know which of these two was in danger, but he could protect Amanda Croker. Protect her and hope that Derek Tonford wasn't the intended victim.

"Thank you, Annie. Now get out of there. I'm organising a warrant to seize that property and a uniform patrol is going to be out there in half an hour. Sooner if he can."

"You don't need to rush, DCI McNeill," said Michael Fielding.

The phone was turned around and Mac saw that Fielding had been the one holding it. Annie stood behind him in thick tartan PJs, biting her nails.

"I'm going to lock the doors and have these boxes put in my office. I'm not going to let Brad Buchanan back in. If you're wrong, then I will ask God's forgiveness. But if you are right, He will not forgive me if I stand by and do nothing."

CHAPTER THIRTY-TWO

MAC HUNG UP. An open box with Amanda Croker's name on it. He couldn't save Derek Tonford, whoever he was, if indeed he was the intended victim. But the fact that the box was open and empty meant that time was running out. If Mac's theory was right, Brad was on his way to his victim. Might be there already, planting the DNA of the other person named on the box. Destroying two lives. He picked up the phone to call Reid, then replaced the receiver. Reid might not be open to Mac's theory, especially if it involved unstitching Akhtar's case against Ash Fenton. Mac felt that Michael Fielding would do his best but it was obvious that followers of Brad's Alpha Brotherhood were present. Fielding and Annie would be out-numbered and in danger. He grabbed his coat from the back of the chair and scrubbed a hand through his hair, checking Amanda Croker's address one more time. As he left the office he called Michael Fielding.

"Mr. Fielding, I'm sending a uniform patrol car out to you

in case Brad comes back. He's got at least one man in there with you. There are probably others."

"You're talking about my brothers, Detective Chief Inspector," Fielding replied, somewhat pompously. "Brothers in Christ. I have faith."

"I don't. And if he comes back wanting to destroy evidence, his Brotherhood will side with him. I'm sure of it."

"Christ's brotherhood is stronger than man's," Fielding said. "You don't know these men as I do, Detective. They are reformed."

"Jesus!" Mac snapped.

"Precisely," Fielding replied without hesitation.

"The police are on their way, right?" Mac said, hanging up.

Next call was to Kai. Mac was stepping out of the lift when he answered. There was a commotion in the background. Sounded like a bar.

"Kai, I need you," Mac said. "How much have you had to drink?"

"Nothing, guv. Honest. Well, a couple of beers but..."

"Grab a bottle of water, take a breath mint and meet me at 2 Allison Drive. It's in Morningside, just off Comiston Road, near the cemetery. A solicitor lives there who's fond of roasting the police in public so for god's sake don't have alcohol on your breath."

"Jeez, guv. Anyone would think I was asking you a favour, eh?"

"I know. Sorry, Kai, but I'm running out of people I can trust, and I'm trying to prevent another murder. Bring your stab vest."

"No bother, guv. I'm leaving now."

Mac caught a female voice in the background, not sounding happy. Kai was brushing her off when he hung up. Mac walked along a corridor and rapped on the door of the duty commander. Opening it, he saw it was Fran Dryden and breathed an inward sigh of relief. Fran was a stickler for protocol but she wouldn't hesitate in an emergency.

"Sorry, ma'am, for barging in. I have reason to believe a murder may be in progress or about to take place. I have a location and I need backup."

Fran had dark hair framing a long face with a strong jaw and thin lips. Her uniform looked like it was brand new. She raised an eyebrow as she picked up the phone.

"How many units do you need and where?" she said in a clipped tone.

Mac gave the address and a summary of the situation. One man believed to be violent and dangerous. The possibility that he had backup himself. Men with a passionate loyalty to him.

"I'll authorize an armed response team in that case. They can be on the road with you in five minutes."

"They need to hang back initially, until I can recce the location," Mac said.

"That's the job of the tactical team, Detective Chief Inspector. I hope you're not proposing to be a hero?"

"Not at all, ma'am. But I think I have this man spooked. He's acting hastily because he knows I'm onto him. If we get there too soon and with lights blazing he may walk away."

"You want to catch him in the act? And endanger a member of the public? No, Detective Chief Inspector. I won't hear of it. Tactical goes in first."

"Ma'am. If he walks away, he has the opportunity to disappear. He might start all over again somewhere else. And we would have no way of predicting where or when. I believe a member of the public is already in danger and could lose her life if I don't get there to stop him. And more people will die unless I take this risk. A personal risk. Please, Ma'am."

Fran pursed her thin lips, tapping a finger nail on the handset of the phone.

"Ok. I'll tell the backup units to hang back and let you go in first. But you'll need an officer with you. I am not letting any officer under my command go into danger with no backup."

"My DS is on his way. He'll have my back."

―――――

Mac walked up Comiston Road. To either side of him were tenement buildings, part of the old Victorian architecture of Edinburgh. In other parts of the city, they were stained black and leprous brown from the acid of vehicle emissions. In this part they were pale and clean, kept that way by expensive sand blasting paid for by factors who collected a fortune in fees from the affluent owners and tenants. Neat hedges gave privacy to the basement level of the buildings. Some windows at the basement or ground level advertised the premises of dentists, solicitors, financial advisors, and accountants. As an equal number of these properties were commercial as residential these days. The occasional lighted window showed high ceilings with elaborate mouldings. Book cases and designer lamp shades. No sign of a flat screen TV on a wall here and no car parked outside smaller than a Tesla Model 3. Mac walked with hands in the pocket of his trousers, coat thrown back. His usual swagger. He had an earpiece connected to a radio in his coat pocket.

Ahead, on the corner of Allison Drive, he could see a figure leaning against a wall, vaping. It was Kai. He had found Mac at the top of Comiston Road, where the backup had set up a road block. Armed response teams were proceeding on foot, throwing a circle around the target property. Their job was to make sure no-one trying to flee the scene got out. More uniformed officers were closing off the other streets leading to Comiston Road, keeping far enough back that no-one inside 2 Allison Drive would be able to see their Hi-Viz attire or blue lights. If Brad wasn't here, Mac was going to look foolish. At the very least. But he didn't care. If it led to a formal complaint for mismanagement of resources from Fran Dryden, followed by a suspension, so be it. Brad had targeted someone Mac cared about. He was becoming a hate figure in Mac's eyes almost equal to Mark Souter. A man who believed he could rampage through someone's life, causing devastation and face no consequences. It was going to stop.

Kai looked around as Mac approached. Like Mac, he wore a stab vest. Unlike Mac, Kai was dressed for a night out. Tight jeans, boots, and a skinny fit short sleeved shirt under the stab vest.

"You not cold, mate?" Mac said quietly.

"Bloody freezing, guv but my jacket wouldn't go on over the stab vest," Kai replied, taking a drag on the vape.

Mac caught a waft of cologne.

"Hope your girlfriend wasn't too upset," he said.

"She's not my girlfriend. Not yet. Don't worry, when I

told her what I was doing, she was very impressed. Thinks I'm a hero. I wasn't doing all that well until you called so..."

Mac grunted, looking from the corner and up Allison Drive. It was a small cul-de-sac consisting of three large villas. Two on either side and one facing Comiston Road. That was number 2.

"Note the white van just down the road," Kai said.

Mac looked. He had to move to the kerb to see beyond the line of trees that ran along both sides of Comiston Road. There it was.

"Took a stroll past it. It's the reg you texted to me and there's no-one inside," Kai said.

He was shivering and hunching his shoulders, but his eyes never left 2 Allison Drive. He looked sharp and ready to go.

"No sign of anyone at the front. Our boy must be round the back," Kai said.

Mac touched the radio in his coat pocket, finding the transmit button.

"McNeill. We have eyes on the target vehicle. White transit van parked twenty yards from Allison Drive. No sign of anyone near it."

"Gold Commander," Fran Dryden replied. "Affirmative. Tac Command, can you confirm eyes on the vehicle?"

"Tac Command, affirmative."

"McNeill. DS Stuart and I are moving in."

"Gold Commander, confirmed."

Mac wanted to be running. To sprint to the house and begin hammering on the door, kicking it in if need be. Brad was there. Amanda Croker might be dead already. But he knew that acting too quickly might get him killed or let Brad through the net. He might end up being arrested for breaking and entering. Or assault with intent. And would be out on the street in a year or two. It wouldn't be justice. Kai kept close to his side. As they approached the house they went from a brisk walk to a jog. The front of the house looked undisturbed. A black wrought-iron gate was closed as was the front door, reached by a set of stone steps and covered by a classical portico supported by fluted columns. A tasteful, minimalist sign on the stone gatepost proclaimed Croker Legal. The logo had a rainbow flag beneath it. A further sign beneath that bore a number of different coloured rainbows presumably covering every spectrum of sexuality and gender. Croker was not shy about her place in the LGBTQ+ community.

The house had a gravel path running back along both sides. Mac had checked it out on a satellite view and it looked like there was access to the rear of the property from both sides. According to Maps, there was a lawn, patio, and garden furniture before a line of trees separating the property from the Morningside Cemetery. He pointed to the left and Kai moved in that direction, keeping to the grass verge to avoid treading on the gravel. Mac took the right, glancing up. The windows were dark and there was no sign of life. He skipped from the grass to the gravel as he went along the side of the house, in order to keep himself pressed against the side of the wall. When he reached the corner he leaned out. Security lights at the back flashed into life. Kai was moving around the far corner, also keeping to the wall, and reaching a bay window, craned to look in. Mac scanned the lawn and patio, seeing nothing moving except Kai. There was another bay window on his side and what looked like French doors in be-tween leading onto the patio. He raised his head to look into his bay window. No broken glass. Dark room.

Mac took a pen torch from his pocket and shone it in. The beam played around an office with tall pot plants, bookcases, a desk and...shit!

"McNeill. Body of a man ground floor..." he tried to ori-entate himself to give directions that would mean something to the tactical squad. "East side. Face down. There's blood. We're going in."

Kai was the first to the doors. He tried the handle, which turned freely. The door opened quietly. Kai slipped inside, Mac behind him. Beyond was a kitchen with a door leading to the office.

"Go check on him," Mac whispered.

Kai slipped into the office, and Mac moved through the kitchen to a hallway beyond. There was a scuffle above and a male voice grunting in pain, then yelling. Then a woman screamed followed by the sound of running footsteps. Mac sprinted for the bottom of the stairs.

"He's breathing. Head injury," Kai's voice came over the open radio channel.

Mac was halfway up the stairs when a woman appeared at the top.

"Police!" Mac shouted.

The woman had short, platinum dyed hair and was bare-foot in a trouser suit and blouse. The blouse was white and Mac could see the blood staining it. She began to run down the stairs but stumbled, her eyes rolling up in her head. Mac braced himself as she fell onto him. She was a well-set woman and her momentum carried him down, braced or not. Mac tried to keep himself between her and the hard floor while trying to keep his head up and avoid his neck being snapped like a twig. Brad appeared at the top of the stairs. He wore a paper forensic suit, hood up and face masked. Mac recognised the eyes. He wore gloves and had a bloodied scalpel in his right hand, index finger laid along the top, hand held out from his side.

"McNeill! Back up required. Officer down!" Mac managed to wheeze.

A babble of voices filled his ear. The go command from Dryden and subsequent command from the leader of the tactical squad. Brad removed the mask, reaching under his hood. He was smiling as he came down the stairs slowly. Amanda Croker was semi-conscious. Mac could feel blood. He shoved her aside brutally and scrambled back on his hands, heels slipping against the floor. Brad jumped the last few steps, grinning. And Kai descended on him from behind. He grabbed Brad's forearm and wrist, twisting it behind and up, as his full weight landed on Brad's shoulder blades. Brad hit the floor face first and his nose burst as Kai shoved his head down with the heel of one hand. With the other he held Brad's knife hand high between his shoulder blades, forcing the fingers to open and the blade dropped. Armed officers burst through the back door proclaiming themselves loudly. Mac was hanging onto the door knob of the front door, holding himself half off the floor. Brad didn't make a sound.

"You're under arrest for assault with a deadly weapon, attempted murder, and assault on a police officer. You do not have to say anything, but it may harm your defence if you do not mention, when questioned something you later rely on in court," Kai shouted above the noise of the tactical unit swarming the house.

Mac grinned, then winced. If he hadn't broken a rib on the stairs at Brad's flat, he thought he might have done now. Kai was grinning back, looking as though he'd like to do it all over again.

CHAPTER THIRTY-THREE

MAC SIPPED HIS COFFEE as he watched Brad through a two-way mirror.

"Seems calm," Mel commented, seated at a table before the mirror.

"Refused a solicitor," Mac said. "Usually tells you something about the person you're dealing with."

"Doesn't realise how deep he's in the..." Kai began.

"Oh, I think he knows. If I'm right, he's bursting to take credit for all three killings," Mac said.

He was operating on about two hours' sleep. After Brad's arrest, he'd gone to A&E and been given pain relief and bandaging around his ribs. There was a fracture but no complete break. Mac couldn't take a deep breath without a stab of pain. The right side of his face was swollen, and he had a headache. Probably another concussion, but he'd refused to be kept in. Siobhan hadn't been on duty. Brad had been left in a cell after being charged and refusing a solicitor. Dryden had spoken to

Reid and sung Mac's praises. Reid had given Mac a verbal slap on the back, then demanded to know how he'd known that a murder was about to take place. Mac had nonchalantly told him it was all part of the Zoe Phillips, Vicky McCourt, and Michael Gaines investigation. Told Reid 'you're welcome' and then hung up.

He'd checked in on Clio, been told she was asleep and that a WPC had sat with her for a while. Mac owed Jim Maxwell big time. Finally, he'd pushed two chairs together in his office and fallen asleep with his head hanging off the back. Noise outside his office had wakened him and he'd emerged to his team arriving for work. Kai looked like he'd had a week's leave, bright eyed and practically bouncing on his toes. Mac had briefed Mel on the events of the night and ignored Akhtar. Then he'd washed in the gents and gone to interview Brad Buchanan.

"Kai, you can come in with me," Mac said. "It's only fair. You made the arrest."

"Cheers, guv," Kai replied.

"You don't want Nari in here with me?" Mel asked, seemingly casual but not fooling Mac.

"No. She's Akhtar's now. I'm recommending Kai for promotion to DS and asking Reid to transfer Nari," Mac said, his voice deprived of emotion.

"You sure about that, guv?" Mel asked. "I mean everyone makes mistakes..."

"Nari jumped ship when it looked like Akhtar was winning. She was thinking of her own career, not the team or the case. I don't need people like that. She's out," Mac said, firmly.

Kai opened his mouth, but Mac just looked at him and he closed it again.

The door to the observation room opened and Reid came in, still in his overcoat.

"This the fella?" he said by way of greeting.

"It is," Mac said.

"And we're charging him with attempted murder."

Reid was looking at Mac with an intensity that could melt concrete. He knew what the charge was and was asking because he was looking to pick a fight.

"That's what we're holding him for," Mac replied. "But I'm going to get more out of him."

"Aye, such as?" Reid's mouth hung open belligerently and his meaty knuckles tapped the tabletop.

"Such as three counts of murder," Mac said levelly.

Reid glared at him, and Mac glared back. He wasn't about to be pushed aside for the sake of politics. Or ordered out of the interview room by the DCC or even the Chief Constable.

"No-one else knows this man like me. I've got him figured out. And if I get the confession out of him that I think he's got in him..."

"Then the DCC will have my backside and Akhtar will be leaking to the press inside of a minute. Just get the attempted murder motive, right? We don't need any more than that."

"Clio Wray needs more than that," Mac said.

"That case is closed, Detective Inspector!" Reid bellowed. "Sorry, did I get the wrong rank? I must have been thinking about tomorrow."

"Kai, with me," Mac snapped, brushing past Reid.

"If you want me out of the room, you'll have to come in personally and drag me out," Mac said as he opened the door.

"Mac!" Reid snapped. "For god's sake, grow up and look at the big picture!"

"I am seeing the big picture, sir, and I don't think I like it. At least not your corner of it," Mac shot back. "Mayhew might have your balls in a vice, sir, but mine are still swinging free."

He was out of the observation room and opening the door of the interview room. Reid's mouth clamped shut over some choice words at high volume. Mac didn't look back and Kai, to his credit, strode in after him in serene confidence.

Kai sat and made the formal introductions into the recorder along with the date and time, then let Mac take over.

"Bhradain Kelso Buchanan," Mac said, taking a seat. "Why did you try to kill Amanda Croker?"

Brad looked alien in his forensic suit, a fresh one given to him in the cells. His head was pale and bald, eyes dark and fathomless. The corners of his mouth tugged into a smile.

"Surely it's obvious? Because she was trying to emasculate every man in this country with her philosophy of feminism and her crusade against so-called toxic masculinity. She wants every boy to be raised by women and eunuchs. To be accepting of fags and their ludicrous idea of changing their sex and living as women. I was doing the world a favour by removing someone like that," Brad said, coldly and precisely. "How long do you think the human race will survive if people like that are the intellectual vanguard of our society? We already have a generation of boys growing up thinking it's fine to surrender their masculinity. To become women or be ruled by women.

Just take a look at what society has grown into. All a man needs to do is glance at a woman and it's harassment. Speak to a woman and its assault. Touch a woman and its rape. I was striking a blow for masculinity."

"That's the philosophy of your Alpha Brotherhood?" Mac asked.

"It is. Not initially. It was just a way of surviving. But when I realised how many men welcomed it. How many men were desperate to get out from under the female thumb, I decided to embrace it fully. To explore it as a philosophy. It's not a crime."

"It isn't," Mac admitted. "I'm sure your father and grandfather would have approved of your beginning a political movement."

Brad sat back, hands in his lap, an appraising look on his face. "Oh, yes, they would indeed. They taught me to understand I am a sovereign individual. I was born into an elite. We don't operate by the same rules as the rest of you. My father was an Alpha, though he didn't have the vocabulary to express it. He refused to be chained by women. He married my mother, but he didn't limit himself to her. Didn't obey any absurd vows designed to empower the wife and emasculate the husband. He chose his partners when he liked. I've lived my life the same way."

"Can't be a great image for a political career, though," Kai observed.

"Any heifer who spoke out got paid off. We are sovereign, you see?"

Brad was warming to his theme now and Mac could tell that he was enjoying holding forth. He was leaning forward, punctuating his words with stabs at the table.

"You're being charged with attempted murder..." Kai said at a signal from Mac.

"Fine," Brad said, looking frustrated he hadn't been allowed to continue holding court.

"...and grievous bodily harm for the assault on Ms. Croker's PA, a Mr. Paul Reisman."

"Yes," Brad said, bored.

"My boss wants me to pin Michael Gaines, Zoe Phillips and Vicky McCourt on you too," Mac said.

Brad laughed. "I'll bet he does. Or, wait a minute, is it really you who wants to do that? Sorry, Detective Chief Inspector. I'll admit to what I did because I don't see it as a crime. But I won't admit to anything else."

"Full co-operation could reduce your sentence," Mac said speculatively.

"So?" Brad crowed. "I go to prison where there are still dozens of alphas waiting to welcome me back. I'm a king in that place. Send me to another prison and I'll be running the place inside of a year. And out in five years for good behaviour thanks to people like Michael Fielding."

"Yes, you're right," Mac said. "I made the mistake of liking you for those three murders, I have to admit. Especially when we found that ring in your pocket. Same ring as was missing from the body of Michael Gaines."

"I happen to like signet rings and that was mine. I found it on the street. Prove otherwise," Brad said.

"I won't bother," Mac replied. "I can see it wasn't you. Not after last night."

Brad sat back, a frown on his face. He started to speak, stopped himself.

"Guv, we can make it stick," Kai said in a low tone. "Think how that'll look. Three murders and an attempted fourth. Come on."

"Exactly what about last night makes you think I couldn't have done the first three," Brad said after a moment.

Mac snorted and saw the flicker of annoyance on Brad's face. "The other killings took place with meticulous planning. Victims were killed in one place and moved to another to create a tableau. An item was removed as a trophy. You clearly hadn't scoped out Amanda Croker like the killer of Michael Gaines did. You show up when there's an able-bodied male in the house to defend her and have to fight him. Then you get interrupted. She fights back. I assume you got a tetanus for that bite." He pointed to the bandage on Brad's left hand. "To be frank, it was like amateur hour. No way you could have got her out of that house and into your van without being seen. There was no planning at all, but I can see how you were trying to make it look. You wanted it to look like the killer of Zoe Phillips, Vicky McCourt, and Michael Gaines. Wanted the prestige. But, Brad, you're not him. You're not clever enough. I don't believe that Ashleigh Fenton or Clio Wray are killers, either. I think we've lost him. He was smart, you see, very smart. Far superior to anything you're capable of. We won't find out who it was. He's gone. Like the Ripper."

Brad was looking increasingly uncomfortable, shifting in his seat, and biting his lip. Mac could see the anger bubbling away. Anger he was struggling to contain. Mac pushed a piece of paper across the table towards Brad.

"This is the statement you wrote last night. Re-read it and if you agree with it, sign, and date it and we're done. You'll be handed over to the Procurator Fiscal's office for prosecution," Mac said, glancing at his watch.

"That's it?" Brad said, sounding surprised.

"Open and shut case, mate," Kai said, turning in his seat to lean on the table with one elbow. It was the epitome of a sloppy, bored policeman. He even bit his fingernails.

"Come on, Brad. Let's not waste each other's time. You'll get your fifteen minutes for this, attacking such a high-profile solicitor. You'll be all over social media for a bit. I've got a backlog of cases longer than a Leonard Cohen song."

Kai snorted. Mac had heard the quip on a TV show and quite liked it.

"I'm not just some flash in the pan. I'm not some disposable reality TV celebrity," Brad growled.

"Yeah, you are, mate," Kai said, dropping the M-word, which Mac believed would trigger a snob like Brad. "By tomorrow, you'll be the same as the flashers and kiddie fiddlers. Moriarty, you ain't."

Mac glanced at Kai and he shrugged. "My ex had a thing for Benedict Cumberbatch. Made me watch the whole thing."

Mac smiled and Brad suddenly slapped the table.

"Stop! How dare you mock me! You're not being fair! This is not fair! I have worked hard..."

Mac looked at him and he trailed off, looking away.

"What's not fair, Brad? You're bang to rights. Even waived your right to a solicitor. I thought you wanted to plead guilty."

"It's not fair that you're dismissing my work! I won't be dismissed. I won't be forgotten!"

"Yeah, you will. We're bored already," Kai said.

"I've got a rape case landed on my desk this morning. I just want rid of you, pal," Mac said, sounding weary. "Just sign the bloody thing so we can pack you off, eh?"

"No!" Brad stood up and Kai was on his feet in a heartbeat. Mac remained seated.

Brad was flushed, eyes wide, breathing hard. Each intake of breath bared his teeth.

"I killed Zoe Phillips. I stabbed her in the back of my van, which I lined with a special forensic tent of my own design. I took her off the street. She was another loud-mouthed female who was building a career belittling and emasculating men. She even treated her own boyfriend like garbage. Like she could get any man she wanted wrapped around her finger. If she'd lived, she would have been another female politician crushing the rights of sovereign, alpha males. I marked her face with areas she should have improved on."

"How did you get her up to Arthur's Seat without anyone seeing?" Kai asked.

"A special backpack. Again, of my own design. My Alpha Brotherhood stood guard and we'd already scoped out the cameras. Easy to avoid if you know where they are."

"And Vicky McCourt?" Mac asked.

"That was Ash's payment. I wanted to see if the DNA was enough on its own to convince the police. I killed her so that he would give a hair that I could plant on Zoe. And it worked. So I went ahead and killed Michael Gaines. That fag was happy to surrender his manhood. He wanted to be a woman and spent his life campaigning for more rights for other fags, just like him! He wanted to turn a generation of boys into women!" Brad roared. "He needed to be put out of his misery. I had a sample of Clio Wray's DNA from the packages she was sending. A skin flake I found under some tape. A hair under another piece. I got close to her daughter online and stole her car and crashed it into his. Just in case the DNA wasn't enough on its own. I knew she was a friend of yours from sweet Maia. The stupid little..."

Brad cussed, insulting Maia with a word that brought Mac to his feet and around the table until Kai intervened. The younger officer was a solid, immovable wall.

"Easy, guv," he whispered, barely at the level of hearing. "Don't you dare screw it up now."

"Why wait until morning to drive Michael Gaines' body away from his house? We know he was killed earlier," Mac said, clenching his fists and walking away. Kai was right. They were so close he couldn't balls it up now.

"Would you believe I fell asleep? Luckily I'd already put him in the car earlier. But Amanda Croker would have been the icing on the cake. A signal to all the emasculators and man-haters out there. A signal that none of them are safe. None! From the retribution of the Alpha! And I would have gone on and on. And you poor saps would have gone on arresting the wrong people, throwing them into jail for nothing!" Brad was laughing now, fingers laced above his head and face joyous. Eyes bright with the crazed shine of a zealot.

"What about the trophies?" Kai asked.

Brad looked at him and smirked. "You'll never find them. They're mine."

"Yea, we will," Kai said. "We'll take apart every place you've ever been, starting with the New Covenant Retreat. Not that it matters, but we don't like loose ends."

"I was onto you," Mac said, re-taking his seat.

"You had nothing. If you hadn't come to the retreat, you wouldn't be any closer now than you were," Brad crowed. "You got lucky."

Kai sat. "Next time, I'll leave the room and you can face the wrath of my guvnor on your own. Sit down," he told Brad.

Brad smirked and took his seat. Mac cleared his throat.

"I did get lucky, but Amanda Croker would have been your last, anyway."

"Oh really? How so, I'm intrigued," Brad said.

"We would have known that Derek Tonford didn't kill her, that his DNA was planted," Mac said.

"How?" Brad said, hands planted on the table, leaning forward with an expression of scorn.

"Because Derek Tonford, Amanda Croker's next-door neighbour with whom she had a long-running and bitter feud, died. Last week," Mac said.

Brad just stared. The scorn flowed from his face and his mouth dropped open. He sat back, looking down.

"He had a heart attack at home. Was found dead by his son the next day. Obviously, this was after you had collected a parcel he was sending and extracted his DNA. It was a model train that he was selling on an auction site, in case you're interested. Like I said. Amateur."

CHAPTER THIRTY-FOUR

THE LATE VICTORIAN TENEMENT BUILDINGS on Leslie Crescent made a canyon shape topped in blue. The air was sharp, but the drizzle and occasional snow of February was giving way to March and the beginning of spring. Mac still wore the uniform of his job and stood with hands in trouser pockets, looking up at the building that was home to Mel and Cazzy Barland. Clio got out of the passenger seat.

"Top floor," Mac said. "No lifts."

"Just lean on me," Clio said with a smile.

"I'm not kidding. I've already been backwards down two flights of stairs. With a overweight woman on top of me for the second one."

"I don't want to know what you get up to in your spare time, Mac," Clio laughed.

Brad had written war and peace, his statement becoming a manifesto for his crazed philosophy. A boy raised in privilege, his misdemeanors covered up by wealthy parents keen not to have their own political and social standing harmed. Mac suspected that Vicky McCourt was not the first woman Brad had killed. She certainly wasn't the first he had hurt. There were girlfriends who had been paid off. Prostitutes whose names he had forgotten. Bodies dumped for him by men of wealth and standing who wanted to protect themselves from the stain of his darkness. Once triggered, Brad hadn't wanted to stop. The charges against Clio had been dropped. It was probable Ashleigh Fenton would be charged with Accessory After the Fact, Complicity and Obstruction of Justice, it would be up to the Procurator Fiscal to determine how much he was coerced by Brad. But he had Fielding's lawyers working on his behalf, hoping for a suspended sentence and rehabilitation at the New Covenant. He was already cooperating fully with the police. The Procurator Fiscal was furious, specifically very angry at DCI Akhtar and DCC Mayhew. Mac didn't care. He wasn't even sure he wanted to remain a copper. He was sick of the corruption. The politics.

Clio put an arm about his waist and gave him a hug that made him wince.

"Sorry. Forgot already. Brace yourself. Maia will want to squeeze you."

"I'll grin and bear it," Mac said.

He led the way up the steps to the clean front door with a shiny brass knob. The names above the intercom buttons were handwritten, each slip of paper decorated individually. It was a nice street in a trendy part of the city, Stockbridge. It felt urban, which made Mac feel at home but without any of the hopeless oppression of places like Liberton or Craighall. Maia answered the buzzer.

"Hello?"

"Police! Open up!" Mac said.

Maia squealed. "Uncle Callum! Is mum with you?"

"Hi, sweetie! I'm here!"

The sound of the buzzer and the click of the door opening were almost drowned by Maia's scream of delight. Clio went through ahead of Mac and began to walk up the stone steps. They were worn in the middle from a hundred years of footfalls. The railing was wrought iron and painted in rainbow colours. Bikes were locked up beneath the stairwell and a boot scraper sat outside one of the ground floor flats. Mac followed slower, hearing mother and daughter greeting each other higher up. When he rounded a corner Clio was hugging Maia fiercely on a landing. When Maia saw Mac she broke away and cannoned down to him. For the third time in three days, Mac was assaulted on a staircase. This time he withstood the onslaught, hugging the girl tightly. She was crying and Mac found that he had a lump in his throat. He blinked several times, not wanting Mel to come down and see him acting the fool.

"Thank you," Maia mumbled into his shoulder.

Mac just smiled and nodded. Clio came down the stairs, putting her arms around Mac and Maia both. The three of them stayed like that for a long while.

DCI McNeill will return soon in book 3

Want to be the first to know when 'Mac is back?' Join the New Crime Club on the website **www.jacquelinenew.com** to get news, updates and more!

Enjoyed the book? It would be a great help if you could leave a brief review on Amazon or the book retailer where you purchased the book.

Thank you

Printed in Great Britain
by Amazon